£2-00

HONOUR

ANN DECTER

PRESS GANG PUBLISHERS / VANCOUVER

First Edition 1996.

The Publisher acknowledges financial assistance from the Canada Council, the Book Publishing Industry Development Program of the Department of Canadian Heritage, and the Cultural Services Branch, Province
of British Columbia.

CANADIAN CATALOGUING IN PUBLICATION DATA

Decter, Ann, 1956–
Honour

ISBN 0-88974-057-7

I. Title.
PS8557.E26H66 1996   C813'.54   C96-910132-5
PR9199.3.D3533H66 1996

Edited by Jennifer Glossop
Copy edited by Nancy Pollak
Cover and text designed by Val Speidel
Cover photographs © 1996 by Louie Ettling
Typeset in Bembo
Printed by Best Book Manufacturers
Printed on acid-free paper ∞
Printed and bound in Canada

Press Gang Publishers
101 - 225 East 17th Avenue
Vancouver, B.C.   V5V 1A6   Canada
TEL: 604 876-7787   FAX: 604 876-7892

HONO

OTHER BOOKS BY ANN DECTER

Insister

Paper, Scissors, Rock

Katie's Alligator Goes to Daycare

FOR UNA

Astounded Souls

This is the silence
of astounded souls

SYLVIA PLATH

OUT ACROSS THE opening ocean, time swallows time. Earth swallows sun and moon, water swallows all. Daylight is blue, is blue on blue. Quietly, I have come to this gentle city, this sweet succulent isle where you first nestled on the belly of a woman. Achingly, I stroll this sea wall, stone of mourning in hand to signal my visit, but no cold proud grave seeks its weight. Your ashes are long since scattered in salt water, awash in sacred seas where solid flesh melts to sorrow, where waterborne, we first crawled to life. We spawn and flood, ebb and flow, tidal women.

The path is steep. Mere sinew and bone, my legs tire on the slope. Breath betrays and teases, air skips out of reach. The sea wind sails through me, challenges me to soar out to where the wind swallows. To become only time and light, sheer particles in motion, to traverse the intimate infinite between human and atomic. A stone's throw from a road tracing the water's curving body, an aching step from welcoming brine. South, ahead, the crisp silver waterway glitters and beckons.

Gulls cry above me. I long to drift. My weary legs have lived too long, walked too many miles in strangers' shoes, stumbled on curbs in too many languages. The path veers away from the ocean. This old body strains. Why persist? Why not abandon flesh for sunshine, dip and crest on rolling waves? Burn light years out of time, a glinting motion, a sunprint on water. Companion to the wind. This driftwood cane bends, the sea wall wobbles. My thickening tongue thirsts. Moisture beads salt sweat. The eye longs to sleep. Breath vanishes, pulse thunders. My knees buckle on a grass mattress. Voices drum flesh and bone, drum earth and sky. And yours among them. Your old soul songs. Sing for me, dear one, I hear you. I ride your lilting melody out into the engulfing blue. Sing for me your honour songs . . .

Shulamit Weiss & Jane Doe 12-93

RAWNESS BLEEDS, BUT an island, no matter how large, is encircled by water. Even when the water is quiet, it keeps summer air genial, mountains distant, sustains a natural moat between provinces and countries. The island's queen city lures tourists and travellers, the tired and the ailing, the hale elderly, pursuing wellness and leisure. Garden city, rain city, healthy city, a good place for the newly minted Dr. Shulamit Weiss. A green city for a green physician. And light, playful air to soothe over-exposed nerves, to reconcile burnt endings and the toll of unac-knowledged history.

Like many before her, Shulamit Weiss had moved west to calm down. To heal and be healed where the sun sets more slowly. Where the sky is pink and gentle.

"I'm a refugee from urban stress," Shulamit explained to Marie as they planned Marie's visit for the following weekend. "Too many years of bucking an elite that just packed the nation's industrial base into a laptop computer and flew south."

"Well, folks come west for a lot of different reasons. Reg-u-lar pioneers arrive every day," Marie responded sarcastically. "But Victoria? Aren't you a little young for retirement?"

"Thanks for the support. I can tell it'll be great to see you," Shulamit whined.

"Simmer down, big bear. You see, that's what I mean . . . you've always seemed so hyp—look, never mind. It'll be good to get together. You'll see."

"I've always seemed so what?"

"So . . . passionate," Marie said quietly. "Uh-oh, somebody at the door. Gotta go. See ya Saturday, Shul, on the dock!"

Shulamit hung up the phone, picked up the car keys and walked out of the house. She wriggled into the small seat of her used Toyota and slammed the door. In her first days in Victoria it had become clear that she needed her own transportation. She flirted with a sturdy Yamaha 400 motorcycle, but opted for practicality and deferred to a geriatric clientele.

It was an evening in late May, damp and pleasant. The air seemed romantically clean after years in southern Ontario, the last four in Hamilton, collapsing steel capital of the country, where, even as free trade closed the mills one by one, Shulamit believed breathing remained a high-risk activity. Carcinogenic dioxins were still regularly detected in the breast milk of nursing women. Shulamit flipped on the radio, the familiar cadence of the CBC evening news filled the car.

"Today, Canada's largest tire manufacturer announced the closing of its last plant in St. Catharines, Ontario. Two thousand workers will be laid off of by—"

"Fuckers," Shulamit blurted, "in search of a more desperate workforce. If they can't find one, they'll create one. They'll be back when the unions have been busted and unemployment insurance gutted and environmental protections removed." She stomped the accelerator.

A moment later her worn tires squealed, braking for the stop sign at the corner of Oswego and Dallas. Ahead lay open water, misty skies above the Strait of Juan de Fuca, a bank of clouds drifting over the peaks of the Olympic Mountains on the Washington coast. In the distance, a rainbow arched into the clouds. Shulamit laughed.

"Nirvana! And soon a pot of gold." She drew deep on pure wet air, fiddled the radio dial until she found the Blue Jays' game. She turned left, following the shoreline along Dallas. Juan Guzman was pitching, top of the fifth. They could repeat, Shulamit thought, remembering the heady days of the 1992 World Series.

In truth, there was nothing about calm that intrinsically attracted Shulamit. It could have been said that moving west was an attempt to overcome her own personality. But it could not have been said by Shulamit, on that damp night in May. She was convinced of the wisdom of reapproaching life in an equally sincere but less driven and combative manner. Like everything else she had undertaken in her thirty-four eventful years, Shulamit embraced her peace-seeking mission deeply, intensely and restlessly. Over the years she had repeatedly generated the only kind of calm she had any affinity for, one nestled in the eye of a storm. Then time and again, Shulamit wrestled toward tranquillity with the grace of an aging prizefighter who knows that winning requires not only slowing the pace of each bout, but choosing them carefully and resting well between.

Shulamit parked by the walk to Holland Point. She listened as Guzman pitched to a 3–2 count. Watched an older woman achingly approach along the path that led away from the sea wall.

"Stee-rike!" the announcer rejoiced.

"Yes!" Shulamit's round fist pounded the steering wheel. She watched the woman veer under generous branches. Watched her turn slowly and collapse toward thick grass. Shulamit flung the door open. Hurried down the path. Arms outstretched to cradle the body as the woman touched grass. Gloria's face popped into view, an unexpected flash from a concealed camera.

There was a gasp before the woman's head fell back, inches from Shulamit's face. Her left arm collapsed across her chest. A stone fell loose.

"Are you okay?" Shulamit struggled to block out the memory of Gloria. "Who are you?"

The word on her lips, before they went silent, was "Honour."

Must be delirious, Shulamit surmised, immediately checking her pulse. Across the grass a chalk-haired white man sat in an immaculate late-model Mercedes sedan.

"Do you have a car phone?" Shulamit hollered.

"Pardon me?" he answered reluctantly.

"A cellular, call an ambulance, I'm a doctor."

Shulamit saw the flat outline of a phone in his hand and quietly, if illogically, cursed privilege. She turned back to the woman on the grass. Her grey hair flopping back, her body a still shadow. Strange that an emergency still became Gloria, nearly three years later. There was no physical resemblance. Gloria would never age and grey, never lie breathing unevenly, well into her seventies, most likely having a stroke a hundred yards from the Pacific Ocean. Shulamit checked her pulse again. Steady but weak. Studied the woman's features, a picture of patient impatience as a siren grew steadily louder. Thick natural eyebrows, eyes that looked large even when closed, a sharp nose, light grey down on the upper lip. Not a woman who would be easily dismissed, Shulamit speculated. Who are you? What had she mumbled? "Honour." An ambulance drew alongside.

"Dr. Weiss," Shula introduced herself curtly to the two ambulance attendants. "No, she's not a patient. I saw her collapse. Her pulse is steady. Looks like she's stroked."

They unloaded a stretcher and transferred her onto it. "Know who she is?" the smaller man asked.

"No," Shulamit shook her head.

"No purse or bag anywhere?" he persisted.

"Not that I noticed," Shulamit answered.

He surveyed the surrounding area, while his larger, older partner gently searched her clothing. "Nothin' here, either, the partner announced. "No wallet, no i.d."

"Look," Shulamit interrupted, irritated with their delay, "I'm here for three months doing a locum for Dr. Killock. I have admitting privileges at Royal Jubilee. Just get her there. I'll follow."

The larger man eyed her suspiciously and slid an oxygen mask over the woman's face. "Nice mustache," he quipped.

Shulamit's hand moved automatically to her upper lip. Gender fascist, she thought, but held her tongue. She was supposed to be calming down, she reminded herself, supposed to be healing in a relaxed, comfortable place. Stay away from crises. Find your inner pain and heal it. Shulamit hastened toward her car. She flipped the ignition.

"Jays lead four to three, top of the eighth," the radio blared.

"All right Jays." Shula's tension dissipated momentarily. "I'd rather find my inner jock and feed her a coupla hot dogs," she announced to no one.

The siren wailed. The ambulance backed onto Dallas. Shula gunned her engine and zipped out. Fuck the traffic, she thought. This is an emergency. Shulamit stayed on the ambulance's bumper, sneaking through red lights, enjoying the power to challenge the authority of the traffic signal and the minor risk of pretending that she, too, had the right of way. In this town, she figured, it just doesn't matter. No one is that itchy. Shulamit missed itchy, missed urban stress the way she missed digging into a grinding argument with her friend Jane.

Jane was still sounding out the big sky above Muddy Water. Shulamit hadn't called her since she had arrived in Victoria. She didn't feel like connecting until she had somewhere to connect from, something that felt like a home. After weeks in a bed and breakfast Shulamit had moved into a rambling house shared by two friends of friends of Marie's. She had been pleased to find a place cheaply and easily, and hadn't bothered too much about her future housemates. Arthur, the guy, seemed young and eager, a retread hippie. The woman hadn't been home when Shulamit dropped by to vet and be vetted. Apparently, Terra was often away on spiritual adventures of one sort or another. Shulamit was sceptical about a crystal-gazing housemate, but however much she was inclined to abhor anything blissed out, her mission included staying open to new influences. Besides, she had a couple of relaxation tapes of her own, loon calls and babbling brooks. Sometimes at night, they eased her toward sleep. The ambulance took a right off Richmond. Shulamit turned, drove around to the back of the hospital. She parked and walked into a cramped, poorly lit emergency room.

Shulamit saw the gurney carrying the woman slip through

swinging doors and followed. At the admitting desk, everything came to a standstill. No insurance number, no identity, still unconscious. Part of the new age in Canada was a tighter line on hospital budgets. If the woman was American, it might well be that no one would pay for her care. If she was a fairly transient Canadian, there could be a problem, Shulamit knew. The admissions clerk and the gender-fascist ambulance attendant fussed over administrative details while an orderly and the triage nurse wheeled the comatose woman down a hallway. Shulamit decided to wield her doctorly queen-of-the-heap wand.

"Admit her as my patient," she said flatly, looking at the admissions clerk. "I'll take responsibility."

"What?" The pert woman looked up, about to dismiss the interruption.

"I'm Dr. Shulamit Weiss, I'm doing a three-month locum for Dr. Killock. You can admit that Jane Doe as my patient, and I'll take responsibility for determining her identity and insurance particulars."

The clerk looked dubious. Doctors did not do administrative work. Shulamit gazed back, unconcerned.

"It could be difficult, you know. We'll have to call the police," the clerk responded behind oversized, plastic-framed glasses. Her skin took on a pink tinge that accentuated red-orange freckles. "People may be looking for her."

Shulamit felt her aggressive self rise happily within, released from an enforced, unwanted sleep. She willed herself to stay controlled. "I certainly hope so," she answered sharply. "Perhaps I'll see her now that she's settled."

"All right," the clerk said, "I'll finish preparing her chart." She managed a small but genuine smile.

The smile brought Shulamit back to her first month interning, when she'd sworn never to adopt the persona of the all-powerful professional, the boss-doctor intimidating hospital staff. Prior years of work immunized her against adopting the belief that possessing and using the skills to save lives raised doctors to the status of deity. Yet, as soon as she became sarcastic, the clerk had responded positively. Shulamit frowned, then deliberately changed her tack.

"I didn't catch your name." Shulamit offered her hand. "I'm Dr. Weiss, Shulamit Weiss. I should have introduced myself properly."

The clerk looked startled for a moment, then shook Shulamit's hand weakly. "Turner, Sharon Turner. Sharon, I mean."

"Shulamit," Shula repeated.

"I'll bring the chart in."

"Thanks."

Down the hall Shulamit pushed aside the curtain and stood over the bed of her very first Jane Doe case. The woman looked much more ill than she had lying quietly on the grass. Shulamit was unfazed. One of the first things she had learned about the practice of medicine was that everyone looks worse in a hospital gown and bed. Sharon Turner slid the curtain back and handed her the chart. Jane Doe 12-93. Shulamit examined the patient carefully, then wrote orders for a battery of tests—complete blood count, blood gases, CT scan—to confirm or contradict her first diagnosis: stroke. If Jane Doe didn't regain consciousness within an hour, the prognosis for a complete recovery would be poor.

Shulamit gently lifted the woman's limp left arm, admiring her long fingers, the plain gold band on her baby finger. Shulamit eased it off. Inside were initials, S.S.W., almost the same as Shulamit's. She slipped the ring back on Jane Doe 12-93's finger. S.S.W. Shulamit made faint additions to the chart in pencil, above Jane Doe. Last Name: W. First Name: S. Middle Initial: S. Sex? Shula took a good look at the woman. Hair trimmed neatly. Short, but full. The undisguised down on her upper lip. The set of her jaw showing years of determination. She circled F, but in her mind she added a definite list toward L. Age? Seventy-plus, she thought. A seventy-plus lesbian. What's your story, S.S.W.?

Jane Doe's clothes hung neatly on a hanger behind the bed. Shulamit felt the pockets for anything else that might identify her. Loose change, and a single key on a ring. A small metal disk hung from the ring, etched with "309." Shula looked at it, looked back at Jane Doe (Lesbian) 12-93 struggling silently in bed. She remembered the clerk saying that she'd have to notify the police. Her promise to resist the arrogance of doctors. Listing toward lesbian. Shulamit slipped the key in her pocket and went to give the test orders to the triage nurse.

Jane Cammen & The Mistresses of History

THE PAST LIES dormant beneath everyday life, an iris germinating beneath warming soil, a mother bear, cubs birthed in a dark season sleep, waking to prowl a budding landscape. Wandering the land while her appetite revives, gradually seeking green grasses, horsetails, wild leeks, skunk cabbage and grubs, foods she can digest after her long fast. Foods for her tender-legged offspring, nursed in slumber for months. And how she behaves depends on whether the land can provide what she and hers need, for she will find what she needs wherever the journey takes her.

With her car idling in the middle of the wide, quiet street, Jane Cammen gazed past the sweeping ash tree at the house of her childhood. Broad steps fronted a limestone foundation. Jane recalled running her hand across the cool rock outline of a fossilized fish below the dining-room window. She thought about spring clichés and rituals, about rebirth and renewal, remembering the one formal Seder conducted around the old oak table, cousins, aunts, uncles spilling over to a second table in the living room. Her mother, Sophia, and Baba Edith spooning matzoh balls into Baba's blue and white Passover dishes. What did it take for Baba to bring her Pesach dishes into the house of her defiant Irish daughter-in-law and her rationalist surgeon son? But Jane knew that with Zeda a decade dead, her father assumed the mantel of head of the family. Phil Cammen, the educated eldest son of immigrant parents, became patriarch to his own mother.

Not so with Sophia. Jane imagined her behind the drapes, opening the glass doors of the oak china cabinet, extracting a bottle of scotch. Heard her rich Dublin voice say, "Perfectly civilized, a drink before dinner," accompanied by the clinking of ice cubes. Dinner, never supper, even when the children ate macaroni and ketchup at the kitchen table. Breakfast, lunch, dinner. Brunch, occasionally. And often dinner "fashionably late," by which Sophia meant considerably after Phil came roaring through the front door at 6:15 and was civilly fended off with the Muddy Water *Free Press* and a cold glass of something—water, pop or whatever Sophia was imbibing.

Sophia brooked no patriarch, husband or son. Sophia, queen of summer at the lakeside cabin, where sweet sloe gin and seven replaced scotch before dinner. Where five days a week she lived with her children, their friends and guests. Slept late, breakfasted on toast lounging in bed or lying on the dock. Washed the kitchen floor only when the children's bare feet began to stick to it, defrosted the freezer in midsummer heat, distributing ice and snow for the children to play with. So white against the dark earth. Signalled silently to a teenage babysitter watching Jane and her brother Gene on the tiny beach, as a mature black bear strolled between cabin and lake. The three tiptoed through low bush to the neighbours' and crawled soundlessly up the steps on all fours. Gene's breath loud in Jane's ears. Then, high above the water, they watched the hulking animal wade gracefully in, swim into deeper water, roll on her back and loll in the summer sun. Without splash or ceremony, concentric ripples crossing the bay.

"I didn't want to make noise," Sophia explained later. "I didn't know if she had cubs with her. Never get between a mother and her cubs. That's when a bear can be dangerous."

Fierce defense. Bonds of life, survival, nurturing. The strange miracle of another being that has grown inside you, the tie to a being you have, unfathomably, lived inside. Love as separation, as unbreakable link. Sophia gone, overnight, as Jane neared thirty. Sudden death became a fault line Jane still struggled to close, half a dozen years on.

Jane shifted the car into drive. Let her mind ramble the rooms of that fossilized house as her hands guided the old station wagon south toward the university. Rooms connected by a web of lives—Sophia and her children, Owen, Jane and Gene; the children and Phil, their father. Even now, Jane found it hard to place her parents in direct relationship to each other, though they were, locked in a direct antagonism spun into a marriage. It couldn't have always been hostile, Jane admitted, rolling across the last patch of open prairie in Muddy Water's south end. Sunshine bathed the city, sweetened the dry air with the fertile scent of damp soil. However bitterly time had soured the pairing, Sophia hadn't travelled five thousand miles, abandoning cosmopolitan London of the early fifties for the dusty flats of Muddy Water, simply to win an argument. Only passion would move a woman that far, Jane thought, spying green shoots in the ditch. And whatever shape her parents' relationship had taken, it had always been passionate. For Sophia, love mutated to hate over a quarter century. Jane grew up in the web of both, inside the fierce black love of an Irish-Canadian bear for her only daughter, and the intricately woven discord that drove Sophia out of the marriage. Bob, husband to her later years, was anything Phil was not. Most importantly, he was simply not Phil.

The big car lurched to a stop at the red light above the south gate to the campus. Lately Jane had come to see the threads of fabric strung directly between herself and Phil, the weave that, unimaginably, did not include Sophia. Connections that withstood Phil's explosions and tantrums, his long, slow death, and Jane's slower reconciliation to it. And later, the surprising emergence of the ways he, too, had shaped her. A deepening link to Jewishness, clearer in the years since his death.

The engine rumbled as Jane pressed the accelerator. Her thoughts returned to Sophia, whose laughter had lifted life in Muddy Water back across an ocean, whose voice quieted year by year in Jane's mind. Jane yearned to hoard the gems her mother had bequeathed, to sift through the sludge of grief and resentment and marvel at an inheritance that continued to provide. Although every mother had a profound effect on her children's lives—through presence, absence and the balance of degrees—Jane doubted that every mother's death resonated so long and so thoroughly. As she mused over why a chasm of loss had dropped so deep in her, Jane heard her childhood voice say proudly, "Mom, you're my best friend." The bond of trust those young words signified became well-buried veins that survived the trouble years, when Jane refused to become the political shaker Sophia expected, while Sophia hardened to bitterness before leaving Phil, the country, the continent, and Jane.

Parking behind the university library, Jane realized she was living in a triangle. Two points belonged in the past: the big house in the south end and the cabin tipping the pre-Cambrian shield. Only her own tentative home in the north end, the home that was everything Sophia's had not been—small, quiet, unassuming, Jane's alone—belonged wholly in the present. And that was enough, as long as the other points on the triangle held. But now, she thought, lugging boxes and watching her awkward reflection in the glass door, there was more absence than sorrow. The chasm had to close. Jane needed convergence, which meant finishing her thesis.

Inside she bumped between the stacks to her study carrel, littered with a mass of books, papers and the odd memento of Sophia's public life. Taped to the shelf was a wallet-sized "vote at" card she had filched from a civic election file at the public archives. The card bore a photo of Sophia in her early forties, vigorous and quite beautiful, wearing a casual shirt dress, still much more European than Canadian. No denim for Sophia, Jane thought, eyeing her own faded jeans and the oversized sweatshirt Shulamit had left on her last visit. "The disappearance of history is the history of disappearance," Shula used to say, filling stark canvases with faces that faded to cold white.

Lately, Jane thought, hands smoothing the spine of Sophia's hardcover copy of *The Second Sex,* Shulamit had offered bits and pieces of her family story, nothing direct, just comments here and there. About the missing and the murdered, Ashkenazi Jews herded for killing in the colossal destruction ordained and organized by German National Socialism. Shulamit had visited the Anne Frank House when in Amsterdam for an AIDS conference. Sent Jane a postcard of Anne's room on Prinsengracht, the one she shared with Mr. Dussel. Walls decorated with photos of family, movie stars and royalty of the era. Ginger Rogers, Princesses Elizabeth and Margaret, Norma Shearer, Ray Milland, Greta Garbo, Heinz Rufmann. Shula wrote:

J.C.—

Today Anne Frank would be 63 years and 13 days old. 13 steps to a landing, 16 steps to the second floor. A map and a bookcase hide the door. On August 14, 1944, 29 steps. Captured.

xxoxx your Shula

Later, two books arrived and a short note. One was the *Diary of Anne Frank,* the other a tourist guide to the Anne Frank House, which Jane learned was not only preserved as the hiding place of the Franks, the Van Daans and Mr. Dussel, but also served as a foundation for anti-racist education. Shula's note said only:

Read these for me. I can't. A steady stream of visitors shuffles through a house where families hid to save their lives from "human-hunters" 50 years ago. How can the world change so much? We thousands meet and talk of this plague and how many it has killed, how long it took for any attention to be paid. How can the world have changed so little? Hitler was a pervert. I am simply a lesbian and a Jew and now, too, proudly, a doctor. Drool. It takes a lot to be a Jew from Europe some days. Other days it's of no consequence. Is there somewhere people die of old age?

Miss you, Shula

Jane read both books carefully, thinking about Shula's lost family, about her own possible cousins. Cammens or Kamens or Kaminskys who stayed in Ukraine and Rumania when her grandparents left, who died at Babi Yar, who hid in attics like the Frank family or in root cellars or carefully covered pits dug in farmers' fields, scrounging to stay alive. Jane imagined an X-ray aerial map of Europe in the 1940s. All over the continent, people lying under piles of bush, huddled in forests, silent in closets and under false floors. Ashkenazi people. Leftists. Lesbians and gays. Jewish children learning to hide body and identity. Shula, a generation and a continent removed, seemed to expect everything of others yet rely almost entirely on herself.

The only time Jane had ever seen Shula lean was during the long fall of Gloria's death, almost three years earlier. As autumn lengthened toward winter, Shula phoned night after night from Hamilton, angry, caustic, cold white fury. Finally, Jane convinced her to take a week off medical school and visit Muddy Water. In the small house on Aikins, Shula raged and was silent, soaked for hours in the tub, jogged for miles through thickening snow, ploughed through mountains of junk food staring at documentaries, sit-coms and videos until two or three or four in the morning. Then she slipped wordlessly under the fading duvet beside Jane and let herself be held. On the last night of her stay, tucked in the safe strength of Jane's arms, her back guarded by her friend's warmth, Shula began to cry.

"I won't." Shula hissed between clenched teeth. Jane woke groggily to Shula fuming. "The bastard killed her, I will not cry. I will hate. I will hate. I will hate." Shula's body jerked. Heaving sobs broke within her. Jane nestled silently around her. "Fucking murdering fucking bastard." Shula curled and clutched her stomach, rocking on waves of tears.

"Let it go," Jane whispered, cocooning her body into Shulamit's curves. "Let it come down, Shula, let it all come down." Jane stroked her hair. "Cry for Gloria, cry because you love her, because you hate what happened to her, because you still want her to be alive, because it's a shitty fucking world that kills a woman like that, that kills any woman. Cry because you loved her and you wanted her. And she loved you." Jane kissed her cheek, lips damp with salt, wiped sticky tears with careful fingers. "And I love you, too."

Shulamit's weeping mingled with Jane's soothing voice in a river of sorrow until the late dawn trickled through frosted panes. When Shulamit quieted, Jane whispered, "Don't worry. I won't tell anyone that tough Shulamit Weiss ever cried for the love of a woman." She heard Shulamit laugh quietly, and then sniffle. "There's tissue on the beside table."

"Thanks," Shula's voice sounded muffled and distant. After a while she asked, "Who held you when Sophia died?"

"Uh, Henry. Remember Henry?"

Shulamit laughed gently. "Yeah. He was kind of nice, if you're into tortoises."

Jane elbowed Shulamit. "And then Marie. Later. I still needed holding when I met Marie." Jane remembered long-ago nights in Toronto, before she left for Muddy Water and Marie chose Vancouver. Accidental nights in a looser life, when dances sparked romance.

"Marie, Marie, I pledge my heart to thee," Shulamit taunted.

"Stop it." Jane whacked her with a pillow.

"But my body stays with me, although you're in B.C."

Jane thumped her again, with less conviction. "Doing who knows what. And with whom." Marie was still fond of rolling the dice of lust, while Jane had long ago lost interest in sex with strangers.

"When was the last time you actually saw her?" Shulamit switched to a serious tone.

"Eighty-seven days."

"And counting . . . What's with the whining? I thought you had an understanding."

Jane laughed. "Yeah, we do. I understand that Marie chases after a bit of sweetness when she gets itchy, and she understands that I don't. Oh hell, we're different, and nothing will make us the same . . . We talk a lot on the phone. I like it here. She likes it there."

"Did you ever think maybe it's not the past that's bothering you, but the present? Maybe you're not still grieving your mother, maybe you're just lonely?"

Jane studied the weave on the pillow in her lap.

"What keeps you here, in the middle of nowhere?" Shula persevered. "I don't understand."

"History, I guess." Jane shrugged off Shulamit's disconcerting comment. "And I like the pace. Besides, it's not the middle of nowhere, it's the middle of the country."

"But it's comfortable on the coast. Marie's there and, I hate to say it, but there's a little more going on."

"No you don't hate to say it . . . And yeah, I always have a great time out there. But I'm not stuck in the middle, going nowhere. There's stuff here I want to do. I'm going to start a masters in history. Women's history. I want to know more about Sophia and her time and who all those women were that I watched when I was a kid."

In the two and a half years since Shulamit's recovery visit, Jane had completed her course work, well supported by Judy Rubin, a dynamic faculty advisor who clashed lustily with the remaining sexist dinosaurs whenever necessary, and occasionally just for sport. Part-time work at her local community centre had supplemented meagre grant funding. During those same years, Shulamit had finished medical school and interned. Then, knowing distance could only help, she transplanted to the West Coast. Exhausted by years of young men thinned to spectres by AIDS, she had chosen geriatrics in the nation's retirement capital. "You know, natural causes," Shula said, and chuckled.

Jane laughed too, wondering how long manic Dr. Shulamit would last in the quiet of Victoria. Jane still waited for Shulamit to remember she was an artist and resume the hardcore urban life she had abandoned so suddenly. She suspected that, in slow-motion Victoria, the personal monsters Shulamit had avoided in her confrontational art would emerge, large as life and ready to prowl.

Jane closed the last box of her research material, walked back to the station wagon, slid it in and slammed the tailgate. It was spring in Muddy Water, a quick heady blooming before the dust of summer. At the cabin, the ice would have cracked and buckled on the meteorite lake, blown on the water until a gale heaved it into the driftwood cove or smashed it against the far cliff. The ground would be damp and ripe, the air pungent with moss and pine. The sun warmed Jane's back. She flexed the loose muscles in her lazy winter arms. Not one more day in that library basement. Time for bush and birch, for listening to crows and watching for the great blue heron, for sharing her mother's land with mother bears. Time to settle lakeside for the summer and drive the flat open highways to the city when she was needed at the community centre. Write the thesis at the apex of the triangle.

The cabin, where Sophia came back so easily. Where Jane would sort history in the pines. Find the roots of this women's world, beyond boundaries drawn by those who dated women's organizing from its institutionalization, from the initiation of the Royal Commission on the Status of Women, or academia's begetting of women's studies. Her unabated longing for Sophia's voice, for Sophia's mind, was the active agent in her research. She hoped that through knowing more about the times that had created Sophia—woman, mother, activist, politician—she might miss her less, that child's best friend. Might fill the chasm with women who made history, women who had organized, created, taught, nurtured, women who explained the world.

Pulling into traffic, Jane began to sing. *I'm a rambler, I'm a gambler, I'm a long way from home,* Phil's driving voice boomed

out of her, loud and off-key, Jane and her brothers accompanying from the back seat. She thought about feminism and Phil,
his attempts to keep up as Sophia scurried down a political path
that lead directly away from their marriage. Phil gobbling books
randomly, always looking, as he said, "for the point." If linearity
is the shortest distance between, therein dwelt Phil, zooming
from one point to another.

Phil devoured any book read by Sophia, or for that matter, by
Jane and her brothers. He read from John Hersey to Doris
Lessing, back across the Atlantic to Mary McCarthy, J. D.
Salinger and Saul Bellow. Norman Mailer and Kate Millett, side
by side on Sophia's bedside table, a critical conjunction. A trail
of Kurt Vonnegut, Richard Brautigan, Jack Kerouac and the
rest of the Beats strewn throughout the house after Owen's hol-
iday visits from college. And of course, then, a Salinger revival.
Mordecai Richler goes without saying. Phil's own man, same
roots. Grew up with a hundred Duddy's, from Fats the gonif to
Izzy the tax chiseller. "And all of them rich bastards now," Phil
would say. He was impressed with *Fear and Loathing on the Campaign Trail,* but *Fear and Loathing in Las Vegas* "didn't have a
point." As Sophia nightly mourned the persistence of her marriage, invariably ending the evening weeping into a glass of
scotch at the living-room coffee table, domestic pressure
mounted for Phil to bend his proud immigrant-kid-who-made-
it identity into something more compassionate and less compet-
itive. He read Studs Terkel's *Working,* Gail Sheehy's original
Passages, and the mid-seventies pop psych manifesto, *I'm OK,
You're OK.* He repeated the phrase like a non-believer's cate-
chism, turning to Jane as he zipped his sports car from lane to
lane, pointing his long index finger at his chest and announcing,
"I'm okay."

"Great. I'm okay too, Dad." Even at seventeen Jane doubted
this would save his marriage.

"No, I'm okay, you're—shit, that bastard cut me off. That
son of a bitch."

"Okay. I'm okay, you're shit that bastard . . ." She imitated Phil's snarl.

"Jesus H. Christ Almighty." Phil gunned the engine. "I'd've made that light if he hadn't cut me off." He braked abruptly.

"Dad, like, maybe you're not quite getting it." Same old Phil.

"What? He bloody well cut me off."

Jane pointed a long index finger at Phil and then at herself.

"Oh." Phil paused. "Okay, I'm okay, you're—"

"The light's green."

"Fuck the whole goddamned thing." He slammed the accelerator.

The memory amused Jane as she crossed the perimeter highway and rolled along the Trans-Canada between ditches brimming with tadpole-breeding water. Bulrushes jutted awkwardly skyward between grey road and rich black fields. Grain elevators, prairie signposts of cultivated land, led up to the evergreens of the Canadian Shield.

Wednesday, not a car in sight, just precious space. The station wagon rode easily on the flat four-lane highway. In just over an hour Jane would turn into an overgrown driveway, greet the ghosts of her growing years with a respectful whoop, and begin to ask questions. She would mull over facts gleaned from books and newspapers, half-remembered stories of those already elderly when they crossed the periphery of her childhood, women who were Sophia's confidantes and co-workers. Political women from Muddy Water, Toronto, Vancouver, Halifax and Montreal, from Europe, Africa and the Caribbean, from Peguis and Grassy Narrows, from Little Grand Rapids and Norway House. The bonds they fostered across their differences, the ones they couldn't. A long rumination with ghosts.

Jane flipped on the radio to the oldies station. Buffy Sainte-Marie's throaty voice crackled over the hum of the engine. *Yesterday a child came out to wander,* Jane sang along, thinking of Sophia, who loved the way this song spun the years round and round, Sophia who knew that life ran in circles and why.

Marie Latouche & The Mothers of Intention

SKY AND SEA are a muted waterscape, shades of grey embracing a liquid city. Rain visits in summer, stays awhile in spring and fall, becomes winter. But on generous mornings graceful mountains peer down, snowy and benign. Sunlight sheers a dazzling sight line across a clear Pacific horizon and the city opens like a lover. Your legs long to pedal through Stanley Park, your feet itch to stroll Beach Avenue and English Bay, your mouth waters for a bowl of wonton soup on East Hastings or fresh sushi in the West End. You are hooked, lushly in love with the city of Vancouver. And if your name is Marie Latouche, you occasionally long for a thick café bol on Montreal's St. Denis or the rhythms of reggae, bhangra, dub and salsa rattling Toronto's Queen Street West. When nights lengthen, you definitely ache for your long-distance lover, stubbornly rooted in the prairie city of Muddy Water—but not enough to ride the wind in an easterly direction. An occasional straying soothes. This watery city has seduced you.

On a grey day at the end of May 1993, Marie Latouche slipped out of the languid arms of Vancouver, and folded her thin body tentatively in the front section of the hoverfoil departing for Victoria. She had hoped to try the teetering hoverfoil service before it collapsed financially. Shulamit's arrival in Victoria provided the perfect prompt.

With effort, Marie ignored the video droning behind her through the morning, closed her eyes and sank back in the seat, anticipating Shulamit. Four years ago, Marie had left Toronto, trysted with Jane in Muddy Water, and flown over the mountains to nestle in coastal charms. Shulamit, the radical artist, spent the same years becoming a doctor. Shula, a doctor with a sad love story. Gloria. Marie struggled for recall, sore facts buried in her clouded mind, which was rapidly becoming a labyrinth of irretrievable information. Something—she had lately named the disruption Mazie the Amazing Mindmaze— was creating heavy static in her memory. Shula had volunteered in a shelter for assaulted women where Gloria worked, and what else? Marie knew they'd been close, and Gloria had died, but when Jane recently retold the tale on the phone, Mazie had cut loose and Marie had slipped into the hostile audience at a horrendous burning at the stake. The name Gloria was imbued with dense, choking smoke, reeked of the searing stench of sizzling human hair. When Marie had finally escaped the Maze, Jane was explaining that Shula had accepted a locum in Victoria, wanting to put Gloria's death firmly behind her and work with older people. Explaining that Shula had never really known her grandparents, just Grand-mère over in France whom she'd seen only four times. She felt the absence of older generations.

"What about her parents?" Marie had asked, fanning away her remembrance of horrible things past.

"Well, that's always been unclear," Jane answered. "For years her mother was so withdrawn. Asthmatic. Didn't like to leave the house, Shula says. All through med school Shula flooded her with drug samples; I don't know if anything helped." Jane sighed. "And Isaac, to use Shula's words, he just *is* . . . I don't know, maybe Shula doesn't see them as old. Happens to a lot of people. They freeze their parents as they knew them in childhood. Then some change breaks the mold. Adult children realize their parents are simply vulnerable human beings."

"It was pretty different for me, I guess. Just with Thérèse, oh she who is so wise," Marie taunted out of habit, exhaling fiery fumes.

"Hey, I've been there."

"You're stuck there." Mind still foggy, Marie resorted automatically to her favourite complaint. "Muddy Water forever. Where a Cammen is born a Cammen must die."

"Very funny. I ain't dead yet. What's bugging you? Lately you sound off."

Marie hesitated, but her struggles with Mazie were hard to explain long distance. She needed reassurance as she talked, to see Jane's face and know. Marie cradled the phone with her neck and wrapped her arms around her shoulders. Shivering bird huddled behind sheltering wings. "Nothing . . . uh, I'm just, uhm . . . feeding my oats."

"You're what?"

"I'm just feeding my oats."

"It's feeling my oats, 'Rie. It's a guy thing. A euphemism for their big hairy balls demanding attention. Or maybe it's about fucking around."

The infidelity dig and pet name eased Marie onto familiar turf. "No, sowing your oats is fucking around," she countered. "You know, horse-talk. Anyway, it's just a joke I make at the store when I fill the oat bin. I'm feeding my oats. Filling in time. I feel like I'm between things, like I'm standing on a new path, but there's a maze around me and I have to find my way out." Marie shuddered.

"Careful, then, 'Rie. Lost in a maze. Writing much?" she asked.

"Some."

"Anything you like?"

"Well, I'm close to something, but I'm not sure what it is exactly. I'm getting interested in history."

"That's the path . . . Told ya so," Jane mimicked a child.

"Yeah, and only about a thousand times," Marie snapped. "But where has all that history got you? You just miss Sophia more. You haven't put her death behind you." Marie stopped, surprised to be speaking long-guarded sentiments. "Sorry. Forget I said that. Anyway, women's history, so you're sort of right. But for me it's not personal."

"How could it not be personal?"

"I said sorry. Just because you're totally into figuring out your mother's life doesn't mean my stuff is personal," Marie insisted. "It's artistic, it's aesthetic, it's imaginary. My mom is a small woman teaching in Montreal."

Marie had been raised alone, by Thérèse, her mother, who offered no evidence of family, extended or otherwise. No mementoes, anecdotes or photos, only an uncomfortable silence in response to Marie's childhood questions. This absence weighed on Jane, but not on Marie. Or not that she acknowledged. Jane drew a breath to restrain herself. Too much time with books and memories, too many nights capped by a mounting tally of beer. "Sorry, sorry, sorry. I know, they're my obsessions. Shut up, Jane," she mumbled.

"Yeah," Marie agreed quietly, "Shut up Jane. Shut up Marie."

They sat, silently linked across half the continent.

"What kind of history, 'Rie?" Jane asked tentatively.

Marie hovered between flight and explanation. "Uh, kind of visual, imagistic. Painterly. I take events from women's history—well-known, almost over-represented events like, like, say the Salem witch trials—and write them from the women's point of view, you know, write the experience." Acrid smells, haunting voices, puzzle memories and nothing written.

Jane hesitated. It sounded so vague. Marie liked precision. "Maybe you'll send me some to read."

"See how it goes. They still need a lot of work."

With stiff reassurances of affection they had disconnected. Marie perched on the stool in her small, tidy kitchen for an hour, a thousand miles and more distant from her lover, staring at her notebook. Waiting for the Maze to open. Determined to trace its paths. Then irritated, she sighed, stripped and stepped behind the black shower curtain. A fine, warm spray rinsed away smoke memories. A thick, pumpkin-orange towel woke sleeping senses. Marie plucked charcoal jeans, a hot pink T-shirt and her over-sized black leather motorcycle jacket from closet hooks, slipped barefoot into Doc Martens. She put a twenty-dollar bill in her front pocket. Downtown, the Lotus was open another two hours. Women drinking and dancing, seeking and sparking. Marie unlocked her bicycle and pedalled toward the bar.

On the hoverfoil, Marie opened the blank notebook in her lap. Waiting. She hadn't written a line of poetry since the Maze first swallowed her. She was obsessed by it, yet too quickly and too fully seized. If there was a noticeable trigger, it eluded her. She munched idly on a bagel from the store leftovers. Working at the food co-op was tolerable. At first she had relished the sensuality, smells, tastes, textures. Healthy fruits of the earth. Gradually saturation diminished her ardour. Still, she could, this late morning, be roused by the grain of the bagel in her hand, the dark moist flavour in her mouth, rye and molasses and sesame blending. Out on the ocean, a figure, standing alone. An older white woman in a plain dark dress, pearl necklace below a stiff neck, solid shoes, no make-up, long grey hair loose in the wind. An apron tied around her waist. She stood, stock still, completely ill at ease. A nuclear family sergeant on stiff parade duty, awaiting inspection. Then behind her, a multitude. A thousand identical women clones in rows, perfectly still on the water.

Marie stared, groped for a pen in her jacket pocket. Her hand moved carefully across the smooth page as the women shape-shifted and danced. A thousand post-middle-age white women multiplied into a throng of women: young and old, children to ancients, Queens Cleopatra and Esther, Bengali women in suits and in sarees, Cree and Anishinabe women in ribbon dresses, buckskin, jeans and jean jackets, white punks in black leather, Victorian housewives in starched collars, pre-historic priestesses wrapped in flowing cotton. Maria, mother of god to some, with gold-brown limbs, obsidian black hair and an uncanny resemblance to Mona Lisa, rocked in the winds of time.

"This is a story," a lone, plaintive voice whispered.

"Told by an echo," another rode on the rising wind.

"A sound that repeats and repeats," an ominous chorus, rallied by drumming to a burgeoning elation, rose like a reign of terror broken open to freedom. Voices in complement and competition cajoled sky and earth. "All blood is our blood." Marie's free hand gripped the arm of her seat, the other scribbled feverishly. The sea rioted in front of her. Women danced and chanted. Twenty, thirty, forty feet above, a towering tidal wave bore down on the front of the craft. Marie tensed to leap from her seat.

"History ends," they shouted.

Instant calm. Marie awash in silence and sweat. Collapsed in her seat.

"Anything to drink?" A young man in a golf shirt loomed politely over her.

Marie forced her left hand to release the arm of the chair. Sucked a slow, quiet breath. "No, uh, no thank you," she mumbled, voice hoarse.

The engine hummed. The craft cruised across a peaceful day on a calm ocean. Marie's right hand stung, still locked on the pen. She eased it open and flexed. The notebook lay in her lap. The writing was cramped and uneven, but decipherable. Marie stared at the title. "The Freewomen's Chorus." Lines scribbled below. She had finally traced the Maze.

> *This is a story*
> *told by an echo*
> *a sound that repeats & repeats*
>
> *this is a song*
> *sung by a woman*

Honour

a cry in the night
a gasp of delight
a long shocking wail of creation

this is a moment
born out of history
a nightmare awakened
millions forsaken
that sharp stunning flash of destruction

this is memory
advancing genetic
bones flesh & blood
hear the freewomen's chorus

ground to ground
soil to sky
because of us
you live & die

All blood is our blood
We have spun this planet round
a million million times
& still you ask
what makes it spin?
still you ask
when does life begin?
still you ask
& now we answer
      this is the beginning of time
      this is the dance of creation
      this is the end of surrender
each woman states her own demands
each woman slaps thunder on this water
the ocean quivers & wakes

a tremendous flooding.
The millennium topples.

History ends.

We are the mothers of intention
ALL CREATION IS OUR INVENTION.

Marie clutched the notebook, mesmerized by her scrawl until the craft slowed to enter the inner harbour at Victoria. She solemnly closed the journal and placed it in her knapsack, as if sealing off a newly discovered sense. Marie had never believed writing arrived as an inspiration delivered by a generous muse. Writing was perception and thought, writing was craft and skill. Writing was desire honed to a razor's edge or conception swollen to bursting birth. It was not bestowed in excruciating psychic flashes, nor hidden away in a mind maze. Exhausted and raw, she clutched her knapsack and waited for the line of departing passengers to clear, fearing the touch of a stranger on her burning skin. She imagined leaping into the cool harbour water, sinking in safe cold. As the line ended, Marie stepped out and halted, staring longingly into the chill water. The damp air soothed her frenzy, a fine drizzle cleansed her face and doused her feverish nerves. She saw a muscular arm wave from the dock, and recognized the bedraggled Blue Jays sweatshirt she had given Shulamit at a raucous birthday party in Toronto. Marie felt the Maze recede, high tide turning on a weathered shoreline, and she a stone eroding under waves of pressure.

"I'll tell Shulamit," Marie vowed, relieved to see the warmth in her friend's knowing eyes. "I *will* tell her," Marie repeated, anticipating, with immeasurable relief, being folded into Shulamit's handsome breasts and lovingly crushed in the mother of all bear hugs.

4

Sophia Barry O'Connell & Miss Impudence

THE DAYS LENGTHENED toward summer solstice. Afternoons shimmered gently into evening, evening drifted lazily into night. The forest chattered through the dinner hour, chipmunks nattering, an old crow cawing overhead, loons calling out on the lake.

Jane hunched over a weathered plywood table set in long grass behind the cabin, reading an editorial on Kim Campbell's ascendence to the office of prime minister. She recalled a T-shirt Sophia had given her nearly twenty years earlier, printed by the federal party women's caucus, bearing the slogan "a woman's place is in the house of commons." Sophia displaying it, in high spirits, as they drove through a green summer evening to the Muddy Water Convention Centre.

"She's the first woman to run for the national leadership. Wait till you meet her, she's marvellous," Sophia gushed.

Through a very political weekend Jane watched Sophia work the convention floor against a clever whisper campaign that agreed the women's caucus candidate would be a great leader of the party, but asserted she could never be elected prime minister.

"They admit she's the better candidate, but say she'll never be accepted by the country," Sophia muttered, handing Jane a borrowed delegate's credential. "So they can't be accused of discrimination, although they're endorsing it. Get out there and talk to people." A firm hand guided Jane onto the convention floor.

"And say what?"

Sophia's eyes flashed blue anger. "Convince them to vote for the best candidate here today, and let her run for prime minister during an election. If they won't go on the first ballot, get them to come over when their candidate drops off. There's Jerry Berman—he can move a lot of votes to us if he wants to." Her eyes followed a short, bearded man, then turned back to Jane. "Talk to anybody wearing a badge for any of these . . ." She thrust a photocopied list at Jane and hurried down the aisle. "Jerry, just a minute there. Jerry!"

Excitement rose as the balloting progressed and the women's caucus candidate held second. During the long afternoon the women began to believe they might win. Delegates from eliminated candidates swelled their ranks. Jane could still picture their beaming faces collapsing as a major industrial union walked in to vote on the last ballot and, to a man, sported buttons supporting the leading candidate.

"White, male, backed by the party establishment." Sophia hissed as the count was announced. "She's worth ten of him." Then forced a smile on her face and went to offer congratulations on a race well-run.

"Could never be elected prime minister," Jane lectured the pines, "because she was a woman. An intelligent, articulate, experienced, Black woman." She turned back to the article. "Kim Campbell, Rita Johnston, Margaret Thatcher—always the wrong woman." Jane tapped out the names with a pencil, noting with irony that feminism appeared to work very well for women who certainly didn't work for feminism. She wondered if Prime Minister Campbell would last any longer in power than Premier Johnston had in British Columbia, or if the ol' boys only allowed a woman in to take the fall for an unpopular government. "Those old boys," she muttered, letting the newspaper drift to the ground.

The table was littered with clippings, reports and old photographs, letters in familiar and unfamiliar handwriting. Sophia's personal papers, boxed seven years since her sudden death. Since Bob, her affable second husband—who had lived on, gradually drowning in rum and remorse—had packed them in two cardboard boxes sealed with electrical tape, scrawled Jane's name and address in thick black marker and shipped them west from the shore of the Atlantic. They sat among Jane's clippings and notes, among books on leftist Canadian political parties and the emerging literature documenting the lives of women in Canada, past and present. Knowledge creeping out book by book. Academics sorting scattered scraps from public and personal archives. Activists taping life stories into oral history. Slowly piecing together a vibrant, layered history that would eventually supplant the flaccid, inaccurate and racist Canadiana served up in public schools. Or so Jane hoped.

Passing crows argued and were silent. Jane resisted plunging into the residue of Sophia's life. Although the material would be directly relevant to her thesis, it would also prompt memories—not Sophia on a new page of history, but Sophia the mother she still missed. Jane nervously broke off a long shoot of grass and chewed.

"If only she'd kept a journal," she gestured at a passing chipmunk. "I could just quote from it. 'Peace, Justice & Other Heirlooms: The Development of Socialist Feminism in Muddy Water 1955–70,' by Jane Cammen, copied from the journals of Sophia Cammen. Thank you very much, Mum." High above, the chipmunk chattered back.

Jane flexed her hands above the table, closed her eyes, reached and selected. Something small and rectangular, a thin leather-bound book. She opened her eyes on the dark green cover of a passport with "Eire" pressed faintly in the leather above the image of a harp. "Ireland" was legible below. On the inside cover was a message, first in Irish, then repeated in English and French. The Minister for External Affairs of Ireland requested "all those whom it may concern to allow the bearer to pass freely," signed, "Sean MacBride." Long-time leader of the

Irish Republican Army, son of Yeats' beloved Maud Gonne and a discarded husband martyred in the Easter Rising of 1916. His mother the guardian angel of Irish political prisoners. It was all in the Yeats that Sophia had treasured, ensconced by the fire on cool summer evenings, reading and smoking over amber scotch.

Jane's patchwork understanding of Irish history was woven from Sophia's random recitals of lines from Yeats' poetry, the plays of Sean O'Casey, a record collection Sophia inherited from her uncle, and facts dropped during Sophia's heated dining-table discussions with Phil. Puzzling details emerged from obituaries clipped out of the *Irish Times* by Granny and mailed to her daughter. Brief but complicated life stories of Sophia's aunts, uncles, and cousins, both first and second, as well as those described as once-, twice- and otherwise-removed. Often by the British police, it seemed to Jane. Like Grandfather, who spent a whole year in Kilmainham jail when he was caught running guns for the IRA.

"Removed?" a just-teenaged Jane asked, as Sophia drove to the Muddy Water International Airport.

"It's generational," Sophia explained, turning onto the new bridge and driving over the slow, brown river. "Niamh is my cousin, but you're her cousin once-removed."

"Why?"

"Because I'm her cousin, and you're my daughter."

"So, it's kind of like, if it's the same distance over, but you have to go down one, then it's called removed." Jane fiddled with the sleepers in her freshly pierced ears.

"Well, that'll do. Get me my cigarettes out of my purse, would you?"

Jane opened the beige leather bag at her feet. "How are you cousins?"

"Her father and my father were brothers."

"Gene says Niamh's father was kidnapped and that started the civil war." She found the pack, pulled out two cigarettes, gave one to Sophia and placed the other between her own lips.

"Yes, he was. As he stepped out the door of the house on Leeson Street. What are you doing?"

"Smoking. Did they ever catch who did it?"

"They always knew who did it. That's who they went to war with. The kidnappers were against the Treaty, De Valera and that bunch, killing for a nation. I always thought I'd quit if any of you were to take it up." Sophia sighed. "Do you smoke?"

"Gene says it was Sean MacBride and you supported him. Maybe."

"Later. I supported him later. Sides change a lot back home. They'd be killing each other one year and in the same cabinet the next. And back at it another year later. When we get to the airport, go in and get her, that way I don't have to park. I wasn't even born when Ginger was kidnapped." The lighter popped out, Sophia lit her cigarette and slid the lighter back in the dash. "What's maybe mean?"

"Ginger?" Jane reached for the lighter, held it to the cigarette in her lips. "What if she's not there. Who's Ginger?"

"Was. Come back, then. Niamh's father. If you're going to light it you have to inhale." Sophia stopped alongside the glass doors to the airport.

Jane inhaled and began to cough. She opened the door and put a foot out. "I tried it when I was a kid." She coughed again. "Just made me feel sick." She dropped the cigarette on the road. "Doesn't seem to have improved any."

"When you were a kid?"

"Grade six." Jane spat on the ground. "Got any gum or mints or anything?"

Sophia shook her head, laughing. "Well, you're certainly no smoker." She fished in her jacket pocket and offered a quarter. "Go on, she'll be here. Buy yourself a pack of something."

Jane entered the baggage area sucking heavily on a mint, as Niamh walked through the gate in sensible shoes and a pant suit, her mischievous smile tilted slightly to the right. Arriving for another summer in the Canadian wild.

"There you are, you cheeky brat. Well, give us a kiss. Hello, hello. Where's your mother? Would you ever carry this bag? There now, thanks. I've another big one. I don't suppose you've brought one of your monstrous brothers to take care of the luggage."

Giggling, Jane delivered the requested kiss. Somehow, Niamh never quite seemed like an adult. "No, no monsters."

"Monstrous, not monsters. Diction is essential, miss."

"Mom's in the car. I'll get a cart, we'll be all right. I can lift a lot." Jane proudly flexed her arms.

Niamh leaned seriously toward her. "Ladies do not display their muscles in public nor in private," she whispered archly, "nor do they brag about how much they can lift."

Jane bubbled with laughter. "You haven't given up, have you? Even Mom has given up." Jane flexed again.

Niamh O'Connell, weary after the long journey from Dublin to Muddy Water via London and Montreal, averted her eyes. "I'm making it my summer project. I shall turn you into a lady."

"If it helps I could kiss a frog," Jane offered. "I might go directly to princess."

"There, Miss Impudence." Niamh nodded at an immense navy suitcase. "My luggage. You may carry it if you wish."

"Might I?" Jane mimicked. "Why, that would be an honour."

"Such progress!" Niamh raised an arm in mock triumph. "And only my first hour. Now, where is your mother? I've got a monstrous bottle of gin."

And so it went through the summer. Sophia, Phil and the children showing Niamh Canadian life. Niamh, for the children at least, representing Irish customs. Gin-and-tonic with Sophia once the sun was high, playing bridge and demon patience till all hours, correcting spoken Canadianisms, and finally, almost inadvertently, teaching Jane one ladylike skill—crochet. At the same cabin where Jane now sat, studying her mother's passport, seeking the threads of that lost time.

Jane focussed again on the document. On the facing page

was written *Sophia Barry O'Connell, Saoranch d'Eirine/Citizen of Ireland, Passport # C61306.* The next page read *Cómharthai Sóirt/ Personal description*:

> Profession: *Ban Ghairmeoir/Horticulturalist*
> Place & Date of Birth: *23 11 1924 Baile Átha Cliath/Dublin*
> Domicile: *Éire/Ireland*
> Colour of eyes: *Gorm/Blue*
> Colour of Hair: *Fionn/Fair*
> Date of Issue: *17 Méan Fómhair 1948/17 September 1948*

Jane stared at the small black-and-white photograph of Sophia, cut crookedly across the top. Sophia at twenty-three, in 1948, a beautiful young woman with a determined gaze, a quiet calm beneath soft pale skin. So soft, even in a bland passport snap. Sophia as she set out for London, looking for a route out of Ireland's Catholic chokehold, escaping the tension of life in a close community, where everyone traced family through a civil war. Where the smallness of the nation cyclically rebirthed hatred.

"So I left," Jane heard her say. Escape was one of Sophia's favourite concepts, and marriage and family were the main jailers from which escape was necessary. Sophia longing to escape her marriage, Sophia advising Jane to escape Muddy Water on graduating high school, Sophia standing at the cooking island in the big remodelled kitchen of the house with the fossilized fish, lighting a menthol cigarette and praising the recent wedding cancellation by a friend's daughter.

"She's lucky to escape," exhaled in a big morning drag.

Lunch time, Jane home from school, Sophia had risen late after an arduous day travelling the province. Sleep in, breakfast in bed, late dinner, argue politics—Sophia's personal heaven.

"Did you ever want to go back?" Jane asked, chewing on an egg salad sandwich.

"To live?" Sophia gazed calculatingly into history. "No," she said finally, "never for longer than the first day of a visit back. After that it always closed around me. Suffocating." In faded blue chiffon-over-satin, loose-zippered housewear she referred to as a dressing gown. Joan Crawford descending a staircase in a satin robe had nothing on Sophia.

Jane studied the worn green passport, pleased to handle an object that belonged to Sophia's single years. Something Sophia's hands had held as a young woman. Jane saw Sophia's signature, the characteristic back slant of her lettering. Only the last name was different. Sophia B. O'Connell. Farther on, a stamp for twelve shillings paid on issuance, and another, three years later, on renewal, 12 July 1951, Irish embassy, London. Permitting travel to "All European Countries, their Possessions and Territories Overseas, Turkey, Syria, Lebanon, Egypt, Cyrenaica, Tripolitania, French North Africa, Spanish Zone of Morocco and Tangier."

Jane imagined Sophia in a matching jacket and trousers, like those she wore in a photo taken as she fed pigeons in Trafalgar Square. Her hair styled like Ingrid Bergman in Casablanca, her lips as full, her skin as soft under the lens, her eyes bigger and steadier. And she'd never fall for a cynical cafe owner with a hidden heart of gold. Sophia preferred a heart worn plainly on the sleeve.

Unlike Bogey's Rick, Sophia was truly a pacifist, and pacifism seemed to have provided her route from upper-middle-class domesticity to socialist feminism. First into the Voice of Women —Canada's sister organization to the American Women Strike for Peace—during cold war nuclear brinkmanship. Then, politicising year by year, from Voice of Women to the Royal Commission on the Status of Women to the activist National Action Committee, whose annual meeting Jane had just skipped for the first time in years. A path traversed by many women, but where did the pacifism root?

Jane searched the pages of the passport for clues. "Sûreté Nationale, Dieppe, Entrée, 22 sep. 1949." What did Dieppe look

like in 1949? "25 sep. Dieppe, Sorte." A weekend? One of those
trips to buy a carefully disguised *Lady Chatterley's Lover* or some
other title banned in England? Or perhaps a crossing with her
Aunt Aggie, who lived on the coast in Brighton, for the wine or
the air or just the adventure. Maybe with Niamh. Wouldn't
Niamh have come to London to visit, if she later came all the way
to Canada? The continent, Sophia always called it. It must have
beckoned even in its destroyed state. Perhaps the weekend in
Dieppe belonged to the affair that a lonely Bob conjured out of
unfinished sentences and memory fragments, after Sophia died.

"Ever notice how she didn't talk much about her life in London?" he said. "I asked about it but she would just kind of trail
off. And she would never go to the opera. Never. She loved
opera. I tried and tried to get her to go, but she completely
refused. I think there must have been someone. Someone she
was in love with, someone she went to the opera with, back in
those days in London. Remember, she went to an Italian community church to hear Beniamino Gigli. How did she know
Gigli would be singing in an Italian community church? Maybe
he was Italian . . ." His mind filled with questions that kept her
alive.

A lover? Why not? Jane thought. Give Sophia a lover for a
weekend in Dieppe, make it September, raining off and on, not
that it bothers Sophia on her first trip to France. He is older
and loves opera, loves doting on a younger woman. Between
caressing, laughing, eating and drinking, the weekend is almost
gone before Sophia notices the surrounding destruction, realizes
the weight of war, sees that her joy is purely personal. That their
happiness is at odds with the evidence of hatred and death. A
selfish love among ruins.

"Too romantic," Jane whispered to a hovering mosquito
before slapping it. She preferred Sophia with Aunt Aggie, sur-
reptitiously reading *Lady Chatterley's Lover,* huddled beneath
plaid wool blankets on the foggy deck of the channel ferry.

The passport contained a series of entry and exit stamps.

Valida para noventa dias en Espana, Londres 20 de Julio 1951. Nine days in Franco's Spain. Sophia in love with a young, lean Phil, having met him that spring at a party in London. Phil, with faint white skin, hair so brown it seemed black, waiting in Germany, conducting physicals for the Canadian government on Europeans who would flee the ruins to populate Canadian suburbia.

Dunkerque 7 aout 1951
Entrée Bundesrepublik Deutschland 8 08 51 Passkontrolle
Republik Osterreich 27 Sep 1951

The trip her parents had taken through Europe, a journey Sophia had always described as their honeymoon. When sixties freedoms spilled into the seventies, and Owen declared he would be moving in with his college girlfriend, Sophia changed her story.

"That trip through Europe. Well, dear," she admitted as they lay on the king-size bed in a late Saturday morning chat. Phil long gone on morning hospital rounds and a five-store grocery shop. "It wasn't really our honeymoon. We were married after the trip," she smiled mischievously. "Get me my cigarettes, would you."

"Never smoke in bed. So you won't care if I do that some-day—live with someone and don't get married?"

Sophia scowled. "Marriage is a trap."

At age fifteen Jane had heard the observation so many times it barely registered. Sophia's incantation short-circuited the usual social messages about the appropriateness of marriage.

"Come on, cigarette." Sophia nudged her. "Never smoke in bed at night, or when you're tired."

"So, noon Saturday is—"

"Perfectly civilized."

"And Phil won't care either?"

"He'll hit the roof. You watch. A son is not a daughter. But

I'll take care of your father when the time comes." A cold determination settled on her face. "You just worry about what's right for you."

The front door slammed. "Gene, Jane, come unload the groceries," Phil hollered up the stairs. "Get your mother out of bed and we'll all have brunch."

Sophia rolled her eyes. "Go on. I'll be down in a minute. Don't worry, you'll do what you need to do . . . And so will I." A quick shared glance confirmed the agreement.

Slowly Jane pieced together countries and dates. Sophia entered France at Dunkirk in August 1951. Perhaps a languid morning after an overnight crossing. Sophia dusting and straightening a simple, well-cut suit. Chatting easily with an older woman in front of her in the line for passport control. Phil might have met her here. More likely, she boarded a train for Germany alone. West German passport control, August 8, 1951. What was happening in Germany? Jane imagined only war and its aftermath, a country of bombed-out buildings, death camps hurriedly burnt to the ground, city after city only rubble. Millions who had been transported to work as slaves for the Reich still wandering the countryside, seeking home or family.

Jane wanted photos, immediately, wanted to see what Sophia saw, perceive the reaction in that fertile mind. Sophia bright and young, travelling to meet a Phil whom she loved, was almost unimaginable to Jane. She wanted to be inside those eyes looking out at the world, seeing the crowds of stateless people Phil examined, walking streets where history had reduced itself to dust.

Or did her resolve form earlier, in August 1945, six years before Sophia visited Germany. Sophia had been twenty, almost twenty-one, studying horticulture in Dublin, living with her aunt and uncle. By her own report, a less than serious student who scheduled her classes so as not to conflict with a thriving social life. A lively young woman waltzing at balls, relishing rebellion and slowly realizing that she needed another, larger world.

What did the *Irish Times* report when the Americans dropped atomic bombs on the citizens of Hiroshima and Nagasaki?

Jane tried to don her mother's skin. Summer in Dublin. Not cool, not hot, often sunny. The war in Europe is over, finally. It marked your teenage years, but your country, unlike those around you, was not invaded or bombed, its citizens were not murdered in the hundreds of thousands, by the millions. Yet in neighbouring countries, families were broken up by forced labour, forced military service and murder. People were shunted in trains to secret destinations, exploitation camps and murder camps, and systematically killed. All of this slowly became clear as you aged from eighteen to nineteen to twenty, twenty-one, twenty-two. As your young mind, already socialist at fifteen, already anti-Catholic, learned the genus, species, life span and growing needs of clematis and lilies, carnations, rose bushes and geranium. All to transplant to a land where gardening is a short-season pastime. Did you need to see Germany in ruins to make a lifelong commitment to pacifism? Was nearby war enough? Did the Easter Rising, the gun-running, your father's imprisonment, the deeply embedded hatreds after the Treaty, convince you that pacifism is the only alternative? Or did it slowly settle into you, during the years in London, as the longer-term effects of Hiroshima and Nagasaki were reported, after you travelled through Europe in the brilliant lovelit August and September of 1951, you and your blue-eyed Jewish lover in a Canadian army jeep, rolling over bloodied earth in love and anguish?

A chipmunk chattered. Jane shook herself from reverie. Evening shade skirted the table. She let a citronella candle for light against darkness and evening mosquitoes, picked up a pen and wrote a short list:

photos — Germany / Austria / Spain / France 1951
newspapers — Irish Times Aug. 1945
London Times July / Aug. 1951
German dailies Aug. 1951

Marshall plan implementation
Owen / Gene — where did Phil work in Germany?

Most of what she gathered might be extraneous to her final thesis, but not to her journey toward it. She returned to the face in the passport photo. Sophia Barry O'Connell, twenty-three, leaving Ireland for London, for theatre in the West End, pubs and restaurants and opera and literature, for the rest of her life. Jane turned the page to a last entry stamp she had not yet recorded:

Canada Immigration, May 16, 1952, Quebec, P.Q.

5

Dr. Cynical & Little Crow

SHULAMIT WATCHED WITH concern as Marie stood eye-ing the harbour water like a road to salvation. Watched Marie wipe a watery eye with the back of her small, bony hand. The gesture echoed to a Sunday, years ago, Shula sketching those hands over and over. Lean and skeletal, palms covering Marie's eyes. Shula gradually began to sketch Marie as birdlike. By the end of the day she had renamed her Crow. "Crow's hands on crow's feet" was the title of the finished painting hanging in Jane's living room in Muddy Water. See no evil, little Crow, Shula thought, waving at her friend. Do no evil, come here to me and we will talk good talk, like in the old days when we were young and unscathed. Marie finally saw her and smiled her sweet bird-smile. She hurried onto the wharf, and flung her arms around Shula's solid body.

"Hi, Doc," Marie mimicked. "What's up?"

"Cute as ever," Shula answered, consciously enfolding the wounded bird in her ample flesh. "Weren't thinking of jumping there were you?"

Marie shuddered.

"Problems?" Shula whispered, releasing her.

"Been a little tense lately," Marie shrugged. "I mean, there's something I'd like to talk to you about, but not here and now. Later." She smiled her sugar smile again and planted a loud kiss on Shulamit's lips. "I'm okay, really."

"Miracle recovery," Shulamit joked. "See, I didn't need all

that education. I am a true and natural healer of the soul, mind and body. Sent to this planet from a dimension beyond knowing. And that is why I live on this distant shore, for it is a green, sentient place, where healers like myself are recognized. Here, our true spiritual natures and amazing mysticism are revered. If a patient calls in the middle of the night I just say, 'Take two capsules of golden seal with a cup of valerian tea, and if you're female and born after 1953 put a teaspoon of live-bacteria yogurt in your vagina. If you don't feel better in the morning, call me.'"

"Yeah, Shul, and pigs have wings. I know you have more respect than that for homeopathic medicine." Marie climbed the steps from the wharf to the road, absently studying her friend's muscular calves. "You forget how long I've known you, Dr. Cynical."

Shula motioned to a car parked down the block, Toronto-style, two tires on the sidewalk, emergency flashers blaring. Marie chuckled.

"I thought Jane said you were on some kind of healing trip out here, calming lifestyle and all that," Marie said coyly.

Shula flushed. "I told you. I am the healer."

"Well, you park like the same revved-up artist I knew on the shitty winter streets of Toronto. Ah, Toronto, the slush, the commotion, the streetcars—"

"The espresso bars—"

"Hours at A-Space and YYZ, lives described by the distance between two artist-run galleries, an Italian cafe and a filthy bar." Marie laughed.

"The Cameron House was not filthy," Shulamit argued, "it was the, the molten core, the sun, the light source, radiating through us."

"Sure it was, but it was also filthy. We didn't notice 'cause of all the black paint."

"I put some of that paint there myself," Shula reminisced. "You remember, the IncreMental Death Free Association Wall-

Writing campaign. Linking cruise missile testing, American funding of Salvadoran death squads and the so-called pro-life movement. 'Pro-life equals no-life, like it? Cruise sex not war.' " She chuckled. "I had to paint black over all the slogans I drafted on the wall of The Cameron . . . We had the kunst then, eh Crow?" Marie noticed a wistfulness in Shula's gaze as she unlocked the passenger door.

"What happened, Shula? Why'd you give it up?"

Shula ignored her and rounded to the driver's side. Her glance met Marie's across the roof of the car. "Art lost its power," she muttered, ducking into the vehicle.

Marie slid into the other seat. "Just for you? Or completely?"

"I don't know. I can't feel it any more. I haven't for . . ." Shula sighed, turned the key in the ignition. The engine rolled over like a blender chewing a wooden spoon. "Well, for a long time."

"You make it sound like sex."

"Gee, I'm so glad you came." Shulamit switched on the radio.

"Today the government of Ontario announced an inquiry into—"

"I thought we were talking." Marie spun the volume knob down.

"We are, but, there's a game on." Shula flicked it back up. ". . . school near Cochrane, Ontario," the announcer's voice continued.

"Hey, that's where my friend Donna practised in the sixties." Shula fiddled the tuning dial looking for the game. "She said there was a Catholic school there that rivalled Mount Cashel in the evil-doings department."

"I'm so glad Thérèse dumped Catholicism when she left those parts," Marie remarked, "and I avoided inculcation."

"Donna might be called, you never know," Shula speculated. "I think she treated kids there."

Strains of the American national anthem filtered into the car and a baseball crowd roared.

"There's the game."

"Okay, but low, then, please?"

"Okay." Shula adjusted the volume, and slipped the car into gear. They lurched forward as Shula pulled off the curb and turned right toward the James Bay neighbourhood.

"About art though," Marie returned to her original subject, "I'd like to hear what you think, because my writing, like, it's changed lately. Anyway, what do you think? Is making art meaningless, so totally self-referential, and unengaged with our, um, our socialness that it's irrelevant? You know, I mean, is it only about art now and not about people?" Marie felt sweat rise on her brow as she spoke. She rarely articulated these questions and was surprised how stale they sounded, as if she already knew the answer, or perhaps, more accurately, the answer knew her.

"Hell, Marie, I really haven't thought about it for years. I shut down a long time ago. I treat patients now. I poke about in other people's bodies the same way you stock the cooler with goat's milk and veggie burgers. True, I understand that they're people—hello, how's the weather, have you heard from your children, grandchildren, great-grandchildren, lately—but, really, I'm trained to look quickly and see. Her colour is fading, there's a tremor in her hand that wasn't there last week. His legs are swollen, circulation is collapsing faster than I thought. Does she have coverage for home care? Probably, only the middle class and wealthier retire here. It's certainly different from assisting boys to die before they're forty, before they're thirty, even. What did you ask? Oh, yeah . . . Art."

Marie studied Shulamit's profile. Eight years ago, Shulamit spent every weekend absorbing the contents of Toronto's downtown and parallel galleries. Immersed in the work created, swimming in dialogue about art, soaking it up. For years, she participated simultaneously in four artist-run spaces, conducted guerilla artfare campaigns, solo and with other paint-happy anarchos, spreading sedition at any and every opportunity.

Marie hadn't seen her since Shula departed for France on her grandmother's death. The next she knew, Shula was a mature student in the medical program at McMaster University. Days gone by like a travelling circus rolling out of town.

"Yeah, art," Marie said quietly, hearing Shula's truth in her drift. It had to be social to matter, whatever the activity, it had to link human beings to be a worthwhile endeavour. Shula turned and braked.

"I'll get into it later. My stuff, I mean," Marie added. Repeatedly raising the topic might actually bring her to discuss it.

"Anytime. I'll just be a minute," Shula answered. "Have to pick up some stuff here." The car door slammed behind her. Flashers blinked.

Marie glanced around. The surrounding foliage was overgrown, hanging thickly above the windshield. She flicked off the radio. In the quiet Marie closed her eyes and listened to a breeze blowing gently, like distant voices calling her. Little crow on the wind, flying back in time, soaring on sound. "Quietly seek us," Marie heard. She clutched the knapsack against her leanness. "Remember." Her ears rode the breeze, her hands fumbled with the bag, reaching for pen and notebook. "Remember," a woman said. Eyes closed, Marie listened and scribbled. "This is your task, look once and remember."

Cautiously, Marie opened her eyes. Around the car, in every direction, women hung from the trees. Hung from the neck, heads bowed, bodies limp. Sarongs and shirtwaists fluttered in the wind, denim overalls and wool skirts cloaked lifeless limbs. In a shared motion, the women raised their heads and opened their eyes. Death stared from all directions. Marie jammed her feet against the floor, sunk her head behind cowering shoulders. "Remember, look now and remember," the women intoned. "We are your burden," they rumbled from the soul of the earth. Marie trembled, the car shook, trees quivered. She tucked tight, tiny and fetal, waiting for the ground to swallow Shula's prized wreck. The rag-doll women dangled in the whipping winds. Nausea gripped her stomach. The earth stilled to an eerie calm. The pendulum women swung to a standstill.

Above appeared the image of a turn-of-the-century Tahitian woman, a floating stereotype lifted from Paul Gauguin's painting *Ia Orana Maria*. She sat in her red sarong with grey and white flowers, a Lady Day white gardenia immaculate in her perfect black hair. She waited. Then, soundlessly she drifted down to the hanging women. The still, hanged women. Carefully she raised a head, brought her lips to kiss death's eyes and lips. Tenderly she nursed each woman, mouth to mouth. Long, slow, life-giving kisses. She lifted each woman's head, fed each woman's bloodless lips. And one by one they wakened. One by one stretched arms to the sky, raised a hand to the rope, yanked it free, loosened the noose and flung it to the sky. Floated down to stand on hallowed ground. The women began to talk and sing, to hug each other. Their chattering grew louder. "Our tongues muscle." The sound built voice by voice. "We are not the womb of your species." A tide of bittersweet liberation rose. "We gave you life." Marie soared on sound waves, riding curl after curl. Unafraid, exulting in a choral euphoria, swept out to sea, past the beachheads of civilization. Alone in an aural hurricane, she surfed that sharp-edged horizon separating justice and revenge. So far out to sea.

In the distance, the crackle of a radio. Marie felt a pen in her hand, a notebook in her lap.

"Marie! Hey—Marie!" It was Shula's voice. "Getting in touch with the muse?" Marie turned. Shula's face contradicted her joking tone. "What is going on with you?"

Marie squinted. The car, the radio, Shulamit, all were beckoning lights on a far shore as she sailed back from that watery frontier.

"Lots, I guess," she finally allowed, sailing, sailing. Then she giggled, still giddy with exultation. Fear had vanished. Marie chuckled again, then struggled to calm herself before Shulamit decided she was off the proverbial rocker. But then, she was. Yanked out of life's ruts by Mazie the magician and her fantastic hallucinations. Laughter bubbled up Crow's long throat. She glanced over. Shulamit was dividing her attention between the road and the notebook, still wide open in Marie's lap. Marie snapped it shut. Two pages had been full. The only words she made out were "Hateful: Permissible."

"That's a powerful muse," Shula said again, wondering if she had any tranquillizers stashed in the house.

"Bottom of the fourth and Morris retires the side," the commentator interrupted.

"All right!" Shula punched the horn and turned off Government.

"All right!" Marie yelled, catching a glimpse of long black spandex striding up the steps of an old hotel. "Who's Morris?"

They laughed together. Shula put a hand firmly on Marie's shoulder as she stopped the car beside a multi-storied wooden house desperate for a new coat of paint. Marie ignored the question put by the gesture.

"Gee, nice place I turned you on to." Marie's friends hadn't mentioned the condition of the house.

"It's fine for now. The inside is in better shape. And the others are hardly around, which I like. I seem to like the feeling of living in a shared place much better than actually hanging around with housemates."

Inside the house was cool and heavy with dark wood. They dropped Marie's bag upstairs in the larger of Shulamit's two rooms, then settled in the kitchen for tea. Shulamit filled a deep-red enamel kettle, put it on to boil and sat down facing Marie.

"So, what's up Marie? You looked pretty strange when I got back to the car and you've been clutching that notebook ever since, like it's your deceased lover's last pair of underwear."

Marie grinned as fire-engine-red bikini briefs flitted through her mind. "Last pair of underwear?" She covered quickly, "Shulamit, who do you spend your time with?"

"No one, mostly. But don't evade."

Marie cradled the notebook, wrapped in little crow wings. "Okay, there's something. And it's confusing, and kind of well, like, easily misunderstood." Her head sunk beneath sheltering feathers. "I want to talk to you about it." She offered one word at a time. "I really do." Unfathomable bird eyes darting away. "But unless you have a few hours now, let's not start until later."

"A few hours?" Shulamit didn't want to wait. Since being almost unable to snap Marie out of her trance, a roll of devastating diagnoses had run through her mind.

"Don't worry. It's not a bad thing. I mean at first it seemed like a problem, but now I think maybe it isn't. Maybe it's okay. Maybe it's good, even."

"Not a bad thing? Crow, I'm flexible, but you sat speechless in the car, staring into space, writing without looking at the page. Now, and do correct me if I'm wrong, you're afraid to look at what you have written. This is not good. Welcome to catatonia, little Crow."

"Uh, afraid might be a little strong . . . You saw all that?" Marie studied Shulamit. Her interest was startling. Mazie somehow became more real and more imagined, in the same moment.

"Yeah. I tried to talk to you. You didn't hear me. Then I threw my stuff in the back, started the car and turned on the radio. Finally, after a few blocks, you tuned in."

"Tuned in . . . tuned out. That's a good way to put it." Marie paused, enchanted by the sense that someone was actually speaking to her, the real Marie, reaching all the way in for the first time since the advent of Mazie. "And, at the time, nothing else seemed strange to you?"

"Isn't that strange enough?"

"No, I mean like . . ." Marie waved her hand in air, as if to point out women hanging from the trees. "Never mind," she murmured. Shulamit hadn't seen them. But were the women in the trees or in her mind? Were the trees in her mind? She could touch the trees . . .

"I'm not letting this go," Shulamit insisted, restraining an impulse to frighten Marie into talking.

Marie twitched and refocussed. "Later. I promise. You know, you're not the most open woman in the world yourself, Shulamit. You ought to understand," she argued back.

"Yeah. But you were gone, Crow. You were so far away . . ." Shulamit detested pressure to open up. "Okay," she said reluctantly, "but, later, without fail."

"I promise. Poet's honour."

"Is there such a thing?"

"Of course. Just like among thieves."

"Honour." Shulamit thought of her Jane Doe. "Okay, mysterious Crow. I have a mystery of my own." She pulled a key out of her pocket, a key and a metal disk on a ring. On the disk was the number 309. She dangled it above Marie's mug of tea. "What's this?"

"A key."

"To what?"

"Number 309."

"Care to go look for it?"

"Shula, care to tell me what's going on?"

"In the car. Two can play at this game. And we need to buy a bed for you. Unless you want to sleep on the floor, or with me. We could always do that."

"Do what?"

"Sleep together," Shula teased.

"Okay." Marie grinned, throwing a mighty crow-wing punch. "But it's more than a game."

"I know. Come on," Shula was ready to move again. "First the mystery. Then to bed or not to bed."

"Anytime."

"But the flesh is not willing."

"I know, sex just doesn't have any meaning any more," Marie needled. "It's just, you know, sticky and fun." She plucked a ripe red strawberry from a basket on the counter and bit in.

"Maybe it never did."

"Love, on the other hand—" Marie wiped her lips with the back of her bony hand "—love is positively dripping." She swallowed the last of the berry and licked her lips. "And sometimes no fun at all."

"Enough . . . let's go." Shula stood at the door motioning to Marie to finish her tea. "Or bring it. This is such a slow town."

"Relax, old Shu. Get into the coastal groove. You're going to kill yourself trying to speed this place up to eastern urban. Anyway, where are we going?"

"To find number 309." Shula dangled the key. "Could be a locker, could be a dormitory, could be a safety deposit box. But I say it's a motel. And you say?"

Marie raised the mug and gulped tea. "Motel," she choked out. "Or hotel. I know one with nice legs."

Shula missed the innuendo. "Let's start where I found the key. And on the way I'll tell you a story."

As they drove toward the water, Shulamit told her tale of coming upon an older woman having a stroke—an older dyke, she suspected, which Marie challenged for lack of evidence—and of admitting the woman as her patient. The woman had regained consciousness in time for a fairly optimistic prognosis, though it appeared she had expressive aphasia, which, Shulamit explained, meant she couldn't speak or write, yet. One side of her body was completely paralysed, for now. She possessed no identification beyond a ring engraved with the initials S.S.W. and the only word Shulamit had ever heard her speak was "honour."

"Nice word." Marie curled her tongue around it. "Honour. Kind of lengthens out and then rolls forward. But what does it mean?"

"Lots of things. We can check the dictionary later."

"Very funny."

"I'm not being funny. We can check the dictionary later. This is a mystery."

"So, what you have is the word 'honour' and the initials S.S.W. and a key to room 309. And you want to know who she is."

"Yep. And a patient, of course. I have the body."

"Shouldn't the police be notified? I mean, she must have family or friends or something. Someone who's worried."

"The hospital would have done that."

"Why didn't they give the police the key?"

"Key?" Shula replied guiltily.

"Shula—" Marie sized her up. "I knew you couldn't have changed that much. This isn't entirely kosher, is it?"

"Well, it's not exactly traif either. I'm her doctor. I'm responsible for her."

Marie eyed her silently.

"Okay," Shula sighed, stopping by a large, stone-walled pond with carved Victorian benches scattered around its edge. "I admit, I shouldn't have taken the key. But the police will take ages and probably turn it into a big mishigass. If I can't find the place, I'll just turn it over to them with some story. No fuss, no muss." She opened the car door. "Come on."

"Where to?"

"Over there. Under that tree. That's where she collapsed." Shula saw the woman falling again, and concentrated on the image. "I want to see if she dropped anything."

Marie followed Shula. They crawled on the grass under the tree for ten minutes before agreeing that there was nothing to be found.

"Which way did she come from?" Marie asked, unconsciously running her hand across soft grass. She picked a blade and rubbed it between her fingers for the aroma, a work habit. Dill, sage and tarragon perfumed her ringed fingers.

"From the path—here—it goes down to the sea wall. It's a

great walk. She was really labouring as she came through here."

"Want to check it out?"

"Might as well."

The path led between full trees, gently sloped down to the left and then disappeared around a curve in the shoreline. Marie's breath danced as she brushed a branch away and gazed out over the strait at the white peaks of the Olympic mountains. "Wow . . . you think I'd be used to it."

"Gorgeous, aren't they. I'm starting to think of the mountains as protectors. They seem so sturdy and constant." Shulamit mimed a body builder raising a weighty barbell aloft. "Like you could lean as far back on them as you needed and they'd stay exactly in place. Undaunted, unflinching even, holding you up."

"Very cool, Shul." Marie winked.

Shulamit studied the range. "I like to walk here. It's about the only altered behaviour I've adopted." Marie put an arm around Shula's shoulder and squeezed gently. They strolled on, watching the ground as it neared sea level.

"How far do you think she walked?" Marie asked.

"Hard to say. She looked so weak, it seems like she couldn't have gone far. But maybe she brought it on by overstraining . . . No, it's more likely she felt weak and didn't walk far. After all, she'd already come here, either by bus or walking from wherever she lived or was staying. There weren't any car keys in her pockets."

"Might have been in a bag or something."

"Yeah, but if a car was towed, the police should have put it together with her collapse by now."

"So let's assume no car. If she was out for a walk, she probably didn't take the bus," Marie surmised.

"True enough. Why would she take the bus, just to walk here? More likely she came from nearby, Sherlock."

"Herlock, please, Dr. Cynical."

"I think there are hotels in the neighbourhood. Of course, the harbour is clogged with them." They had turned back and were making their way up the incline. "It is a little taxing." Shula breathed the comment out heavily.

"It's also a little beautiful." Marie nodded toward the expanse of white-blue water. The sky fading pale blue, distant and easy. "I saw an old hotel as we turned onto your street."

"That's right. The St. James. First stop." Shula watched the sunlight catch Marie's prism earring and refracted a full spectrum across her feathery neck.

Before getting in the car Shula paused again. Replayed in her mind the scene of Jane Doe collapsing. Nothing had fallen away from the woman's body. There had been no other words or sounds, just "honour."

"I don't think we've missed anything," she said, half to herself, opening the door.

"She wasn't unconscious when you found her, was she?"

"No, I saw her fall and I ran from the car, and I saw, I mean I had a flash of—of Gloria's face." Shulamit shifted uncomfortably. "Then I asked if she was okay, and what her name was. And all she said was 'honour.' "

"You didn't mention asking her name before."

"Sorry I—"

"No, I mean, maybe she answered your question."

"What? 'Honour' is her name?"

"Yeah, Honor is a name. Like Honor Blackman—quite the handle for a white woman—the first Mrs. Peel, in *The Avengers*, before Diana Rigg." She wolf-whistled. "Black leather from nape to stiletto. It's a British name."

"She told me her name? I don't know . . . she was pretty far gone. I don't think she even heard me. And what about the initials in the ring?"

"Maybe you heard wrong, maybe it sounds like Honor."

"Yeah, like maybe her name was Donner, or Blitzen for that matter."

"Honor . . . Donner . . . Sauna . . . Shawna," Marie chanted.

"*Shawna, Shawna bo-bonna*," Shula sang, drumming on

the steering wheel, "*-bo-nana-fana-bo-bonna, fee fi fo fawna, sha-awna!*" She tapped the horn as she finished.

Marie pinched her round cheek. "Very cute, Shula. Well, keep it in mind, it's still a possibility. Honor. I like it. Nice sound. Well, that hotel then, Dr. Cynical?" Marie asked.

"The St. James," Shulamit replied, backing the car onto Dallas.

An hour later they had tried unsuccessfully to match the key at the St. James and a half-dozen other hotels near the inner harbour. Shulamit had exhausted her limited patience and was inclining toward delivering the key to the local police station. Marie yawned drowsily and considered the possibility of a power nap, a habit she indulged with increasing frequency. Mazie's adventures were draining. Dispirited, they drove along the curve of Dallas Road, rolling beside a blue canopy of sky and water. They almost overlooked the small square building on the city side of the road, a dozen white metal balconies hanging on grey stucco. The Surf Motel, blinking vacancies.

The lobby was small and panelled in wood. It belonged somewhere in a California of '49 or '56 or maybe even '62. A bottle-blond woman in a turquoise sweatsuit and pink headband listened to Shulamit's story of finding the key on a patient who'd arrived unconscious at the hospital.

"She collapsed near here, so we thought maybe . . ." Shulamit laid the key on the counter for the woman to see.

"That's ours, all right. 309, 309, 309," she cracked her gum smartly. "Yeah, I thought so. Older woman. Kinda quiet. Sarah S. Wise. Toronto, Ontario. Ms." Shulamit flashed Marie an I-told-you-so glance. "Too bad."

"Too bad?" Shulamit asked politely.

"The address. She didn't fill it out completely. Just says Toronto, Ontario."

"I should be able to get more information through the health-care system."

"Just how sick is she? I mean she booked for a week, but we just took the one night payment in advance. She comin' back?"

"No, she's not likely to leave hospital this week."

"Why you looking into this anyway? You sure you're a doctor? How do I know? Why aren't the police lookin' after this?" Marie giggled.

"I assure you, I am Dr. Shulamit Weiss, fully qualified general practitioner. The police have been notified, but I found the key later. I'll be happy to pass it on to them," she offered benignly.

"Now I can do that myself," the woman snatched the key off the counter as Shulamit reached out. "You just have them call me and verify all this so I can clean out her room in good conscience." Shulamit seethed, a grizzly writhing deep in her spirit.

"What do you normally do with belongings left behind?" Marie asked, separating the antagonists. Shulamit drummed the counter loudly with her thick fingers, glared at the woman, clenched her teeth.

"Well, normally it's just a toothbrush or a pair a panty hose, maybe a lost sock. Single earrings. Used to get a lot of cufflinks but no one wears them any more. This is different though. Guess we should turn it over to the police, let them find the owner."

"But—" Shulamit started.

"I guess," Marie cut her off, "it might be best if the woman, I mean Ms. Wise, if she had the things with her at the hospital. You'd think she'd want them as she recovers."

"Guess so. Yeah, that sounds right."

"So maybe Dr. Weiss could come back for them, after you've had a chance to get them together."

"Maybe she could bring a note, or something saying it's okay." The woman eyed Shulamit with hostility. "Can't give away a guest's belongings to anybody who finds a key in the ground and comes in with a story. Maybe the police could give you a note."

"A note? From the police?" Shulamit's voice trilled a piercing register.

"Well, sure, I guess we could get them to give you a call or something. Just to be on the safe side," Marie said in complicity, enjoying Shula's frustration. "You keep that key and we'll get someone in authority to call you Ms.—?"

"Donald, Mrs. Donald. You just have them call the Surf Motel. I'll be here."

"We'll do that," Marie promised, linking her arm through Shulamit's and backing away. "Let's just leave," she whispered to Shula. "Most of the time I don't believe you're a doctor either. So come quietly." Marie waved and smiled pleasantly, guiding Shulamit through the glass doors. Outside she collapsed in laughter as Shulamit raised a tight fist to smack the sky.

6

Sarah S. Wise & The Old Grey Mare

"Hateful: Permissible." In the cafeteria of the Royal Jubilee Hospital, Marie waited for Shulamit to finish her rounds, fingers tracing words in her notebook, sensing for meaning like a new lover mapping old scars. "Hateful: Permissible." She pictured the women hanging again, a vivid memory in conscious recall, sipped her tea and continued reading.

We are no longer dirt & stone
no more the dust of time blowing
we are unearthed & howling
our lives & deaths the same
hanging by a thin rope
from the tree of our betrayal

We are the dead awakened
& cannot be mourned
we are the dead restored
the women you scorned

Tongues sliced from us
restored
breath choked from us
restored
life bled from us
restored

Our tongues muscle speech
in defiance

We are not the womb of your species
you are
> *the mechanism of ours*

Arise
the millennium of destruction ends
Awake
see the line of time bend
Rise up
the murdered & betrayed
for now
debts must be paid

> *WE SHELTERED YOUR BODY*
> *WE NURSED YOUR BREATH*
> *WE GAVE YOU LIFE*
> *YOU GAVE US DEATH*

"Well, it has a cheery ending, anyway, that bit," Shula announced, peering over Marie's shoulder.

Marie looked up, startled. Shula's slightly anxious face hovered above her.

"You'll get hypertension, flinching like that every time I speak to you. Could develop nervous tics, psychosomatic allergies, insomnia. It's a quick sharp slope to complete emotional dysfunction. Even a sharp crow can plunge down it."

"Thank you doctor know-it-all . . ." Marie pouted, slumped in the orange plastic chair. "I hate hospitals."

"Why? What's to hate?" Shula raised an arm and gazed benignly on the almost empty cafeteria. She had little patience with squeamishness.

"People get sick here, people die here," Marie squawked.

"There are body parts being stored for garbage. Pans full of piss and shit and vials of blood —"

"I hate to break it to you," Shula cut in sharply, "but that's what all that wonderful healthy food you sell is for. To make piss and shit and blood and spit and all the other lovely substances that sustain us. It's all organic, Marie. You'd have to shelve it with your overpriced organic grains. 'Course, it might keep better in a cooler, say between the rennetless cheese and the tofu. A little plastic container labelled 'human fecal matter, low-fat high-fibre diet, nine ninety-nine for a hundred grams.' " Shula began to giggle.

Marie hunched between protective wings. "It's so aggressive and diagnostic and linear. It's so re-*ductive*." She spat the word out.

"What is? Shit? Piss? Blood? How about a little pus or mucous thrown in?" Shula whispered angrily, conscious of their location.

"No, allopathic medicine." Marie stared at her, coal eyes densely determined.

Shulamit relished Marie's passion. A long-lost engine of desire, slumbering within, stirred slightly. "Watch it, Crow, you're outnumbered here," she taunted quietly.

"You know what I mean, Shula, I don't believe you don't know what I mean." Marie inhaled sharply. "Allopathic medicine treats the body part and not the body and most certainly not the person." She waved an emphatic index finger. "It totally ignores prevention and fights tooth and nail—no, scalpel and claw—against any kind of devolution of medical authority to people with other approaches." She was leaning across the table, her thin, sculpted face inches from Shula's.

The buried beast of lust woke fully. Shula's teeth pulled on her bottom lip. Damn, that feels good, she realized. Her eyes roamed the curve of Marie's cheekbones, the clean line of her lips. She put a hand heavily on Marie's left shoulder.

"Crow, I learned to be a doctor; I didn't change into some-one else."

"People always change, Shula," Marie said quietly. "Jane believes everything we do, everything we live through, changes us."

"Jane is enamoured of process, Crow. Take her as an example. She says everything changes us, but she always has and always will say that. She doesn't change. That's just what she notices, what she focusses on. The processes we go through. I might have been an artist last time we met, and that might seem like a lifetime ago to both of us, but I still think in the same way about things. I just think about different topics. It feels the same, only less abstract."

"Do you like it better, being less abstract?"

"Better?" She paused. "Yeah, I guess I do. It's not just that I feel more directly useful, it's, I guess, hands on, is the way to say it. I feel dug into the core of life. The human groove." The bear within relaxed again. She was Shula reassuring the pensive Crow.

"Human groove. I think I'm going in that direction myself. I've been thinking about whether I'd like to be a midwife."

"The woman groove. Great, Crow. And was that the source of the tirade?"

Marie shivered. "No." She gave a nod toward the notebook. "General tension."

"So?" Shula waited.

"Later. I promise. Later." Marie picked up the book and slid it into her backpack. "All done? Can we go?"

"Actually, I want to check on that Jane Doe. You know, our mystery patient, Sarah S. Wise. Come with me. I want you to meet her, as much as that is possible. Then we're outta here."

Marie sighed. "All right, I admit, I'm curious."

Sarah Wise was on a medical ward, in a double room. Shula scooted off to the nurses' station by the elevator. Marie hesitated at the door to the room, feeling intrusive. Being bedridden in hospital was like being on display in a showcase; you couldn't prevent anyone from peering in. Shulamit was standing at the nurses' station, looking serious and intent, for all the world like a respectable professional. It wasn't just the white lab coat and name tag, it was also the take-charge manner she adopted.

Marie edged into the room. A second bed, by the window, was unoccupied. A curtain was half-drawn around the bed near the door. An older woman lay with her eyes closed, her left hand across her chest, her right wrapped around the bed railing. Marie wandered over to the window, looked out on a swampy field, then shivered, feeling watched. She turned to face the woman's bed. Her eyes were open. Bright and brown and wide open.

"I'm sorry. I don't mean to intrude. I'm just here with my friend. She's your doctor, at least, here, for now, she's your doctor."

What had Shula said? "She can hear, but what exactly she hears, we don't know. No one can say for certain what this woman, what Sarah, is perceiving."

Nonetheless, Marie thought, I should introduce myself. "I'm Marie Latouche."

The woman's right eye twitched.

"Are you Sarah?"

Her right eye flickered again.

"My friend, Shulamit Weiss, she's your doctor. She's very nice. Very good, I mean, at least, I don't she why she wouldn't be very good. She was an excellent artist before she decided to become a doctor. So, looked at that way, you're being cared for by an excellent, socially committed feminist former painter and conceptual artist. Oh sorry, I get off track sometimes."

Marie heard a throaty chortle. The woman, Sarah, had not moved. No sound came from her. She gazed around the room. Outside, a bank of grey clouds drifted toward the city. Somewhere in the room, the sound of laughter. Marie paced, worried one of her flashes would start. Again, a gentle, woman's laugh, older, generous and calm. Relief expressed without words, a musical note running coolly in a mountain stream. Agitated, Marie paused by the bed and leaned on the bed rail. A chuckle echoed above her. She looked up to the ceiling and watched it dissolve into open sky. She tightened her grip on the railing. A rock face and waterfall appeared. Glacial water tumbled down a thousand feet, toward her. At the top of the falls sat a woman with pale pink–white skin and large, smart grey eyes. Her lank hair fell loose from a careless bun at the nape of her neck. She wore a sleeveless gingham dress, with a full skirt, two top buttons open. Her bare feet dangled pinkish in the roaring water. Marie perceived the detail as if there was no distance between them. Her lips were red and full.

The old grey mare she ain't what she used to be, Marie heard the laughing voice sing clearly. *Ain't what she used to be, ain't what she used to be.* Crisp notes sparkled in the flood. *The old grey mare she ain't what she used to be, many long years . . .* Her dangling feet, her legs, dress, arms, neck, and hair melted into the water flowing over the high, narrow falls . . . *ago-o-o-o-o-o-o.* Song and face cascaded down. Marie stiffened, bracing for the harrowing sound of the woman's agony. But there was only the fresh hush of falling water, a cooling sensation showering her inside and out. And then a calm within, and a strange aliveness, a quickening in her body as she looked back toward the woman in the bed. Almost euphoria, that gentle euphoria of childhood love. She stretched her hands and arms, gazed timidly at the ceiling. Only plain white paint, with a sheet of paper taped on it. Marie read the word WOMAN above the word BOARD and then the letters

       w

           a

              t

                  e

                     r

She turned away, then furtively glanced back. The paper was still there. She stared. It must be real. Real as in verifiable, visible to other humans, to Shulamit, even, who couldn't still be gabbing at the nurses' station.

Marie relaxed, laid a hand on the bed rail. Those lively brown eyes blinked uncontrollably, then closed. Marie took a tissue from the bedside table and wiped the water gathering on Sarah Wise's face. She tried to imagine the frustration of being suddenly immobilized. Alive and aware and yet unable to communicate. She shoved the tissue in her pocket.

"Okay," Marie said. "If I'm not mistaken, you can blink your right eye when you want to. That means we can talk a little bit, if you can hear me, or if what I say makes sense to you. I'll ask you a question. If your answer is yes, blink your right eye once. If it's no, blink it twice, close together or pretty close together. Okay?"

Sarah's right eye blinked once. Then after a long pause, came a flutter, almost a spasm.

"I'll take that as a yes, okay?"

She blinked once.

"Okay, my name is Marie. If you know what my name is, blink once for yes."

The woman shut her eye hard, like a child learning to wink, and then opened it. Immediately it began to flutter again.

"Well, let's say that's a yes."

Sarah slowly closed both eyes, her face slackened into slumber.

Marie was standing at the window imagining wriggling tadpoles and buried earthworms when Shulamit returned, chattering avidly with a physiotherapist named Todd about the Jays' chances of repeating and the possible sexual orientation of various major league baseball stars. Marie saw a small stud in Todd's ear below carefully trimmed sideburns. How many gay physiotherapists could there be in this town? She mused, and enjoyed Shula's knack of surrounding herself with enchanted beings. Lesbians, gays, bisexuals, their parents, their friends, their children, Shula seemed to draw them to her in a swath of subversive magnetism.

"Todd, Marie. Marie, Todd," Shula rattled off a quick introduction.

Shula was right and Jane was right, Marie thought, shaking Todd's firm hand. Somehow, people change constantly without changing at all.

Todd ambled bedside and studied the sleeping woman.

"How is she?" Shula asked Marie.

Marie shrugged. "You tell me, you're the doctor."

"We can run tests till hell freezes over," Shula said, "and certainly she needs to work with O.T. and physio as soon as she can, but it's really people that'll make the difference. Company, contact, caring. Touch can be a great healer in these cases. I've seen it. She's probably confused, scared and lonely right about now."

"Well, I did try to communicate with her and it seemed to be working, but then she was too tired. She went to sleep. Before that she seemed to be trying to answer my questions by blinking. But her eyes would get tired and spasm."

"Really?" Todd was totally attentive.

"Spasm—where'd you pick that term up?" Shulamit laughed.

"Oh, I've had a few." Marie giggled.

"Lower back," Todd cut in.

"Yep, bending from the waist at work." She demonstrated a luxurious deep-knee bend.

"Excellent." Todd gave a mock applause.

"Months of exercise. I have the thighs of a downhill racer."

"You certainly do," Shula cajoled.

"Now girls, no flirting in the office."

"Pay no attention. She gave up sex in a crisis of doubt. It lost meaning." Marie teased, relaxed.

"I think I'll stay away from that one." Todd waved her off, smiling.

"What's that on the ceiling?" Marie asked quickly. "That paper." She looked up quickly to check it was still there.

"Where?" said Shula.

"Is that still here?" Todd craned his neck. "God, that's been there for months now. Those are word puzzles. A patient's family asked that we tack that paper up there and someone obliged. I guess no one took it down. If you study them you'll see what I mean."

"What? Oh there," Shula saw the page of writing on the ceiling. "Woman," she read out, "woman above board, woman over a board—woman over board." She laughed.

Marie gaped.

"And w-a-t-e-r," Shulamit read each letter aloud. "Water, water falling . . ."

"Waterfalls." Marie said quietly. "Shul, I think I need some fresh air."

"You're pale as a white man's ghost," Todd winked, and Marie noticed the Haida engraving on his silver bracelet. "Gift from a grateful patient." He winked again, broadly, backing toward the door.

"I'm done," Shula said. "Sorry I kept you so long, Marie. Todd, you'll look in on her? We'll work on this?"

"Yes. Yes. Call anytime. Better get her some air before you have to pinch those cheeks." He turned, waved and was gone. Marie grasped Shulamit's white coat firmly and followed.

7

Sophia Cammen & Neely O'Hara

PINE SHADOWS STOLE across the wooden table, covering Jane's arms and neck as she lay catnapping on her books and papers. As she lay dreaming of Sophia, in basic black and pearls, lips ruby red, blond hair a helmet of sprayed curls, a period image of white womanhood from Chez Hélène to Juliette, from Ozzie's Harriet to Mr. B.'s Hazel. Dreaming of a party in full flow, adults chatting and drinking throughout the broad ground floor of the house with the fossilized fish. A big man with a Santa Claus belly, hair and beard leaned on the piano.

"Ah, but women," he said smiling, "women have always been part of things. Women are threaded through our daily lives, women are the thread that holds our lives together."

"Thread! Your lives!" Sophia flung her arms in the air. "Don't you see what you're saying? Thread that holds your life together?"

"Sophia, that's the way it's always been. I'm not saying things can't change. Even though our generation is strongly influenced by what we experience growing up, Sigga and I both work."

"Certainly," Sophia retorted, "and you've built a career with the knowledge that you'll always work and that your work comes first. While Sigga works between raising kids and running the house and taking care of things for you. It's hardly equality."

"No," Santa Claus agreed easily, "it's not equality."

"Well, it's time for a change," Sophia maintained.

"To change!" Santa Claus raised his glass high.

Then Santa Claus settled in at the piano and a crowd gathered around him, singing the "Mountains of Morne" and "Danny Boy" and finally "Somewhere Over the Rainbow," and Sophia floated around the room, chanting the exit lines of her marriage. "Nowhere has to be like home . . . The arrogance of the man . . . Marriage is a trap . . . Women get more radical with age . . . Nowhere has to be like home . . . When the house sells, I'm leaving . . . Nowhere has to be like home . . ." Slowly quieting to a whisper.

Waking, Jane felt the rough wood of the table on her cheek, yawned and stretched. "History is personal," she said, seeing Sophia in a cocktail dress hovering among shadowed evergreens. "At least the history we need is." She faced Sophia and the image faded. Jane stood awkwardly, stiff from napping in the chair. Strolled through the long grass of the unkempt driveway.

Was this land like anywhere Sophia had lived growing up? Jane had visited some of Ireland. There was a similarity in the northerness of the places, but nothing more. This land had not been cultivated or tamed, only inhabited. Jane wandered up the sloping driveway to the gravel sideroad known as Crescent Beach Road, knees brushing blooming yellow avens. Caragana bush had spread along Crescent Beach Road during the years of its neglect. After the summer of intense cutting in 1989, Jane sheared erratically, only enough to control the regrowth. Regular dousings with a liquid poison had shrivelled the neighbour's overgrowth to twigs. But Jane would not pour poison, however weak, on this land. To her, that was sacrilege.

Sacrilege, like escape, was quintessential Sophia. As she stepped from the gravel of Crescent Beach Road to the cracking pavement of the old highway to Muddy Water, Jane recalled agnostic Sophia muttering indignantly, "That's sacrilege."

"What's sacrilege mean?" a young Jane had asked over lunch.

"Well," Sophia paused, "it means a violation of the church or religion." Jane pictured her pouring freeze-dried chicken noodle soup into their lunch bowls as she replied.

"Religion?" Jane asked. Sophia was a long-rebelling Catholic.

"Yes, well, I don't mean it religiously. I don't use it religiously. What I mean is, it goes against the essence of the thing, against the nature and spirit of it. It violates the spirit."

"You do use it religiously," teenaged Owen pointed out, lounging in a kitchen chair. "As I recall, just this week the decision on South Indian Lake was a sacrilege, reading *Coles Notes* on Yeats was a sacrilege, and Dad putting mayonnaise instead of sour cream on his baked potato was a sacrilege."

"No, South Indian Lake was a travesty, and your father was simply gilding the lily," Sophia countered.

"So what does religiously mean?" Jane asked, blowing on a spoonful of soup.

"It means all the time," Gene cut in, holding his spoon in front of his mouth.

"It also means having to do with religion," Sophia explained. "Watch, it's hot," she placed a bowl in front of Owen.

Sophia paused as she ladled a bowl out for herself. "While you're all here I want to discuss something. Even though the party leadership didn't go the way we wanted, I still intend to run in the provincial election. I'm seeking the nomination in River Elm."

Owen was alert. "Why River Elm?"

"Well," she put the soup on the table and went back to the cooking island in the middle of the room for a cigarette. "Hans Ziegler wants The Woods. And Fort Oaks—it's too far from here. It's bad enough I'm parachuting, but at least River Elm or The Woods have areas comparable to here." She stopped to light her cigarette. "I can't suddenly purport to represent the working class. Not with all this—" She waved her hand grandly at the encumbering opulence.

It was 1969. Sophia was no longer the woman who had eagerly selected the pine panelling and double sinks, the cooking island and dishwasher. She had spent years becoming more than a weaver who spun a home. She was planning a campaign for a seat in the legislature and dragging hard on a menthol cigarette.

A few weeks later Sophia had secured her nomination in River Elm, a bellwether riding, known for consistently electing a member of the party that won the election. The election writ was dropped the same week. Owen and Gene disappeared into the campaign headquarters along with Sophia.

"Can I come to the campaign office now?" Jane remembered asking one day after school, as Sophia rushed in to throw together a casserole. Sophia flinched and offered Jane a beseeching look. Jane glared, hands firmly on her twelve-year-old hips. "Why not?" she repeated. "I know Owen's older but Gene's younger than I am and his grades aren't any better than mine. And they're always there."

"You know why, Jane," Sophia said softly. "It's because of your father."

"Well, can't he turn the oven on to 375 degrees for an hour by himself? I could make the salad now and the dressing too and just leave him a note. I could do that every day. It's more interesting than being stuck at home."

"I know you could, dear," Sophia said soothingly. "But think about your father."

"I don't want to think about my father."

"Jane," Sophia said calmly, "he will make my life hell if someone isn't here to give him his dinner. I won't be able to run. You know what he's like. Most nights he comes through the front door hollering for his supper."

"I know," Jane mumbled, relenting. "And an ice-cold glass of something and today's newspaper. The boys ignore him and I bring the drink while you make dinner. But that's not fair. When he's in a bad mood I hate eating with him. There isn't any good reason that I always stay home and serve dinner and Gene never does." She whipped open a cupboard door and slammed it shut.

Sophia grabbed the door as Jane yanked it open again.

"You're right, Jane," she said softly. "It's not fair, and that's the whole point. That's why I'm running, to make everything more fair. For lots of people, but definitely for women. For women first and foremost."

"What about girls?" Jane kicked the door.

"Jane, listen," Sophia grasped her arm firmly, then coaxed her into the sensuous comfort of smoke and perfume. "I know this probably won't be much consolation now, but I'll say it anyway. If women like me can't get elected, can't hold positions in government, we haven't got a hope in hell of making things fair. For women or for girls. And I'm really sorry, but your father expects a female here to serve him dinner when he gets home from work. That means you or me. I'd really appreciate it if you did that for me, so I can keep working to get elected." Sophia sighed heavily at the irony of the situation. "I'll get Gene to stay home for dinner more often," she promised.

"Couldn't I come down after dinner? Dad could give me a ride."

Sophia winced. She had invested considerable effort in keeping Phil and his domineering temperament out of the campaign office. She ran a hand through Jane's short hair. "It's nice like this," she said idly. "You have such a happy face, keep it happy. I'll think of something for your father. There must be some task where his belligerence would be an asset." She sighed again. "I'm sorry it has to be this way, Jane. You can be down there all weekend. On weekends he can fend for himself. He likes to cook all those brunches anyway."

Jane hugged Sophia, and Sophia ruffled Jane's hair again. Then she hurried out to the station wagon with campaign signs taped to the doors. "CAMMEN" blared in loud, orange ink. Jane waved, then retreated reluctantly to the kitchen, where she rummaged in the fridge for anything remotely saladlike. Dying leaf lettuce, a couple of half-bruised tomatoes, one partially shrivelled green pepper, an inch of cucumber. She cut carefully, removing bruises, dents and discolouration and tossing the rot into the left-hand sink where the garberator would grind it for sewage.

As Jane cut she tried not to think about her father. Sophia had spent years inadvertently teaching her how to manage Phil.

"See what your father wants, will you?"

"Go help your father start the pump, would you?" an annual request to assist Phil prime the water pump at the cabin. "He's already lost his temper at Owen and Gene." The gratitude in Sophia's eyes marched Jane down the path to the water, where she filled the old red kettle each time Phil asked, saying nothing as she did so. Usually by the time she was asked to do a boy's chore, both her brothers were pouting somewhere, and Phil was beginning to feel contrite. Jane understood that the quieter she stayed, the calmer Phil would become.

Sophia did not realize that Jane was probably a little too mature and accommodating to be true to the feelings of a twelve-year-old girl. Sophia had always talked to Jane about the world, about their community, taught her things she couldn't really comprehend. Like how to placate Phil, an explosive man. Avoid triggering his outbursts. Jane often acted as Sophia's agent in her marriage. Holding the fort for her, while Sophia sought a place in the public world.

"Holding the fort," Jane muttered, tripping down the grassy steps leading from the old highway to the beach, "a domestic military metaphor." Fuschia sky radiated above the western shoreline. Tiny shards of rose quartz glistened in the lapping water. Jane kicked off her shoes, pondering how, in those days, responsibility for the home belonged to womanwifemother. For making a house a home. Homemakers and housewives. She remembered remarking to Sophia in her late teens, "House-wife—it's like you're married to a house."

"Exactly," Sophia nodded in approval.

In Jane's everyday life there was no household of expecta-tions. With the simple phone call she was about to make from the phone booth across the old highway, she could keep home and work in order from a hundred miles away. The same was true, in one way or another, for most of her friends. Was it a reaction to their mothers?

Jane dusted the sand from her feet and slid on her runners. A Parks pick-up truck rolled by as Jane returned to the top of the steps. Colin, who had lived all his life lakeside, waved at Jane. "Where's those brothers of yours?" he shouted without stopping.

Jane waved back, crossing the badly patched blacktop to the phone booth. The sunset deepened to crimson, an easy breeze rippled the water beyond the quiet beach. Jane lifted the receiver and pressed eight numbers to Muddy Water, fourteen more for her long-distance calling card and another six, with pauses, to trigger the messages on her answering machine in the kitchen on Aikins. She was mulling over the ludicrous power of her index finger when her cousin Masha's voice burst happily down the line.

"Hey, Jane. We're comin' home. Well, almost home. We're heading to Kenora for a while, till at least the end of July, probably middle of August. Yesterday we stopped to see petroglyphs. Micah nearly slid into Lake Superior. Hear him giggling in the background? Charlie says hi. Actually he says nothing but he means hi. Maybe you're at the cabin and we can drop in. Anyway we've got a few stops to make, a few days canoeing in Quetico, see if we can spot an eagle. Then visit folks in Sioux Narrows. Anyway, it's Thursday, by the end of next weekend we'll be in Kenora, I'll call back with the number. Wow. Your machine really takes a long message, I hope. See you soon baboon."

"Soon, baboon," Jane whispered their playtime salutation.

The machine beeped and Harry, the executive director at the community centre came on the line, informing her of an emergency board meeting about gang activity in the neighbourhood and the development of "a coordinated, multi-agency response."

"Nice jargon, Harry. How about some family services?" She'd have to call in.

Then, unexpectedly, Marie. "Hi, it's me. I, uh, I guess I just missed you and I thought I'd call even though you're at the cabin. Well, you know, we should talk. Not about anything. Just talk. Je t'aime, Janey. Salut."

Jane scuffed the sandy shoulder. Marie's voice betrayed the tone of satisfied disappointment, that mix of I-got-what-I-wanted-but-I-wish-it-had-been-you that Jane heard as fling, loud and clear. Jane knew the pattern of Marie's flirtations. Alone and restless, a quick bike ride to dance at the Lotus, then, well, it didn't pay to think about it, as Jane had discovered. After so long together-apart, she almost wished 'Rie well in her adventures, almost believed Marie's insistence that distance was the sole cause of her excursions, though in four years Jane had never sought the single-night solution. They were different people, and both of them knew it. Jane sometimes thought distance was the reason they had lasted four years. Space alone resolved differences in expectations. Space enough not to mind, Jane thought.

Returning to the cabin, Jane crossed back over the old highway and cut through the site of the old fish hatchery to a lakeside path. Her memory still scented the great metal tubs that had run with a constant flow of fresh water, loaded with perch, trout and pickerel, minnows for stocking the surrounding lakes. The path climbed above the lake. Jane followed the footworn trail across the front of properties that backed on Crescent Beach Road, checking for small changes in cabins, boat houses and docks. She chewed a stem of grass and thought back to pleading with Sophia, to that June night when she was twelve, slicing the vegetables smaller and smaller in frustration.

Finally, Jane had stopped cutting, and shovelled the vegetables from the cutting board into an aging wooden salad bowl. She mixed oil and vinegar three to one, added salt and pepper, a sprinkle of mustard powder and a pinch of oregano and mixed it thoroughly. Wandering around the house, she flipped through the mail on the polished oak dining-room table, picked out two publications, *Medical Aspects of Human Sexuality* and the *Cana-*

dian Jewish News, and lay down on the couch to read.

The phone rang at five to six, Phil's nightly call to Sophia to see if there was anything they needed for dinner.

"No, she's at the campaign office. Everything's ready. I'm just waiting for you," Jane said, heavily engrossed in an article on tumorous growths in women's reproductive organs. She suggested Phil bring something for dessert, then checked on the casserole.

Phil arrived home fifteen minutes later and announced that he hadn't brought dessert, as they could "just as well have ice cream over at that place by the campaign office. How about a glass of ice-cold water?"

Jane nodded noncommittally, aware of what he had said, but preoccupied with possible distortions of the organs that had been solemnly outlined in a girls-only grade six health class two years earlier. Jane had ignored the details and lost the take-home brochure "Growing Up and Liking It." Young for her grade, she had simply taken it on faith that tubes, eggs and accoutrements existed somewhere in her guts, and had crossed her fingers against the early onset of menstruation. Now, she read with interest as she trooped between the kitchen and dining room, setting the table.

"What's a hys-ter-ectomy, exactly?" she called to Phil, who was adjusting the newspaper and sliding into a chair in the living room.

"What's for dinner?" he yelled.

"A hyster-ectomy," Jane repeated, arriving in the living room with his water. "Sorry," she said. "It's the magazine."

"That's a helluva thing to offer for dinner," Phil said, fence-sitting between amusement and anger.

"Oh, Mom made it," she joked lightly. "I just made the salad." Then she laughed and he laughed and it was a safe, good moment, like the dawn after a long night of bad dreams or sliding into a warm bath after a muddy football game. "It's just what I'm reading," Jane said finally, displaying the magazine.

A more conservative, less scientific father might have sug-

gested that articles on physically anomalous genitalia and reproductive organs were not the best material for an inquiring
young mind. But Phil meant to be progressive. His wife was a
feminist. He believed in equality. She was running for the legislature and the bastards were running two women against her,
goddammit. The bastards. Phil's eyebrows descended into a
scowl.

Jane reacted automatically. "Some kind of chicken casserole,
you know, chicken cacciatore à la Sophia," she gushed. Raised on
Rumanian Jewish home-cooking—roast chicken and strudel,
home dills and knishes—Phil did not respond well to the canned-
soup casseroles on Sophia's hold-the-fort menu. "So what is a
hyster-ectomy, exactly?" Jane asked again. "And is this the reason
you made me stop playing football even though Gene still gets to
play?" She pointed to a diagram showing ovaries, fallopian tubes,
uterus and cervix. "I was only winded. Not hurt. I've done it
to him a hundred times. He just likes to tackle head first."

Phil tried vainly to recall the discussion.

"You know," Jane prompted him, "you and Mom told me I
shouldn't play football because my organs for making babies
might get damaged. These are them, right?" she asked again,
holding the magazine up.

"Yes, basically," Phil nodded. "Those are female reproductive
organs."

"Re-pro-ductive organs," Jane repeated. "What about boys?"
she continued, still holding up the magazine.

"What about boys? I'm getting hungry. Can we discuss this
over dinner?"

"Promise?" She eyed him solemnly.

Phil nodded, amused.

"I'll get the chicken chuckatory," she said and Phil laughed
again. "Hold this," she handed him the magazine and then
froze. She had bossed Phil. Instantly, her back and neck tensed,
waiting for a holler to rip the evening tranquillity. But Phil had
taken the magazine from her hand and was strolling to the table.

Jane hurried to the kitchen and lifted the casserole from the oven with a partially charred oven mitt. Phil ladled heaping portions on each of their plates while she fetched the salad. Jane sat and ate, waiting for Phil to pause.

"Nice chuckatory," he said finally.

"So?" said Jane.

"You're like Baba," said Phil. "Say it in Yiddish, like the old folks do. Say 'Nu?' "

"New?" said Jane.

"No, not new, 'nu?' " Phil repeated. "More like moo."

"Noo?" said Jane. "What about boys?"

"What about boys?" Phil asked her.

"Boys' reproductive organs."

"What about them?"

"Do boys have organs inside that might get wrecked if they play football and then they couldn't have kids?"

"No." Phil shook his head and speared a loose piece of chicken skin floating in sauce. "You know, boys have testicles."

"Test-tickles."

"Balls," said Phil.

"Nuts," said Jane and Phil laughed. "No skin off my nuts," Jane added and they howled with laughter. Phil's eyes were watering.

"It's a good thing your mother isn't here." He sighed, fingering his eyes.

"Yes, it is," Jane answered, surprised at herself. "So that's why I got in so much trouble when I kicked Robbie Jones by accident in the, uh, test-tickles. Popsicles, test-tickles, Don Rickles."

"You kicked a boy?"

Jane nodded. "It was an accident. I wasn't trying to kick him, just to make him back away. Besides, who'd have believed he'd tell his mother and she'd phone here. I mean, he's almost the same age as Owen. What a suck."

Phil chortled, then caught himself. "Still, maybe you

shouldn't be doing that. Kicking boys, I mean."

"Well, they're boys. They're always bragging about being so tough. Besides, it was an accident. Why do boys get so upset about their test-tickles anyway? I don't suppose they're worried about having kids?" She gulped half a glass of milk.

"No," Phil chuckled. "It's the pain. Any bread to mop this sauce with?"

"I'll check." She returned with two slightly aged onion buns. "What's so special about the pain?" she asked.

"Hurts like hell," Phil said, tearing a piece of the bun off and sliding it through the sauce on his plate.

Jane imitated Phil's movements with her own bread. Despite Sophia's derisive comments on the crudeness of Phil's eating habits, Jane knew a lot of them were delicious. "Well, boys always act like it's the worst pain in the world. Like as if all the pains anyone had ever felt in all of history had been rated and the worst one was the time some boy got socked in the nuts in the schoolyard. I bet it hurts worse to have a baby."

"Socked in the nuts?"

"That's what Mash says," Jane referred to her cousin. "Keeps boys off when they're trying to grab you. She says 'sock 'em in the nuts.' I bet it works, too. Only they'd probably tell the principal and then the girl would get suspended."

"Jane, if boys bother you, you should tell a teacher. You and Masha can't be running around punching boys in the testicles."

"Oh, don't worry. I don't. And she's much smaller than me. I'm sure she's just talking tough. So, I mean, nu," she ventured, "if boys' test-tickles are on the outside, and they hurt like crazy when they get socked, and they're for making babies, it doesn't make sense that Gene can play football and I can't. It's discrimination." She patched together words and phrases that tumbled daily from Sophia's smoky lips. "It's sexism, isn't it?"

"Maybe."

"I want to play football. If Gene can, so can I. If he doesn't have to have kids, neither do I."

"No." Phil chuckled again. "You certainly don't have to have kids. We just wanted you to be able to."

"Well, don't you want Gene to be able to?"

"Yes, sure. I want all you kids to have kids, if that's what you want."

"So?"

"Nu?"

"Nu, shouldn't he stop playing football? He doesn't even like it really."

"He stops or you start?"

"Right." Jane stacked the dishes for clearing.

"I'll speak to your mother."

"Nothing like catching the long bomb." She grinned, standing and piling the cutlery on the stacked plates. Phil licked the sauce from his knife and handed it to her.

"Anyway, what about hyster-ectomy? I can't understand this article."

"The article is for medical practitioners. You're not supposed to be able to understand it."

"But what exactly is a hysterectomy?" She finally got her tongue around it. "Didn't Mrs. Greenfield have one and die?"

Phil scowled. Then he was quiet. Finally he said, "Janulah, they made a mistake. It was something that should have been checked. The hysterectomy didn't kill her. It was the anesthetic. Doctors make mistakes, Jane. They hardly ever get caught, because they won't testify in court against each other. It'd push the malpractice insurance rates up and a lot of them are cheap sons of bitches. But doctors are like other workers. We make mistakes. Thing is, when we make mistakes, someone gets very badly hurt. Maybe even dies. That's what happened to Shelley Greenfield. Thirty-two years old. Given an anesthetic that reacts if you have a certain disease that no one knew she had." His voice trailed off. After a minute he asked, "Do you still want to know what a hysterectomy is?"

Jane shrugged. "I wanted to know about her."

"Ice cream?" Phil asked.

"Ice cream," Jane nodded. "But I have to load the dish-washer." Phil would obviously go to the campaign office after-ward. Well, too bad, she married him, I never told her to, Jane thought, debating butterscotch ripple in a cone versus a hot fudge sundae as she rinsed the dishes.

The lakeside path ended at the public pump, where Sophia had often sent her children to fetch a pail of cool spring water. Jane pumped the long wooden handle, yielding only warm air. Then she cut across the pine needles and weathered roots of a neighbouring lot back to the worn sandy gravel of Crescent Beach Road. She remembered 1969 again, feeling puberty lurk beneath the buzz of Sophia's campaign, researching reproduc-tion and sexuality in Phil's medical textbooks to ease her anxiety.

Phil's books contained fascinating see-through pages, detailing human anatomy layer by layer. An initial skeleton was covered, page by transparent page, with organs, nerves, muscles, veins and arteries. Viewed alone, each page illustrated a single system. Jane discerned that the heart was not heart-shaped, but that kidneys, beans and Hollywood swimming pools were definitely related. The nervous system resembled wiring for sound, light and move-ment. And all the detail in the world didn't alleviate her worry as the age of thirteen approached. Jane's fingers remained fully crossed against the arrival of her first period.

One sunny Saturday morning a few months later, Jane was relishing her first trash culture novel, languishing in the *Valley of the Dolls*. She gobbled her cereal immersed in the troubles of Neely-pillhead-O'Hara, as Neely soaked in a hot bath willing it to bring on her period and prove she wasn't pregnant. That evening, Jane ran her bath too hot. Easing herself in slowly, she thought jokingly, maybe it'll bring my period on, like Neely O'Hara. Strangely enough it did. Tomboy Jane was astounded, then dismal. A defeated but busy Sophia gave her a thick pad to stuff between her legs and a ridiculous elastic contraption to hold it up. The pad felt like a pillow for a king-size bed, protruding between her muscular legs. Walking became waddling. Under the influence of Jacqueline Susann, the curse of womanhood was all too real. Life was over. And just turned thirteen. Jane retreated to her bed in tears. While there, she noticed that she didn't feel any pain. After a morose night and morning, she rolled out of bed, stuffed the elastic belt in the box of pads and shoved it to the back of a shelf in her parents' bathroom. She folded some toilet paper neatly and laid it in her underpants.

"Worse than a sock in the nuts," she said to the mirror. Then she went outside and built an obstacle course with Gene and his friend Joey and for hours she ran over tires and climbed up trees and crawled under benches, always rushing to be the fastest, the strongest, the bravest.

A couple of days later Sophia asked how she was doing with the pads.

"Hate them," Jane answered. "I just use a little toilet paper."

Sophia flinched. Later that week a box of tampons appeared in Jane's room.

"Does she want everybody to know?" Jane asked the mirror and quickly shoved them in a drawer.

As the second onslaught trickled in, she found herself sitting on the toilet, then standing with one leg raised awkwardly, studying the little diagram provided in the box, a tampon in one hand, the other hand searching for an opening. Jane closed her eyes, shoved the tampon in and threw the inserting tube in the garbage. It rebounded off the rim and scored.

Jane pulled her legs together and didn't feel a thing. Ecstatic, she leapt up on the toilet seat and down again. Still nothing. She twirled on the spot, flash-kicked an imaginary opponent. Nothing. Freedom. Life was not over at thirteen. "Sophia must be crazy to use those gross things," she told the mirror, then she noticed the tube in the garbage basket. She plucked it out, wrapped it in a mass of toilet paper and dropped it back in the basket. She soaked her hands in lukewarm water and went to find Gene.

He was lying on the rug in the den reading the encyclopedia.

"Arm wrestle," said Jane.

"No, I'm reading."

She jumped on his back. "Arm wrestle or I'll pound you."

"Get off me." He rolled over and shoved. "Get off." Determined, Jane remained firmly in place. "Okay," he said finally, "arm wrestle."

They lay face to face, clenched hands and pushed. Jane had him most of the way down but he wasn't giving. She realized that at the rate he was growing this could be the last time in her life she would ever defeat Gene in an arm wrestle. She mentally cursed puberty, grunted and drove his hand to the carpet.

"Arrrgh!" She bounced up and raised her arms in the air, triumphant.

"You're such a tomboy," he sneered, turning back to his reading.

"So what. You're just a boy, period. And all you got is, is— Don Rickles," Jane retorted, wondering what tomboys became when they grew up.

"You're nuts," Gene called over his shoulder as she walked away.

"Nope." Jane snickered. "Your nuts." Could she really be a tomboy *and* be a woman, like Neely-show-biz-O'Hara or Sophia? There had to be a way. Jane crossed her fingers securely, scooted into her parents' bedroom and opened Sophia's closet. She spent the rest of the afternoon in a T-shirt, cut-off jeans and spike heels.

The gravel road succumbed to nightfall. Jane ambled back down the driveway to the table in the grass. Sophia had seemed to become more distant as Jane entered her teens. Busy with politics, longing to leave Phil, perhaps even deliberately giving her daughter room to grow, trusting her to make her own choices and have her own secrets, Jane reasoned. She relit the citronella candle. Memory was so expansive. It was hard to confine her thoughts to the history relevant to her thesis. She yearned to write about how those women, for whom the world had changed radically but not radically enough, had raised their children. Jane thought back to Sophia sitting beside her at an awards ceremony, just the two of them, the first academic award Jane ever received. Sophia insisting on a new outfit, tomboy Jane uncomfortable in a boldly coloured dress with matching gloves. Now she understood. What would please a feminist mother, educated in a gender-segregated convent school system, more than a daughter outsmarting the males at her school?

The two old fighting crows cawed loudly. Jane loaded boxes, clearing the table top. The crows evoked Phil and Sophia, arguing, daily and nightly. Shadows swallowed the landscape like lives disappearing in smoke. A quiet rustle revealed an old doe poised at the top of the hill, watching her. Jane bowed courteously, piled the boxes and doused the candle with a breath. She heard the doe come toward her, then veer off to the south. A quarter moon cast a path of light through the forest. Starry whiteness littered a navy sky. Jane toted the boxes into the cabin, set them down and flicked on the radio.

"NDP leader Audrey McLaughlin criticized Prime Minister Campbell's recent remarks on unemployment in a speech today," a fluid Caribbean voice delivered the hourly national news. "Speaking in Muddy Water, Ms. McLaughlin called the prime minister's comments unthinking and a poor excuse for national policy."

Jane twisted the cap off a Black Label and raised the bottle in a toast. "Well, Soph, it's not all you hoped for, but you had your impact. As 'Rie would say, 'Salut, maman.' It is most certainly a different time." Jane's guzzle was long and satisfying.

8

Anne Frank & Gloria Johnston

ANNE FRANK'S DIARY lay on the wood floor of Shulamit's bedroom in the rambling house. Shula rocked in a weathered cane rocker, peacefully exhausted and thoroughly relaxed for the first time since she arrived on the sprawling island. Most of her favourite things had been delivered that afternoon, hauled by semi-trailer over Canadian Shield and across prairie, through the Rockies, Crow's Nest Pass and the interior ranges to the coast and, finally, by ferry to the island.

"Stuff for you in the living room," Art had mumbled, ambling out the front door in a thick red toque over scraggy, white-boy pseudo-dreadlocks as Shulamit came in from work. Sliding the oak door aside, Shula made a mental note to discuss the uncoolness of Art's hair with him someday. The room was crowded with boxes addressed to Dr. S. Weiss, 577 Toronto Street, Victoria, B.C., sevens carefully crossed in her mother's European hand.

Carefulness spoke Helen clearly across the miles. Through Shulamit's childhood, Helen had covered the living-room furniture with plastic so stiff that crinkling accompanied any movement. Helen wound basting thread back onto spools. Helen flattened tinfoil and wax paper and filled drawers with it, long before recycling. Helen smoothed and folded newspapers after Isaac read and rumpled them. Helen filed the Jewish monthlies, and every issue of the Yiddish papers until their demise, by date and place of publication. Helen sat and read and struggled for breath in a spotless, dust-free house. Helen vaporized in the cold season, humidified when the snow fell and dehumidified when tropical winds blew north. She sealed each window against pollen and smog, lived on shallow breaths of well-conditioned air. Helen's was an interior life.

As a child Shulamit stayed by her side, protecting the shadow mother, bringing home news of the strange country outside. It seemed odd to Helen that Shulamit, a child born of her and Isaac, could understand this new land so well, could be so much a part of it. Sometime during high school Shulamit abandoned the sad indoor mother, departed emotionally for the world beyond. Helen sighed with relief, thankful that her daughter had stepped so easily beyond the legacy. When Shula abandoned art for medical school, Helen began to worry again. From inside that island house in a comfortable, fairly Jewish suburb, Helen watched Shulamit sink deeper into the grief of others, searching for lives to save. Sorrow shadows burrowed beneath her eyes. As visits became rarer, Helen longed to reach out and stroke her daughter's face, longed to step out the front door and breathe deeply on fresh air. Once and only once, during that silent winter when Shulamit's friend was killed, Helen asked quietly if Shulamit could find out anything about new treatments for her condition. Her intention was to distract her daughter, but she wouldn't have denied harbouring a hope that Shulamit might unlock the prison surrounding her chest.

At first Shula took the request as lightly as it had been given. Soon, though, she found herself sitting in on extra classes on the respiratory system, showing up for grand rounds conducted by specialists, combing magazines and journals for research developments. By the end of her schooling Shulamit was supplying Helen and her doctor, Sheila Hanover, with the names of new treatments as they came on the market. Helen's breathing was still a problem, but she experienced occasional respites. New drugs often proved effective for a short time, then Helen would relapse or develop side effects. Shula cautioned against ending up on a treadmill of drugs, each one treating the side effect of another.

Helen's breathing improved, enhancing her days. During a good spell, Helen had been known to check the Weather Network's air quality report. If the report was favourable, she would take a measured walk to the kosher meat market north of Lawrence Avenue and select a special cut for dinner. Once, when the latest miracle potion relaxed her lungs fully, she and Isaac had gone swimming at the uptown Jewish Community Centre, not far from their home. Although her lungs slowly constricted again, Shulamit noticed Helen's determination remained constant. She continued to try any and every new treatment suggested by Shula or Dr. Hanover, and was doggedly consuming a new round of medication as she carefully crossed the sevens on the labels for Shulamit's basement boxes.

"Send the boxes piled at the far end," Shula had said.

"The west end, you mean." Helen wanted to be clear.

"Yeah. Not the art supplies. They are in the laundry room. Just the boxes and furniture clogging the rec room."

And here it was, cluttering Shulamit's living room.

Two hours later Shula leaned back and listened to the comforting sound of cane runners creaking on a maple floor. T-shirts, shorts, underwear and socks lined the multi-coloured dresser she had painted in art school. Sculptures and art-in-facts, as they'd called them, work by those contemporaries who had not leapt totally into conceptualism, lay scattered around the room. A gorgeous sequined womanikin from Dez's—aka Dezaster—"Akin to Skin" series glittered in the light of an "Aquwhere-i-am," Lenny Feinstein's self-portrait of a light-fed land mammal. A gas station giveaway tiger tail collected for Dez's project dangled from the back of the rocker. On the window ledge, a jar of pastel-coloured Toronto beach glass, discarded shards smoothed by the waves of Lake Ontario, separated two similarly eroded red bricks. Shula had moved in.

Books and records surrounded her, foothills encircling the woman mountain. She held a short note from Helen:

*More new medication, and feeling better. If I had any mazl,
this one will last, after so many tries. If I had any luck, well,
even for bad luck you need luck. But maybe this time, who
knows?*

> *Love, Helen*

Maybe, Shulamit thought, gazing at the books piled on Anne
Frank's diary. *The Last of the Just,* Elie Wiesel, Primo Levi, Hannah Arendt's *Eichmann in Jerusalem,* Aahron Appelfeld, Rebecca
West on the Nuremburg trials, Irena Klepfisz, *Babi Yar*—histories, biographies, journalism, poetry, memoirs purchased
steadily over the last few years. Through her reaction to Gloria's
violent death, through working with assaulted women in shel-
ters and peers with AIDS, Shulamit had begun to perceive the
shape and depth of her ferocious internal wall. A solid iron will
encasing the pain of history. Always an activist, Shulamit was
nonetheless surprised when anger was her consistent grief
response.

"The bastard killed her." Words still captive within her, as the
chair slid more rapidly on the dusty floor. The bastards hadn't
really killed Gloria. Shulamit's foot jangled as the chair rolled.
One had fired and the rest simply hadn't saved her. They could
have, and they didn't. Not enough time, Shulamit thought, not
enough time because the fucking police were too slow to
believe a resident was being stalked, doubting the urgency of a
shelter worker whose voice echoed the hills of Jamaica.

Shulamit stopped the chair abruptly. For more than two years
she had been rocking the same frustration. The ruts wore down
to this literature, these lives, whether history or novel, autobiog-
raphy or reportage. Shulamit had not read a word of it. Nor had
she ever explained to Gloria the crucial difference she made to
Shula's daily struggles. It was just one of those moments that
never arrived. One of those understandings that didn't need to
be said. Now it was buried with all the other unspokens.

By the end of her first year of training, medical school had become a dry deluge of information circulating in a claustro-phobic atmosphere. Needing a broader community, Shula located a shelter for assaulted women and their children, and offered to do medical support work. She dropped by once a week and checked the bodies of confused children for scrapes and bruises, coughs, colds and ear infections. If anything looked potentially serious she referred them to Donna Murdoch, a nearly retired general practitioner brave enough to have endured medical school in the 1940s. The arrangement allowed women whose safety depended on anonymity to abandon their family doctors without resorting to hospital emergency services. Shulamit learned from the residents and from Donna. There, at the shelter, she met Gloria.

Gloria was a joy. Smart, caring, self-reliant, the most efficient worker Shulamit had ever met. Walking through the door, Shulamit could tell whether Gloria was on shift. A liveliness would permeate the house. Or maybe the liveliness was in Shula. Gloria was warm and warming. Distressed children trusted her calm confidence. She could reassure a traumatized resident across a multi-continent language gap, shift the most intransigent bureaucrat to action or stare down a cold commit-tee of elected officials. In Shulamit's admiring mind, Gloria was magical. She convinced Shulamit to rethink more than one issue, and repeatedly pointed her toward her own history, whenever Shulamit resisted the obvious.

"Read yourself. Know yourself. Know your people," Gloria said, as they sat late at night, talking. Those nights when Shu-lamit drove aimlessly, trying to shed insomnia in the streets of Hamilton, listening to the music of alternative Toronto, songs like "Dis Ya Mumma Earth" or "Dancing at the Feet of the Moon" or painful favourites like "Troubled Child." Joni Mitchell serenading the night, Shulamit listening, wandering back to those growing years she could barely remember. To the unasked questions, religious training burrowed deep in the bur-geoning Jewish community at Bathurst and Lawrence. Years in complete ignorance of her parents' histories. Years when she began to suspect and avoid, inhaling the end of high school and the beginning of art college in a marijuana-induced euphoria. Gradually art, the freedom to create and to comment on creation, took root. Shula lost interest in joints and nickel bags, Thai sticks and Afghani black hash, and enthusiastically decorated the city with wilder and wilder projects. Bushes with ribbons streaming in the breeze. On each ribbon the name of a missing daughter or son, copied from the scarves worn by the mothers of the Plaza de Mayo as they walked the square in Buenos Aires. The night she and Lenny and Dez, with Marie and Jane for back-up, tied helium balloons to the fence along the front of the South African consulate on University Avenue, each bearing the name of someone who had died in police detention. The next morning they distributed press releases at the St. Patrick subway station, dedicating the event to the future of Azania and commemorating the Yippie attempt to levitate the Pentagon. Shulamit was everywhere. She knew everyone, attended every event in the downtown political-cultural community.

All the while, though, she had a sense of living out of place. Bathurst and Lawrence—home—held secrets that began to surface unbidden. Unwanted images in paintings that became increasingly difficult to finish. Telling phrases in Yiddish, French, English that undercut her titles. Mid-performance of the piece "Quoi est maman?" Shulamit realized it was not only the abstract, analytic feminist work she had intended. Names and images repeated in dreams, hinting at secrets she had always known, in some way.

Stories of the Jews of Europe, in the 1930s and '40s. Stories that belonged to her like the gates of the Warsaw Ghetto, the paving stones of Buda, photographs of Jewish bodies piled, emaciated and naked, in mass graves. Shula had raised a hand to block them from her sight in the Anne Frank House on that visit to attend the AIDS conference. Unable to look directly at them as she had walked through. Inwardly, she had keened and wept. Outwardly, her bulky body had shuffled in the steady line of tourists, up the stairs to the landing, up again and she stood in the first room of the tiny attic. Shula stepped out of line abruptly and walked to the back window. *I am Anne Frank,* she thought, *these are the rooms I live in, day by day. No, I am only her possible daughter,* Shulamit struggled back from the abyss, *the real daughter of Isaac and Helen Weiss, Yitzhak and Hélène.* She pressed thumb and forefinger into her thigh, *the real daughter,* turned and rejoined the line. *And this legacy of hate and hiding, it is mine. My mother and father lived it. And their parents, brothers and sisters, aunts, uncles and cousins. They died it.*

Outside the Anne Frank House and Museum at 263/265 Prinsengracht, Shulamit had slumped on the low stone wall of the canal, clutching her bag of books and postcards, peered into the black water and imagined Gloria's serious face.

"Read yourself," she recalled Gloria's advice, "know yourself, know your people." Shula knew Gloria had visited a house in St. Catharines that had received freedom-seeking Africans escaping America in the 1840s and 1850s. Her grandmother's grandmother had been welcomed there after a harsh journey north. And Gloria rued the fact that the name she carried— Johnston—traced back to a Euro-American slave owner. Shula could still hear her say, "I wear that name. That racist's name. Instead of my people's."

Sitting on that low stone wall, Shula had finally finished the conversation. Okay, she thought, when medical school is done. Then she would open the door Gloria had pointed to those nights when Shula's aimless driving brought her to the shelter, knowing Gloria would be on the shift known as "overnight awake." Nights their voices plied desperation into affection, nights their minds danced through, remaking the world and each other, and never once did Shulamit acknowledge that lust, too, could be part of this knowing. Never once did she let herself even feel it, afraid to shift something so valuable outside the context in which it worked, afraid it might come crashing down on all the points of difference and similarity, and she would lose that vital, sustaining communication. Lose a lifeline.

Then Gloria died, and every risk seemed worth taking. Gloria died on the yellowing front lawn of a nondescript house in a Hamilton suburb, as Shulamit pulled into the corner donut shop for a coffee and walnut cruller before a routine visit to the shelter. Turning into the parking lot, Shulamit noticed the police cordon and swerved back out. Halting at the do-not-cross ribbon, Shulamit recognized Gloria, and bolted from her car. She shoved aside two constables, dropped to her knees and felt in vain for a pulse, until lifted off by two gargantuan officers. Paced the grounds uselessly as commotion raged on. Then she was sitting on a swing at the back of the house, and Tina, a young woman whose coked-up husband once shoved her out of a speeding car, offered her a cup of tea. Shulamit reached across a haze of dissociation and felt the mug warm her hand.

The numbness persisted through the inquiry and the hearing, Shulamit's iceberg thickening in the legal chill. She appeared anywhere and everywhere, never telling the lurid story the journalists promoted, never giving the police the pardon they sought.

"Her death was preventable," Shula announced, on radio and television, in the newspapers and, finally, at the coroner's inquest. "The first request for police assistance was received more than fifteen minutes before the police arrived. The dispatcher was told the man was armed. The second call, to which the police appear to have responded, indicated the man was threatening to shoot. Had the police arrived earlier they could have halted the situation before Ms. Johnston was killed."

Shula was almost oblivious to her behaviour. She was vaguely aware of her voice droning on implacably, a leaden, factual monotone expounding beyond her cool cocoon. The voice lobbied the criminal lawyer on the shelter's board to find out what kind of bullet killed Gloria. The voice speculated publicly that it had been fired by the police and that Mr. Larry Williams, deceased, had never fired at all. The voice expressed no shock when the police discovered Heritage Front propaganda in Larry Williams' house. "Sexism and racism are forms of violence, there is no surprise here," the voice announced. "A rise in unemployment brings a rise in social violence."

The voice ceased haranguing all and sundry only after physical evidence verified that Larry Williams fired the single shot that violated Gloria's chest and the second that shattered his head before police bullets ripped his abdomen. The dissonant cloud thickened. The iceberg hardened. Shulamit listened through cotton wool, Shulamit lived a hundred feet beneath the sea, submerged below everyday currents, bottom-feeding on loss.

Daily life flickered hazily by on a distant television screen. Gloria became a ten-second graphic, a random image on the nightly litany of shot his lover of eight years who had left him a week earlier, shot his wife and three children before turning the gun on himself, shot fourteen female engineering students at l'école Polytechnique, ". . . shot Gloria Johnston, 29, counsellor at a local shelter for women. A divorced father of two, Mr. Williams was a former boyfriend of a shelter resident who had previously charged him with assault. He had been laid off last spring from an auto parts plant in nearby St. Catharines. Ms. Johnston left the house to warn the woman Williams sought, who was approaching the house after an outing. Other residents of the shelter told the coroner's inquiry that Ms. Johnston was talking calmly to a tense Williams, who refused to believe his girlfriend was not in the shelter. When he saw Ms. Johnston signal to someone behind him, he panicked and fired. Ms. Johnston was shot once in the chest as she dove to the ground."

Shula couldn't look at Gloria, small on the screen. She trained her eyes on the blurry photo of Williams. A few days' growth of beard covering the ashen skin on his pallid face. "Bastard." The word chipping off the glacier of her frozen jaw. "Momzer," Shula repeated. "Waste of your mother's womb." An avalanche rumbled. Her hands trembled. Tremors crept up both arms, her body pitched and heaved, Shulamit rolled heavily to the floor of her small apartment and lay jerking, her body weeping dry tears. Convulsing, she thought in a small, clear voice. On the floor of an idiosyncratically decorated apartment in a working-class section of Hamilton, a woman is lying on brown indoor-outdoor carpeting, convulsing. That woman is me. Shulamit Weiss. Please, Shulamit, she prayed to herself, stay conscious.

Gradually, ice flesh melted to liquid. She lifted an arm. The phone was on a low table beside her. She knocked it to the floor and yanked it within reach. *Puh-lease hangup and tryyyyyor call again,* Shula heard. *Puhleeazzzz hang upand . . .* As she walked her hand across the thin carpet, willing her fingers to become ants and carry a hundred times their own weight, Shula's flip card memory recited the possible causes of this physiological crisis, none of them appealing. Her best bet was a wild, medically inexplicable, emotional burn-out as a result of suppressed grief. She dialled, elongated fingers moving across ten digits. Once, twice, three times she dialled the ten numbers it took to reach a tidy house in the North End of Muddy Water. She waited through long seconds. Finally, ringing flooded her chest, curled at the base of her throat.

"Hello." Jane's voice, crisp and clear.

Shula heard it, heard the TV still droning in the living room. "J-j-aane." Shula gulped for air.

"Shula?"

"Just . . . talk . . . to . . . me."

And Jane began to talk, quiet, gentle rambling talk about this and that, understanding that Shula would speak when she could, understanding that her voice carved a path for Shulamit. Jane talked about the events of her day, about life in Muddy Water, about her work at the community centre. About Sophia and her political career, how she had lost in the election of 1969 though her party won, and missed out on a chance at a cabinet post, but had been appointed to chair the Social Assistance Appeal Board. Which meant she travelled the province, by car and by plane, listening to the lives of deprivation amid wealth.

"The thing was," Jane said, immersed in her own obsessions, "she never just saw the poverty. She never reduced the people who appeared before the board to simply their problems. And so she never just came home with the anger, she almost always had a story sparkling with the foibles of humanity. She'd sit at this coffee table we had, smoking and sipping on coffee or booze and you could see her joy in life bubbling from her eyes.

"One time she arrived home from a trip up north with a large soapstone carving. But she wouldn't take it out of the bag. 'I've done a terrible thing,c" she said, ominously. 'You know how carvings are so much cheaper if you buy them up north, and of course, a lot more of the money goes directly to the artist. Well, we just had a few minutes before the plane, so I grabbed this carving and bought it. I wasn't wearing my glasses. Then we get to the plane and the deputy minister says, "Sophia, what did you buy?" Well, I handed him the bag, and the next thing I know he's holding it up for everyone on the plane saying, "Look, everyone, take a look at Cammen's obscenity" Well, I put on my glasses and well,' she tried to be serious but burst into laughter. 'It was a carving of two individuals in parkas, having anal intercourse.'

"So, of course Sophia had to generate an analysis of the situation. She used to go on about lonely men out on the traplines, needing relief. I guess she never heard about Two-Spiritedness." Jane sighed, more conscious of Shula's state as her story dwindled. She searched for another anecdote, wanting to keep her voice flowing until Shula responded.

Shulamit heard words drifting at her, dropping slowly like balloons in winter.

"You know, when I was a kid I didn't always appreciate her activities," Jane reminisced. "Given the neighbourhood we lived in, being 'half-Jewish' and really, child atheists, her political stuff just made us more oddball. I usually kept it under wraps. Like singing along with the Christmas carols but never bowing my head during the Lord's Prayer. Of course, always having dried out sandwiches wrapped in wax paper was harder to hide. Eventually I explained that we didn't use plastic wrap because it was made by the same company that made napalm. Didn't go over that big. There was a small network of kids with like-minded parents, but none of them were into sports like I was.

"Then one day Sophia lets on that my phys ed teacher is the daughter of a Ukrainian communist school trustee. I read her obituary the other day, the school trustee's. She was on the board for decades, elected from the north end. Sophia was on the school board with her for a few years. Muddy Water had a long tradition of electing communists. School boards, city council, even the provincial legislature."

Jane paused, but there was only Shulamit's even breathing. She rambled on. "Anyway, I'd always liked that phys ed teacher. She was quiet and fair. One weekend we had hosted a volleyball tournament at the school and two of us went with the gym teacher on a cold dark morning to pick up six dozen freshly glazed yeast donuts at the bakery on the corner where the big-bosomed baker always had time for a harsh word. In the car on the way back we each ate one, still warm, the cooling honey glaze melting into light bread. I was a fish in water, eating that donut. The socialist's daughter under the wing of the communist's daughter. She knew what it was like to hear all about politics and justice and world affairs at home and then stuff it away completely at school and pretend you agreed with everyone else. And she liked sports."

Shula noticed she could wiggle her faraway toes. Her ankles loosened. She drew her knees up. Words flowed into sentences. Something about Sophia and sculptures, traplines and statues. Sophia's face dangled momentarily in front of Shula. She pressed her feet on the floor and shifted her rear. A wave of relief rolled over her. She eased her shoulders free, shook out her arms. Jane's voice slowed.

"I felt a bit better in the world," she said.

"I hate the world," Shula hissed back. "I just fuckin' hate the whole goddamn world."

Jane stopped. The previous night, Shulamit had spoken with all the enthusiasm of a pre-taped weather forecast. Now she was spitting fury.

"Shul, uhm, maybe you'd come out here for a few days? I could have a ticket waiting for you at the airport. We could just take some time out."

Shula struggled to respond, to wade through her anger and speak. There was a long silence. Jane waited it out.

"I'm lying on the floor here, J.C. I had some kind of episode. I couldn't move. For a moment, for a while, I guess."

"Shula, you're fried. Past it. Basket case. Can you move now?"

"Yeah, I can move everything, thanks to communists and donuts."

"You're scaring me. You have to get past this. It's not pleasant to say, and maybe it's too early for you to hear, but you can't help her now. You have to help yourself. Never mind."

"Never mind what?"

"Never mind about the ticket, I'll come there myself."

Shula was stunned. "Look," she said quietly, "I'll come. You're right. It's just I . . . I can't cry. It's choking me. If I go near it at all, I'm raving. I don't know where to go when I can't sleep. She's all jumbled up with the shit I've been ignoring for years. Oy vey is meer. I feel like a cigarette and I don't smoke. I feel like a whole pack. I won't say I don't need help. But maybe Donna Murdoch wouldn't mind a guest for a few days. I'll come soon."

"Okay, but only if she'll run you a bath and make you hot milk and put you to bed."

"That's her all over. Plus she can write prescriptions and diagnose. I'll call her."

Jane talked as Shulamit heaved upright, wooden feet shuffling a small circle on the brown carpet. The sea within rose and fell, churned and was quiet. The iceberg floated on open water. Shula shuffled over to the television, turned it off, sea-legs swaying as she leaned down.

"Shul," said Jane, "could you sleep?"

"Yeah," Shula grunted, "I'm for bed." Shulamit took her own pulse, pronounced it within normal range, poured a glass of water and downed a tranquillizer.

"I'll have to hang up. That tranquillizer's going to kick in and I'll crash."

"Promise you'll phone Donna?"

"Promise. First thing in the morning."

"Love you, Shul."

"And you."

"Now, get some sleep."

The sheets cloaked her skin and she slumbered.

After that evening Shula resigned from the shelter, later joining a committee organizing a local hospice for people with AIDS. She was soon juggling her studies and the compelling demands of HIV/AIDS support work. Stress became her remedy for distress. Two years later, she sat on the stone wall overlooking the canal in front of the house that sheltered the Frank family, the Van Daans and Mr. Dussel, and promised the memory of Gloria Johnston that she would learn her own history. Her people's history. A year after that promise, she sat amid stacks of Holocaust literature, in a rambling house five blocks from the ocean, rocking in a soothing rhythm, easing toward the pillars of unopened books. She thought back to Marie's visit, her poems and her episodes. Shulamit suspected that Jane and Marie were no longer in love, she even doubted whether they were still lovers. They seemed stuck, that happiness they had fuelled in each other long vanished. Not excited, just friends. It was their business, she knew. She also knew she'd stick her nose in, even though she'd been the queen of reticence since Gloria—well, even with Gloria, to be honest. Since immersing herself in medicine, really. And what about Marie's wandering with Mazie, as she liked to call it? Maybe it sprang from a magnificent muse. Maybe Marie was cracking up, though she didn't seem to be. Shulamit had offered some tricks for staying more aware of the outside world.

"Hold on to something. Use other senses to clue you outside the hallucination. Use your left hand to clue you to the world. But you can't drive a car if you're having these spells."

"I don't drive."

"Or ride a bike."

"It never happens when I'm on my bike."

"It might."

Marie shrugged. "I don't think so. Anyway, now I can kind of tell when Mazie's coming, so I have time to stop."

"Maybe walk or bus it for a while, Crow," Shula tried hard to sound sweet.

"Why Shulamit Weiss, whenever did you learn to speak like Shirley Temple?"

Shulamit laughed. "I'll try anything I think will work." She teased Marie. She liked to tease Marie. It was fun. Old tired Shulamit seeking out the elderly, burdened by the dead, could still work up a little fun. All was not lost. Maybe retreating to the land of spectacular beauty had been a good idea after all.

Shula rocked as she thought, cane runners pressing on northern hardwood. Sarah Wise's recovery was entirely possible. What she needed was steady personal attention and company. Shula hadn't produced a note for Mrs. Donald at the Surf Motel. Obnoxious woman. Shula had informed the hospital administration that Jane Doe 12-93 was one Sarah Wise of Toronto, Ontario. They would have written for her billing number. Her hand brushed a stack of books. Shula lifted the top one off the pile, *Children of the Holocaust*. She shivered. Maybe

Marie would come again soon. Her hands opened the small paperback. Wary eyes skimmed the title page. Fingers turned thin paper, to the opening words of the introduction: *For years it lay in an iron box inside me.* Shula slipped along a razor edge. *Thirty-five million died in that war.* Shula bounced between paragraphs. *Five million were political prisoners, dissidents, anti-fascists, homosexuals.* Shula balanced precariously on commas and semicolons. *Six million were Jews—civilian Jews. There had been nine million Jews in Europe before the war, three million escaped murder. Some died of old age, some fled to Russia or Shanghai; half a million survived in labour camps or passing as Christians or hiding in secret attics or cellars.* Shula rocked through the litany.

In secret attics or cellars. Otto and Edith and Margot and Anne Frank. And Helen, Shulamit's mother, a child with rigid self-control. *Passing as Christians.* Isaac, her father, a massive boy surviving as a roving farmhand. Sisters and aunts, brothers and uncles, mothers and grandmothers, how can you tie six million ribbons to a tree? How can you float six million balloons? Shula's hands had frozen, her imagination chilled, her art came to rest within, stone cold iron lodged in the soul. The cane chair rocked. The pages turned. Shulamit forced her eyes from word to word with that same ferocious iron determination. The rocker creaked rhythmically late into the night.

9

Thérèse Latouche & The Statue of Liberty

THERE ARE DREAMS and there are dreamers. Some say dreams are only about the dreamer, some believe dreams are pathways to eternity. And waking life is a temporary escape from the wild, infinite multiverse to a concrete universe where we relish predictability and order—from the fixity of stars in our stable heavens to the seven days of the week endlessly repeating, from astrological predictions to television series in perpetual rerun.

Marie entertained all possibilities, seeking to transform her lingering disquiet over Mazie's visitations into productive curiosity. Gradually, she realized that she was unnerved because no one else saw the women. Watching their magical acts and hearing the prophetic incantations, being whisked away on a hurricane of sensation was exhilarating, a magnificent woman-high. But their continual practice of appearing only to Marie threw her off balance. She needed others to see them. Needed to create them outside her mind, visual images to complement the chanted verse. Shulamit, already in on the secret, was her first choice. She had to convince her to paint again.

Late on a warm July evening, Marie curled on the fold-out futon couch in her crowded living room, drafting a letter to the Association of Ontario Midwives. "Birth," she wrote, "is the substance of . . ." She paused, crossed out "substance of" and paused again, fingering the woven bracelets on her left wrist. She brushed aside a vine from a nest of plants dangling above her, then added "essence of human creativity."

"Think you've taken a broad enough approach?" Shulamit asked, later, when Marie read the line over the phone. "You're inquiring about midwifery training—you sound like an apprentice to god."

"-ess"

"What?"

"An apprentice to goddess. I sound like an—"

"You sound like Lynn fucking Andrews, that fake white shaman."

"-ess. Shulamit fucking Weiss. Fake shaman*ess*."

"Shit, Crow. You don't actually stick diminutives on words to make them female, do you?"

"Sure. Like man, maness, jerk, jerkess, creep, creepette, wolf, wolfette—*ahhh-ooooo,* I'm a howlin' wolfette. Come on, let me read you this thing, you bulless, or would you rather be a bull moose or better yet, a bull moosette." Marie slipped off her stool perch and paced the kitchen.

"Okay, read. But realize that I am not only your loving friendette, but a licensed doctoress, and subject to the biases of the profession."

Marie crisscrossed the black and white tiles, reading a carefully worded explanation of her political, emotional, intellectual and artistic commitment to birth as the essence of humanity's creative capacities. "It is our magic," she exhorted, "not ours alone as a species, but ours as one species occupying this planet. It is the process of creating life itself, both the most profound and the most mundane fact of our existence. I believe that birth must not be organized on a disease model of care, but reintegrated into our homes, and our lives, as the healthy, purposeful event that it is, with, of course, ready access to appropriate medical technology, should the need arise."

Shulamit rocked pleasantly in her cane rocker. Marie enjoyed the mountains' dark beauty through her kitchen window as she outlined her analysis of how patriarchy medicalized birth. Shulamit pronounced Marie's critique excessive for a letter of inquiry, but agreed that the dominance of scientific medicine had severed birthing traditions.

"How about, 'We need to retrieve the knowledge our mothers escaped,' " Marie suggested, adjusting a postcard photo of Amelia Earhart on her bulletin board.

" 'The knowledge of our grandmothers' might sound better," Shula answered.

" 'Our grandmothers' knowledge and skills,' " Marie countered. "Not that I have any. Grandmothers, that is."

"Sounds good. Me neither, any more."

For both Shulamit and Marie, generational links were almost untraceable. While Shulamit hesitantly examined the severed cords, Marie lived in a kind of surface peace with the silence passed to her by Thérèse, her mother. Marie had no siblings, had met no father, no aunts, uncles, cousins or grandparents. Thérèse, a Franco-Ontarian raised a good half-day north of Sudbury, was Marie's entire family. Thérèse never spoke of other family. Marie clearly recalled the shiver occasioned by childhood questions about Grand-mère and Grand-père.

"Ils sont morts." Thérèse ceased washing the dishes and moved unsteadily toward a chair.

"Everyone?" Marie asked, carefully drying a Melmac plate. Although Thérèse spoke only French to Marie until she was ten, Marie decided that Toronto was English, and spoke English in response. Marie climbed on a chair and placed the plate on the shelf.

"Oui. Toute la famille." Thérèse pulled off a rubber glove and ran her hand through hairspray curls. She watched her daughter climb down off the chair and pick up another plate to dry. "Toute la famille," she repeated, "sauf moi." She daubed a tearing eye with the back of her hand, sighed and put the rubber glove on again. Thérèse moved slowly back to the sink and resumed scrubbing a frying pan.

Marie became disinclined to ask. She knew that her mother grew up near a town called Smooth Rock Falls. Thérèse pronounced it Smoodroc Falls and claimed everyone else did too. Adding only that she hated Catholic boarding schools in general and one in particular—St. Jude's—and she should have settled in Montreal instead of Toronto, if only she'd known more when she was young, but then if she'd known more when she was young she wouldn't have had Marie, and Marie was the best thing Thérèse could have imagined happening. So, perhaps, after all, it was better this way. "Comme il faut," Thérèse would say, and Marie would wonder how it all connected.

For the most part Marie was content in the cosy apartment with Thérèse. Her mother was young and kind, and loved to spend time with her daughter. As Marie grew up they went to movies and concerts. Through the seventies they enjoyed the renaissance of English-language Canadian theatre at Sunday afternoon pay-what-you-can matinées. Often they laughed outrageously at all the wrong moments; other times they sat rivetted by the generation of new playwrights. "La renaissance, peut-être la vraie naissance," Thérèse said of home-grown Toronto theatre.

Marie did not envy her schoolmates who lived in two-parent families. Family was a small concept to her. Marie and Thérèse. Experience had taught her it was very different for others. Family seemed to be a rigid set of rules that her friends spent their evenings and weekends bending or breaking. Family was a woman and a man and a house and sisters or brothers or both. Many times, Marie saw her friends' fathers rise like awesome giants, poised between the family and the outside world. Guardian kings of their castles, or so it seemed to a girl who lived comfortably and modestly with Thérèse Latouche as Thérèse aged from her twenties to her thirties, scraping through university, then teaching, growing from flip curls and Maurice Richard to flower power, Trudeaumania, hot pants and marijuana, through the quiet revolution, the FLQ, bilingualism and Canadian nationalism; explaining all these phenomena to Marie as she would to any inquiring young girl. Marie grew from child to teenager and finally, young woman. Then, life became more difficult. Hard to pull away, to both continue growing, without conflict. Hard to have conflict without a third person to help them make peace.

Thérèse had occasionally dated men, but never seriously enough to involve a third person in the family. It was only as Marie neared her thirtieth birthday that she began to wonder if that was a deliberate decision. Lately, too, she had begun to wonder about Smoodroc Falls, whether Thérèse might explain now, whether there might be an obituary in an old newspaper somewhere. Isn't there always an obituary when someone dies? Did they all die at one time, the whole family in one cataclysm? It might have been a lot of people. Then again, she was in Vancouver, and her mind was always drifting to oceans and chants, masses of women doing goddess-knows-what. Smoodroc Falls was not very present.

A father, though, a father had been an intriguing question. For many years all Thérèse offered was "Il est très gentil et il demeure très, très loin de nous." Marie believed he must have wavy hair, blond or light brown, as hers was light brown and tended to curl, while, unadulterated, Thérèse's hair hung straight and sleek, a brown as dark as black. In the hippie years Marie loved to brush the shine into it, long strokes down the length of Thérèse's back. Watch it sway, full and dark with the rhythm of her mother's movements. But for the hair and her bone thinness—Thérèse was small but gently curving—Marie might have been spawned by parthenogenesis or hatched like a baby crow from an egg. But for the name on her birth certificate: Paul Latouche. Once upon a teenage time she had tried to obtain Paul Latouche's birth certificate from the provincial registrar, but they had no record for the birthdate she invented, nor any near it.

Most of the time Marie didn't care, but in her early teens, she had pestered Thérèse, until one day Thérèse finally hollered in English "What do you want me to say? It's true, he is a very nice man, or he was, and he lives very far away. Would it be better if I said he is a horrible creep rotting in prison? Or very handsome and very cruel and he lives three blocks away so I can't tell you his name? Would it? Would it? You're still too young, but you're so interested, I'll tell you anyway."

She sat down abruptly at the kitchen table. "I was very lonely, very tired. I was nineteen and I'd been living on my own for three years. No family. It was very hard, here in the city. I got a job, finally, a fairly good job, in a nice restaurant off Bloor Street. Keep quiet, look nice, smile at the customers, good tips. I could save for university. I was going to be a nurse. One night, a very nice-looking man comes in. I mean nice-looking, his face and body, but also nice, uhmm, kind-looking. A relaxed, far-off look in his eye. And the way he dressed. Just a little different from all those blue suits and white shirts and plain ties. I thought he was old, but I guess he was maybe thirty-five, if that. And he was friendly. He ordered and ate, and each time I went by the table he chatted longer. He stayed, having coffee and dessert and I don't know what else. And when it was closing time he left, and he left me a very good tip. And it was just nice. A good customer. Nothing.

"I wouldn't have even remembered it, but the next day, Monday, was my day off. Most of the restaurants closed Mondays in those days. I was walking on Bloor in the evening, and there he was. Waiting to cross at Avenue Road. He recognized me and we chatted, and then he asked me if I would like to have a drink with him in the hotel. Well, I knew they had a beautiful lounge on the roof, where you could see the whole city. But I could never afford it. And I trusted him somehow. He was just so—what can I say, it sounds boring—he was just kind and pleasant. I was nineteen and that was all I wanted, kindness from a calm, respectful man. We had a drink, two, I think, but I was quite clear-headed. He invited me to stay with him that night. And I said yes. I thought, tonight I will not be alone. And I tried to be afraid of him and I couldn't. And I tried to worry about getting pregnant, and when I did, all I thought was how I wouldn't be alone." Thérèse stopped.

Marie looked across the table at her mother. "And his name is Paul Latouche."

Thérèse laughed. "No, no. There is no Paul Latouche, at least none that I know. I am Latouche, and so you are and so your father had to be. It was just easier. I lied a bit here and there. It wasn't easy, arranging all that you know. They liked to think of women's children as bastards then . . . But what was his name?"

Marie gasped. "You don't even know his name?"

"Oh yes, I know it. I'm sure I know it," Thérèse said earnestly, studying the tile floor as if the past was written there in a detailed narrative. "It was a strange name to me. A silly name, I thought. It didn't suit him at all. Henri? Henry? Ha-Hank. That was it. That was the funny thing he said. 'Call me Hank,' like a cowboy. But then he was so nice. And so nice to just go away forever and leave us to get along."

"You didn't mind?"

"What?"

"Being alone. Without money. There couldn't have been many single parents then."

"Well, more than you'd think. The first years were hard. I worked at the restaurant until they realized. And by then I had applied for university, and for every loan or scholarship I could find. I lied whenever necessary. Whatever they wanted on those forms, that's what I put. I started university in the fall of 1963. You were two months old. We shared a house with Peggy McLean, whose husband was killed building that old Bank of Montreal that used to be the tallest building in town. Remember Peggy?"

Marie nodded. She pictured a round face, with thick red hair tangled around it, a woman laughing, lots of teeth.

"She had a daughter a year older than you."

"Polly."

"And we lived there until I graduated as a teacher. The

summer of 1967. Of course I owed enough money to buy a small house, but who cared then?"

"I remember that stuff, but before, weren't you mad at the guy? Or lonely? Or afraid?"

"Mad? Angry? No, never. I had a sense that night that I might get pregnant. I suppose it was just my lonely dream. And if I was I just wanted him to be as far away as possible. So, I was glad he wasn't Canadian."

"A-ha!"

"Merde, Marie. You are obsessed." Thérèse stared at her fourteen-year-old daughter. "Get dressed."

"I am dressed."

"Not dressed—dressed up."

"Why?"

"Because we are going out. You and me. Toute la famille. Parce que cette famille, c'est Thérèse et Marie, Marie et Thérèse, et seulement Marie et Thérèse." Thérèse glared at Marie. Marie did as she asked.

They took a subway to the hotel with the roof-top lounge. Thick, red carpets, waiters in white shirts and jackets. The ribbon lights running north on Avenue Road. Thérèse led Marie to a corner table by the window. The waiter approached soundlessly. Thérèse ordered a glass of white wine for herself and a juice for Marie. The city spread out below, a spun web of white light. Marie saw sparklers and fireworks glittering. The drinks arrived silently, footsteps absorbed in plush wool.

"Now," Thérèse's voice drew Marie away from the window, "you have the whole story. Maybe most of it doesn't make sense to you, maybe you don't like it, right now. But, you must understand that I was alone in the world, and you're not. There's no reason for you to have a child to cure loneliness. Because you always have me. Now, we toast the man who made you possible, an American from Boston or Philadelphia or Dallas or San Francisco, who might have said his name was Henry or Hank or maybe 'My friends call me Hank.' You and me, we'll call him Hank the Yank. And we will be glad he was here and glad he didn't come back." Thérèse raised her glass determinedly.

Marie mirrored her mother's gesture, but shakily.

"Salut, Hank," Thérèse said, her eyes drank in her daughter and began to water, "merci, merci, merci." She touched her glass against Marie's.

At fourteen Marie was not altogether pleased with this version of her conception. Paul Latouche, a putative father, had been replaced by a one-night stand with an American cartoon character. He would never exist, never show up to claim Marie as a daughter. He would never become a giant standing between her and the world.

But as the years went by, Marie accepted that relaxing in a quiet, comfortable room at a table that looked out over the city was all the paternal comfort available to her. Gradually, she came to consider the entire hotel as set in a parental stance toward her. When life became difficult, when she and Thérèse began to fight and she needed to live on her own, she was very pleased to sip an overpriced soda, a glass of smooth wine or an imported beer at her paternal table and amend her perspective on life. Rather than feeling fatherless, she became a perennial salmon able to return, as needed, to her spawning ground and regenerate.

When she became a feminist, Marie initiated a special celebration of her conception day. Whatever city she was in, she found a quiet bar with thick carpets and a wonderful view. As twilight became darkness, she did not think about a stranger named Hank with wavy hair lighter than her mother's, but of Thérèse, young and lonely, of Thérèse, thirty-three, with a teenage daughter, toasting a father shed like an outgrown coat. She toasted Thérèse, her strength and determination, raised a glass to all that Thérèse had taught her, and thanked her deeply for sharing it.

So it came, not long after Marie had visited Shulamit, that she sat in the bar of the Sylvia Hotel, looking out on English

Bay, and lifting a wine glass to Thérèse. To her good sense thirty years earlier. "Salut, Maman!" she whispered, "salut, chère femme avec tes mystères." Marie drank slowly, relishing the nectar of life.

Light shifted on the water. Marie set the glass down and slipped a pen from the pocket of her oversized black suit jacket. Traced circles on the place mat. Circles and circles, side by side. Out on the water, women gathered. The dancers. She knew them. Women from everywhere. A night pane, sheet black water, figures shimmering, round and round. Marie reaching for the notebook. Women holding hands, tracing great circles, dancers in tutus and tights, brown ankles with singing silver anklets, the ageless, nameless, faceless guérillères rising from the water, brilliant dykes in all shapes and sizes, beauty queen butches and frivolous nuns, holding each other by the hand, swinging round in great arcs, circles and circles and circles, whirling, breaking into a whip of women. Girls of ten, eleven, twelve winding in patterns that wove night into star cloths, spinning a great silver-grey sky web. Water rushing above them, a great wall of water rolling toward the beach and the sky glittering as the women shed their many skins, shed their flesh down to dancing bones, clashing, grinding, smashing, flaking into air. Marie weeping quietly at her table as a shining shroud engulfed the city. Above it, in ashes, only a word remained: *INSURRECTION.*

Marie closed her eyes and rested. Sipped the wine and drew a heavy breath. Looked down. The napkin, place mat and paper coaster were covered in circles, spirals, figure eights. The word "circle" scribbled everywhere. In the notebook, she read:

> *We were the dead*
> *now we have woken*
> *we were the dead*
> *now we have spoken*

Break the circle & dance
child of the water
break the circle & dance
daughter of the daughter
break the circle & dance
in the darkness of creation
break the circle & dance
through the murdering light

We are women of all the ages
we are the spirit that woke you at birth
Go home to your birthplace
& look on creation
home to your birthplace
instead of salvation
We offer history one last chance
break the circle & dance
the millennium's ending
break the circle & dance
there's no more defending
break the circle & dance
in the harrowing light
break the circle & dance
murder history tonight

Marie drained the wine glass. She placed the napkin, place mat and coaster in her notebook and closed it. She rubbed her eyes and squinted at the darkened beach on English Bay. The still water beyond, the outlines of a few freighters lolling at anchor in the harbour. Her bicycle was locked outside.

As she pedalled through the West End, Marie realized that her calm was anchored in having explained her visions to Shulamit. She could ride her bike across downtown and pick up the bicycle trail on Adanac. A few blocks more and she could be home, dialling Shulamit, talking it out, talking herself down.

Safe from dreams, fantasies, visions and hallucinations. From the amazing madness of the Maze. Real, not real. She couldn't answer that. Feet pressing on pedals, her mind returned to the last afternoon of her weekend visit with Shulamit in Victoria.

"Does it matter?" Shulamit had challenged her in the big empty kitchen in Victoria.

"Well, if they are messages, shouldn't I be doing something? I mean, they're kind of apocalyptic. Shouldn't I be re-ordering my beliefs, at the very least?"

"I guess that depends on what you believe. On the other hand, you are doing something."

"What?"

"Writing it down. If you come to believe that they really are messages, from, like, some mystical wormhole of women past to women future, then it's all recorded, word for word in Little Crow scrawl. So, really, you're doing all you can. You said you had a sense that it was received, didn't you?"

"Yeah."

"And that lessened as you began to write?"

"Uh-huh."

"So maybe that sense was because you weren't writing. Maybe it was all blocked up in your head or your spleen or wherever it is you write from."

Marie nodded.

"On the other hand, Crow, maybe this is the end of history, and all the wronged women of all time are out dancing on the seas every night."

"It is." Marie giggled. "They are. I see them, Shula. And they dance like, like, women enchanted with lust and revenge and power and liberation. Like freewomen." Marie grabbed Shulamit and they two-stepped playfully around the kitchen.

"Up the insurrection!" Shula yelled.

A bear, waking slowly from a lengthy hibernation, danced with a little crow. And if a crow could kiss a bear she would have, and joined that insurrection, that joyful internal emancipation. So much history, so bound by history they hadn't lived. And if a bear, well, if a bear could kiss a crow without taking a delicious bite, that would definitely change the order of things.

Marie rolled to a stop and locked her bike outside the attractive wood and glass women's co-op. Sea air wafted on the night breeze, carrying thoughts of water, of Sarah Wise and waterfalls that gushed from ceilings. She would go back to Victoria soon. Back to the sprawling house, that old bear's warm lair, with a request and maybe even some canvas. Marie hurried up the steps, a chill brushing her spine. Saw her reflection flash in the glass doors, and behind it, like a memory that will no longer stay out of sight, Jane's face. Marie shivered. It was time to explain Mazie to Jane, before everything spun beyond their years. Shulamit was more than a tasty night.

"Mazie?" A half-hour later, Jane's voice drifted to a higher register. "What do you mean, a mind maze?"

"Well, it's a nickname, really. Sort of captures how I feel. Lost but intrigued. I, uh, I see things, people. I mean, I see women." Marie wriggled on the kitchen phone stool, struggling to convey fleeting impressions. "Women dancing, drumming, singing and chanting. The chanting—it's so powerful. No, it's more than powerful. 'Power-filled' captures it better."

"And they're not there? The women, they're not really there, wherever it is you see them."

"Well, I see them. But other people don't. So, I don't know where they are exactly, just they're suddenly present to me but not to others."

"Either only you can see them, or they're not really there."

"No." Marie hunched in frustration.

"What do you mean, no?"

"I mean stop. Right this minute it doesn't matter. I just want to tell you this is happening. I want you to know about it, to know this is what I write about. It's strange, and frightening, but it's fantastic. Excellent fantastic. I couldn't have dreamed it better. To me it's not real or unreal, any more, it's just something that happens, that I live with, that I work with." Marie blurted and exhaled, straightening.

"Any more?" Jane murmured. "Has this been happening for a while?" she asked quietly.

"Yeah."

"How long, 'Rie?"

"Couple months, now, I guess. It's, uh, it's just been too hard to tell you over the phone or in a letter. It's hard enough to tell someone face to face." Marie recalled her isolation prior to the Victoria weekend. Her thin neck stiffened, bony shoulders hunched again, winglike. "I didn't tell anyone until Shulamit noticed."

Jane was silent, silence that became sixteen hundred unbridgeable miles from Muddy Water to Vancouver, became the soundless acknowledgement of the separating distance.

"I'm sorry," Jane said after a time.

"Sorry?"

"I wasn't there. I couldn't help. You've been going through something big and we're too far apart for me to even know about it."

The silent miles stretched again. Marie slipped off the stool. Listened to the distance. Rested her head against the cluttered bulletin board. Finally she spoke.

"We are far apart," Marie said weakly, but clearly. Then, gathering courage, she asked, "Do you ever wonder what it would be like to be involved with someone close by?"

"More than a fling, you mean?"

"Yeah, Jane. Involved, something that mattered, someone who mattered." Marie's anger peaked and subsided. "Someone to do things with and talk to face to face, meet for breakfast on a workday, wake up with in the morning any day at all. You know what I mean, don't you? Somebody present."

"Back at the beginning I used to wish you were here. I used to imagine you somewhere in Muddy Water, at work or studying, and maybe I would meet you at the end of the day, for dinner or a movie, or just a quiet night on the couch. But, I guess I stopped. I got used to being here on my own. Now, I'm just here, and you're there and that's how it is. I don't think about it, I guess."

"What if you did? Don't you think you might be happier?" Marie fiddled with a tiny Guatemalan cloth doll lying on the kitchen table.

"I don't want to think about it." Jane pouted, then relaxed. "Well, yeah, I could be happier, I guess. You could say I'm sort of in a rut, I mean, some might say. Hell, Shulamit even does say. But I'm not desperately unhappy, either."

"Well, would you think about it? It feels like a rut to me. I'm not moving to Muddy Water and you're not moving here. So this is what we have. Maybe we both deserve more." Marie knew she had succeeded in planting the question in Jane. They talked a little longer, Jane asking to see her writing, Marie promising to send some, and to call soon.

When they disconnected, Marie immersed herself in a bathtub dense with essence of thyme. Comfortably supported by an inflatable Minnie Mouse pillow, she soaked in the scent of change, of belated endings spawning new romance. Marie soaped her skin thoroughly with a fist-sized loofah sponge, and doused baptismally, flexing tense shoulders. Wrapped in her favourite orange towel, she perched on the bed, clipping and filing her toenails, massaging dewberry cream into her calves and thighs. Then she slipped into an oversized Thelma loves Louise T-shirt and between leopard-print sheets, wrapped her arms around a worn satin pillow and sailed to sleep. Visions of Shulamit danced in her head.

Kiss the Spirit

To kiss the spirits:
now this is what it is really like

HOLLIS SIGLER

Ruby Gottisfeld & The Voices of Women

SUMMER CONTINUED COOL and moody, good working weather. When the sun broke through to warm the lake, Jane broke too, lolled in the small bay, idle in a canoe adrift on calm water. Sophia clouded her mind. Sophia doling out green foil harps and Irish ten shilling notes, gifts for St. Patrick's Day from Granny. Sophia laughing and smoking with Ruby Gottisfeld, distributing buttons printed with "Otto Lang is 2 4-letter words" after a sexist remark by the then-minister of justice. And laughing and smoking.

Sophia carefully explaining to Jane and Gene the peaceful coexistence of the tooth fairy and nuclear fallout. Fallout landed on grass where cows grazed, farmers milked the cows and children drank the milk, which, when digested, knitted into their bones and teeth.

"With strontium 90, scientists can test your old teeth for fallout, or traces of a nuclear bomb," Sophia said. "And the tooth fairy will still leave a quarter under your pillow."

Gene was sceptical. "If the tooth isn't there?"

"Fairies know everything," Sophia insisted. "You don't cross a fairy. In parts of Ireland people turn their jackets inside out to avoid being captured by the fairies." Sophia nodded seriously.

"Why turn your jacket inside out?" Jane wondered.

"Then the fairies can't see you."

"Why don't you want them to see you?"

Sophia leaned down and whispered. "Fairies are very mischievous. They're not all sugary sweet like Tinkerbell. If they capture you, there's no telling what they'll do to amuse themselves."

Sophia ensconced at the dining-room table, struggling to shred a gold and white credit card with curved nail scissors.

"Try these." Jane handed her a pair of sewing shears.

"Now, where do you keep those?" Sophia asked.

"In the sewing basket. Remember, we had to buy one for home ec."

"But that was years ago." Sophia sliced the card in half. "You still use it?"

"Sure. I keep my sewing stuff in it, you know, pins and needles, fabric scissors." Jane peered over her mother's shoulder at a letter laying flat on the table. "What have they done now?"

Sophia slid her letter into Jane's view.

" 'I am mortified,' " Jane read aloud, " 'by the blatant sexism in your advertisement on page 12 of the Muddy Water *Free Press,* Tuesday, May 15. I am closing my account and returning my credit card in protest.' "

Sophia chuckled, outrage giving way to a moment of pleasure. Then she was on the phone, reading the letter to Ruby, summoning the network that would send similar letters. Followed by a call to the store's publicity director, one of many similar messages he would receive that afternoon. Wafts of smoke curling up from the telephone corner, Sophia's central switchboard, until well into the dinner hour.

"Jane," Sophia called, pouring herself a quick sloe gin-and-seven, and rushing to cook, "would you set the table?"

"Sure, dining room?"

"Of course. At least if the table's set it'll look like dinner's on its way." Sophia tossed onions, mushrooms and chicken into an electric frying pan.

"What's cooking?"

"Chicken something-or-other. I'll name it by dinner time."

"Oh, let me. Should I make a salad?"

"Do we need it if we have rice?"

"I could slice some tomatoes and cukes. What's brown and crawls up your leg?"

Sophia grimaced. "Slice an onion thin as well and I'll make the rosemary dressing. Dear me, what?"

"Uncle Ben's perverted rice." Jane chuckled, pleased to assist, to talk as they worked together. Kitchen talks with Sophia were the best times. "Sorry. So do you think it'll work?"

"The point is to get them to withdraw the ad," Sophia explained, "by exerting economic pressure. Chicken Extraordinaire . . . Open a can of consommé for me, would you? You know, it isn't brown."

"Chicken Ordinaire, sounds more like it. What isn't brown?" Jane rummaged in the can cupboard. "Consommé . . . here, try this." She handed Sophia a tin of peaches along with the soup broth. "Chicken Del Monte," she laughed.

"Uncle Ben's Converted Rice, it isn't brown." Sophia looked dubiously at the tin of peaches.

"It works in that shish kebab thingy you make. Why not with chicken?" Jane pulled a box of Uncle Ben's rice out of the cupboard and checked inside. "Beige."

"Hell's bells—it's six o'clock. Open the can. But don't name it Del Monte. Something southern. The thing is, we have to connect our politics with our purchasing power."

"How about California, Chicken California, then it can be wacky. Or some place in California. How about San Diego? Chicken San Diego, that sounds good." Jane noticed the brown-skinned figure of Uncle Ben on the front of the rice. "Uh-oh."

"Uh-oh what? . . . Chicken San Diego? If you think he'll buy it . . ."

"Leave it to me. Politics and purchasing power?" She handed Sophia the can of peaches.

"Yes. If we can connect them, they'll get the message. If they didn't already understand that women do most of the shopping, they wouldn't be aiming their disgusting advertising at us."

"Speaking of which, did you ever notice that Uncle Ben is a Black man?"

"No." Sophia blanched. "You'd better drop that joke." She waved a greasy metal flipper at Jane.

"Done," Jane answered, embarrassed. "But, uhm, what about us buying it, or Aunt Jemima for that matter. Is that racist?"

"I'll have to think about it. Right now, your father's due—"

"I'm home," Phil called, slamming the front door. Jane hurried to set salt and pepper shakers in the middle of the table.

"Damn," Sophia muttered. She shoved the chicken around the pan, dumped in the can of peaches, then tipped in the remainder of her drink.

"Hi Dad," Jane called, running interference. "Like a drink? Dinner won't be for a few minutes."

"Fetch me a cold glass of Seven-Up and the paper. And put the ice in first, so the liquid runs over it and cools. Where's your mother?"

"Kitchen."

"What smells so good?"

"Chicken San Diego. It's the latest." Jane winked at Sophia through the door to the kitchen.

The ad in question never ran again in the Muddy Water *Free Press*. Chicken San Diego became a Cammen family staple.

Politics and peace, peace and politics. Jane mused, drifting in silence. Peace and how to achieve it. Float in a canoe or protest, rally, organize? Jane's generation had rallied when Reagan heightened nuclear fever in the early eighties. A hundred thousand walked through Vancouver to protest cruise missile testing, a quarter million lined the streets of Berlin. Was it possible to be other than pacifist in a nuclear world? Cirrus stretched like cotton candy above her. Obviously, it was. Was it moral? Jane wondered. Of course not, but ethics were out of fashion. Jane dipped a hand in cool water, rolled over the gunnel and flopped into the lake, sending the empty canoe skidding. She wriggled underwater, somersaulted onto her back and exhaled gently, watching the bubbles rise through the water to the liquid blue sky. A swift flutter kick broke surface, languorous breast stroke brought her alongside the chipped green canoe. Peace in our time, the peace movement, peace, love and Woodstock, peaceniks—words bouncing pebbles through the decades.

"Snow peace," Jane gurgled into the water, then lay on her back. The wide sky trailed tufts of white on the periphery of her vision. "There's no peace like home," she said plainly. "There's no peace like home, there's no peace like home." Touched her heels together soundlessly three times in the water. Sophia's face floated above her, not the handsome young woman of photographs and memories, but those same generous eyes in an older woman's face, her cheeks puffy, bloated skin beneath her eyes. Jane's sorrow staring back at her. The swollen hand that waved a final farewell through the reflecting glass of the airport outside Halifax. Sorrow linked not so much to her death, any more, but to her withdrawal from life before dying. When she escaped her first marriage, Sophia abandoned her public life. With only domestic peace to lean on, she gradually lost her balance. Jane shoved the canoe hard toward shore and swam away from the story of Sophia's last years.

Back in the cabin she heated the kettle for tea, mentally organizing the sheaf of clippings on the wooden table that crowded the tile hearth. She could remember Sophia laying the tiny tiles one by one. Two tiles in the front row had come loose annually, Sophia refastened them every July. The ends of the mantelpiece were guarded by two Irish goblets Sophia neither explained nor used, just stared at longingly, windows across an ocean. In between, a stuffed and mounted twenty-pound pickerel won by Phil in the last Wabigoon Fishing Derby before mercury poisoning suspended fishing in the river system. Sophia pronouncing it a "disgusting old thing."

Tea in hand, Jane settled down to Sophia's papers: no longer the detritus of her mother's life, but, along with other documents

Jane had recovered, tools of reconstructed history. Photocopied microfilm of newspaper articles on Sophia's activities, the major headlines that motivated her life and the minor ones that documented it. And Ruby—Jane held an obituary clipped from the Muddy Water *Free Press* two years after Sophia died. Ruby, smiling directly in the camera, bottom lip curling ironically, the way it would have the night she phoned Sophia from Ottawa. Ruby had coordinated a gala evening at the National Arts Centre celebrating the province's centennial.

"Not a single soul so much as glanced at my dress," Ruby howled. "The hours we spent looking for it. The money I wasted. Trudeau waltzes in with Streisand on his arm, and she's the only woman in the room. If I'd stood there naked, no one would have noticed." Sophia laughing till her eyes watered.

Sophia smoking and laughing with Ruby, talking, smoking and laughing. Jane, Gene and Ruby's boys silk-screening orange and black signs, political colours too ugly to be anything but honest, for Ruby's run at city council. Jane stared again at Ruby's steady grin from the obituary page, then picked up two pages with a note across the top in Bob's traditional printing. Grace, charm, manners, Bob was a man who knew how and when to be quiet. Sophia felt she had found it all in Bob, the retired teacher who read every word of Proust's *Remembrance of Things Past* to her night by night as the Atlantic lapped outside the window. Who recited Hamlet's soliloquies at random, booming out every line, who bellowed in a terrible imitation cockney when he was blowing a few rums to the wind. Bob, the second husband and the single pillar of the life that grew so unbalanced. The second pillar, Jane finally had to admit, had been a bottle of gin. Or rather, many bottles.

"Remarks of Ruby Gottisfeld at Sophia's Memorial Service." Immediately after her death, a lonely Bob kept Sophia present in his life by extending the memorial service to a far-flung network of friends, mailing photocopies of Ruby's speech and the Yeats poetry that Jane and her brothers had read across Canada and the United States, to a small village on Crete, to all of his extended family on the Isle of Wight and throughout Great Britain, and, of course, to Dublin. Jane, herself, received several sets as poor Bob wandered in a forest of grief.

"We met through the Voice of Women," Jane read. "We were committed socialists, committed feminists before that word was recoined by the present women's movement . . . Sophia once said to me, when we were talking about our over-whelming need to be involved in making change, that 'many care but few have the guts and the gall necessary to do' . . . She made the serious attempt to give her children a world at peace. She tried to give them individual freedom, to grow up independently. Yet she provided them with help and encouragement when they needed it . . . Her goals, dreams and aspirations have not died with her. In each of us who have been privileged to be part of her life, they live on."

"And yours, Ruby," Jane said, picturing Ruby's long, clean-shaven legs rising from high-heeled sandals as she flipped a dozen eggs one by one in the pan in the cabin kitchen. Ruby snarling, "Breakfast is ready, you rotten kids. Get in here and eat it," at her gentle sons.

Ruby and Sophia in earnest, late-night conversation over the direction of the fledgling government in 1969. How left would it be? How would they keep it honest? How would they wrest advances for women from an all-male cabinet? Sophia and Ruby and their cronies birthing the Women's Liaison Commit-tee in the living room of the house with the fossilized fish, plan-ning strategies to lobby the men they had supported.

And what we have flows from that, Jane thought, mourning the power that could have existed had Sophia and Ruby sur-vived to share her adult life. The inheritance of more than a dream, more than a fighting spirit and ghosts cheering her on. Hovering at the edge of grief's chasm, Jane quickly stood and stretched, noticing a small photo of Marie leaning on the trophy pickerel. Marie. It wasn't time for Marie. Her schedule was research from late morning until dinner. The sun had arched over the cabin, but there was still an hour or more before a dinner break was justifiable. Marie and all that went with her would wait. This was Sophia's time, time to trace the narrative of her political development, then write the chasm closed. Even broaching the notion of closure brought Jane some calm. She flipped Marie's photo face down and plunked stiffly back into the chair.

"We met through the Voice of Women." Jane reread Ruby's line, casting her mind back to childhood. A small wooden bowl that sat for years on a side table in the living room, a gift from "the Rushin Women." Four Soviet women invited to Canada by the Voice of Women—the vow Sophia called it—the national women's peace group spawned by the fear that followed Khrushchev's stormy departure from summit talks with Eisenhower in 1960. Initially a groundswell collection of Mrs. Who's Whos, vow members slowly set aside luncheon hats and kid gloves. The organization shed the Mrs. Lester Pearsons and Mrs. Front Page Challenges, along with its nonpartisan coat, and radicalized, emboldened by a note from its president on how to respond to "the communist smear."

Jane pictured the four Soviet women on the wide steps of the house with the limestone front, wearing dramatic dark-rimmed glasses, hair swept away from their faces, quiet voices, distant gazes. Was it 1963 or '64? Still cold war years, and the vow forging an international women's peace network. Jane opened a package of photocopies from the provincial archives where she had spent many intense, exhilarating days. Floor to ceiling windows looked out on the cenotaph. Sophia had stood there with other vows through the night on Mother's Day peace vigils. She imagined the women standing there still, as she combed through boxes of newsletters saved and donated by history-conscious members. Reports of travel missions through the Iron Curtain, copies of urgent night letters:

CABINET DECISION ON WARHEADS DEFERRED
UNTIL FRIDAY. JUDGE T. SAYS ALMOST COMPLETE
LACK OF LETTERS TO CABINET. SILENCE TAKEN AS
CONSENT. IF SUFFICIENT WIRES GO TODAY OUR
CONCERN CAN REGISTER EFFECTIVE FOLLOW-UP
TO MAJOR POWERS TEST BAN.
                    CHARLOTTE

Who was Judge T. and how had he become a cabinet insider?

Memos on conference organizing and proceedings, updates on special liaison projects. In quiet living rooms, women knitting green, brown and grey sleepers for Vietnamese children.

"They only use dark colours—" Sophia spilled boiled macaroni from a strainer onto lunchtime plates, "so American planes on bombing missions can't spot the babies."

"Why do they want to spot the babies?" Jane kneaded her frostbitten cheeks and slipped into her regular chair.

"Not babies." Gene smeared his noodles with cottage cheese and ketchup. "Baby communists."

"Better dead than red," Owen added.

"How anyone could drop a bomb on a baby," Sophia fumed, puffing away as she served the plates. "Inhuman."

Rooting through the material, Jane halted at a newsletter cover photo of a glass bowl engraved with a naked woman cradling her child; for several years all the newsletter covers featured mother-child images. On page eight, she read the caption, "Our Russian Visitors" and their names: Zoya Mironova, chemical engineer, leader of the delegation and deputy mayor of Moscow; Natalia Sladkevich, engineer, economist and industrial planner; Marina Bantsekina, surgeon and researcher in neurophysiology. "Dr. Bantsekina and the others were delighted to shop for clothes in Montreal," Jane read and laughed. Ludmilla Doilnitsyn, associate professor of English at the Moscow Foreign Language Institute, wife of the Soviet ambassador, was a late addition following the cancellation of a school principal from Ukraine, due to the sudden death of her husband. Zoya Mironova, Natalia Sladkevich, Marina Bantsekina, Ludmilla Doilnitsyn, an accompanying photo captioned each one. After all these years, names for the Rushin Women.

Jane skimmed the newsletters for threads of an underlying narrative, treading carefully between personal memory and public events that formed the crucible of political development for women who sparked second-wave feminism in Canada. "Mulford Q. Sibley," she read. The Sibley Affair.

Sophia had been a brisk wind doling out chores to ready the house for a post-speech reception. Jane cleaned windows and dusted, spraying cleanser graffiti on windows and tables, smearing and buffing until they glistened in the cold Muddy Water sunlight. Tables, sills and door frames gleamed with a mean Lemon Pledge coating.

"Silver?" Jane called from the dining room, spraying a peace symbol on the glass door of the china cabinet.

"No, it's just a coffee and dessert, maybe a bit of cheese and fruit, well—" the phone interrupted Sophia's mulling.

"Mom, it's for you," Gene called from upstairs where he lay buried in *The Hardy Boys Detective Manual,* learning how to tail a suspect. When spring later greened the city he practised out of doors, lurking behind blossoming crab apple trees and sweet lilac bushes in sunglasses and Phil's old fishing hat. He scurried from telephone pole to fire hydrant behind older neighbours out for a nightly stroll. He particularly liked to follow a slow-moving supreme court justice and a retired premier, their careers adding to the intrigue. This occasioned polite phone calls by Sophia, explaining that it was just her son "going through a phase. No cause for alarm." While Jane polished and dusted, Gene stretched out on a rug memorizing the routines of a good detective, and postponed taking out the garbage and sweeping snow off the front steps.

"Mulford Q. Sibley's been stopped at the border," Sophia announced from the kitchen phone. Jane hurried in.

"Well, we knew this might happen," Sophia added, dialling out.

"We did?"

"We had a warning." She raised her eyebrows for silence. "Hi, Sophia Cammen, is Ruby Gottisfeld there?" She glanced again at Jane.

"Why was he—" Jane began to ask.

"Undesirable, advocating violent overthrow of the government—Ruby? No, oh, okay, I'll try her there." She dialled again.

"Really?"

"Of course not. Pure crap. The man's a Quaker. Ruby Gottisfeld, please."

Party preparations ceased. A whirlwind began. Phone calls, meetings, press conferences, radio and television appearances, lobbying in Ottawa and Muddy Water, women in motion. Jane had it all in front of her, a detailed chronological sequence of events written by Ruby, publicist for Mulford Sibley's cancelled speech, appended to the minutes of the meeting of the Muddy Water VOW, March 25, 1965. The story behind Jane's childhood memory was a primer in basic political organizing, a short set-piece with all the right moves and immaculate timing. A phoned warning the night before, followed by an immediate call to their legal contact, who advised that Mr. Sibley had to actually arrive and be turned away to create a case; telegrams and phone calls to the federal minister and the VOW national office; a demonstration, legal counsel and press at the airport when Mr. Sibley was refused entry; a meeting carried on in his absence with speakers and folksingers—it was 1965—denouncing the government decision; and before the week was out, a meeting with the minister of immigration, in Muddy Water. The case was built for an appeal hearing, including letters of reference from the president of the University of Minnesota and the governor of Minnesota. Two months later Jane was back on house-preparation detail, smearing a fierce-smelling liquid over silver bowls and lids, watching it dry to a milky coating, then scrubbing until her distorted face shone in the reflection.

"Look, it's worse than the toaster," Jane giggled. "I gotta schnoz the size of the Umpire State Building."

"Empire State Building." Owen set a bag of party groceries from Phil's car on the counter.

"Witch Hazel," Gene hissed his regular taunt at Jane.

"Look who's talking, Jimmy Durante." Jane smirked. "Still, father's nose best." Gene nodded in agreement.

"Sssh, he'll hear you," Owen admonished.

A handwritten notation on the vow minutes indicated that the immigration minister promised to ensure that vow would be "exonerated from the smear." The comment led Jane back to another document, an internal memo from the national office titled "Voice of Women and the Communist Smear":

> Some of our members have been very worried during the past months, in fact, ever since the Voice of Women was founded, that Voice of Women might get a reputation as a "Communist infiltrated" or "leftist" group and lose its effectiveness in taking action for peace and international co-operation. This fear is bound to weaken many social reform, peace or civil rights groups. All through history those who want to keep things as they are have labelled advocates of change as "subversives," "outsiders" and "traitors."

And politically correct, Jane sighed. Her stomach grumbled. Dinner time. "Good night, Sophia," she whispered, "good night, you good women." She stood and stretched again. Picked up the small photo of Marie on the mantel.

"Marie, Marie, I pledge my love to thee," she mimicked

Shulamit. Maybe Shula was right, it was over, a fait accompli. Maybe it had been convenient to love Marie part-time, long distance. It didn't affect her life in Muddy Water or at the cabin. And if they hadn't been in different cities, would she have shrugged off Marie's liaisons? Heights of passion notwithstanding, Marie had been her occasional lover, not a live-in, entwined-lives partner. And a very good friend. Now it seemed that the proverbial woman of bounty was belting the final aria. She slipped the photograph in her pocket and pushed the screen door open.

Outside, the air was warm and inviting. What if she had a lover here, with her? Someone to talk to, someone to go for a walk with, at this very minute. To marvel at the sunset above the cliff, pitch stones at the beach, climb the hill above the lake and behold the panorama. What if that lover wasn't Marie? Jane scratched her scalp, attacking the itching thought. It wasn't her idea, but it was hers to ponder, now that Marie had spoken it.

Helen Weiss & Hannah Senesh

AFTER A HECTIC morning of patients in her downtown office and a dry tuna sandwich from the hospital cafeteria, Shulamit idled on a yellow bench on the very green grounds of the Royal Jubilee Hospital. Her foot tapped incessantly on the concrete sidewalk. She was reading. Since first tiptoeing her balking nerves into *Children of the Holocaust* she had read voraciously, her mind horror-tripping through the Ashkenazi genocide, the gates of perception flooded. Every story offered another nuance of government-required murder; every tale painted another section on Shula's iron wall with human faces, actions and sorrows. Shulamit lay the book *Hannah Senesh: Her Life and Diary* across her lap. She closed her eyes, saw Anne Frank's healthy face grow gaunt with typhoid, and opened her eyes abruptly. Afternoon shadows cast a lacey pattern on rich green grass. Shulamit squinted and the shading fused into black lace over vibrant growth, recalling the lace draping women's heads in the synagogues of her childhood. Her mother quiet beside her, silently encouraging Shulamit to blend her voice into the communal prayer of the congregation, though she herself never did. Until recently, Helen had preferred to pass unnoticed, to watch rather than join social activities, living adjacent to daily life rather than in it.

Now Shulamit was hearing better news. Through three postcards and a surprise phone call the most recent medication had remained effective. Helen had returned to swim at the spacious Jewish Community Centre set in the suburban ravine, sometimes with Isaac, sometimes on her own. Helen walked well-paced laps of the quarter-mile track behind the buildings, nodding politely at the many older heart patients making the same trek. After one such walk Helen wandered into the on-site art gallery and was awed by glorious silk screens of biblical women —Esther, Sarah and Rachel, Naomi and Ruth. The plastic covers came off the living-room furniture, the spotless end tables gradually piled up with flyers and brochures about Jewish women's organizing, about readings of Yiddish literature, about Torah study and midrash, about working in solidarity with Palestinian women. Strengthened by her walking, Helen had taken to exploring the city beyond her familiar suburban corner.

She'd been downtown to the women's bookstore where she sat on a stool and read at will, gradually purchasing every title on the three shelves devoted to Jewish women, from *The Tribe of Dina* to back issues of *Bridges* and *Lilith*. Back up to the old downtown branch of the Jewish Community Centre, where she shared the whirlpool with two red-haired women recently arrived from Russia, smiling and nodding as the water bubbled over their round pink flesh. And Helen, though still small and thin, finally did not feel frail and tentative, did not hover anxiously in anticipation of a tightening at the base of her throat, a shallowing of her breath followed by ragged chest pain that pinned her to the nearest chair. She sank into the warm water, eyed the other women's largeness, her own smallness, and enjoyed it all. On her way out she checked the bulletin board and saw a notice for Keshet Sholom, a gay and lesbian congregation. Crossed Spadina to a cafe where she rejuvenated with fresh carrot juice, a bagel with cream cheese and a decaffeinated coffee, perusing a free newspaper called *Xtra: Toronto's Gay & Lesbian Biweekly,* equally fascinated by the bustling news of a realm she had never imagined and the array of shining men's bodies bulging from its pages.

Another day she walked determinedly down to Yonge Street

searching for the bookstore that sold only books by gay men and women like her Shulamit, always with the pants and the short hair, never even a whisper about marriage, girlfriends who seem like more than friends, and a broken heart hidden from a fragile mother. Everything hidden from her fragile mother. In the crowded store at the top of a rickety staircase she would not have looked up a year ago, let alone climbed, Helen read the spines of book after book, awed by the breadth, and occasionally the focus, of the literature. Where had she been while all this has happened? While Shulamit grew from a rambunctious young girl to a doctor, almost a stranger, nurturing sadness on the other side of the country. Where had she been? At home, all those years, waiting for the pain. Afraid of the fear.

As mid-summer air thickened to paste, Helen visited the liberated zone, where gay men, and less so, lesbians, dominated a small area of downtown. In and out of card shops and video stores, past green grocers, delicatessens, hairdressers and rows of men who lined the cement steps of the coffee shop, appraising each other. Intently reading the flyers posted in the community centre, trying to snare in decades, determined to catch up to a world that had spun beyond the range of her fears and swallowed up her daughter. For thirty-odd years Helen lived in a city she had never even visited.

One very humid afternoon she called on Isaac at his office at the university sports complex, striding briskly in her mauve walking shorts, colour-coordinated track shoes and purple T-shirt with a small white women's symbol on the collar. His office door was open and she stepped in. He turned, and for an immeasurable instant they were not Helen and Isaac, thirty-seven unchanging years on opposite sides of a shared bed, nor even Hélène and Yitzhak, bewildered survivors of a continental scourge scraping together sparks of life. They were strangers, distantly assessing each other on first meeting. Before it passed, both recognized the moment and its surprising conclusion. Attraction. Helen saw a large, weathered man, greying hair a little too long and receding slightly, thickened all over by age, handsomely comfortable in loose, rumpled clothes, apparently comfortable in his life. Isaac smiled warmly at the sinewy woman in front of him, her intent brown eyes and sculpted face quickened his pulse. Helen drew a deep, satisfying breath.

"Shulamit is a lesbian." She spoke the fresh sentence across new air, a bridge between repetition and change. She watched his lips purse in amusement, watched all he knew that verified her statement coalesce in his mind.

"Yes," he said finally, "I would think that she is."

"Are you working much longer?" Helen asked "There's a film about a Jewish pig farmer I'd like to see. And the air conditioning is excellent at the cinema."

"I can leave anytime," Isaac answered, reaching for her hand as they left the office.

During her adventures Helen bought postcards and mailed Shula short health bulletins. It took more courage to pen the letter that rested in Shulamit's breast pocket as she read of the poet Hannah Senesh departing Palestine, parachuting into Yugoslavia, crossing into fascist Hungary in search of her mother. The letter Shulamit had carefully buttoned into her pocket each morning before work, as she slowly digested her mother's awakening to the contemporary world. Carried like a talisman, a positive omen of a future event. For many years Shulamit's greatest desire had been to receive Helen's sincere, undivided attention. Now, she realized with a shock, she was long accustomed to the lack. She was, in some aspects, shaped by it, and awkwardly unprepared for Helen's renaissance. Each morning Shulamit reread the astonishing letter:

> *So many years I have been here and not present. I'm sorry to have been so far away, so unreachable. I know something hurt you very badly, and I have been too far away for you to be able to tell me. But I have been walking and reading and out in the city like a young woman, exploring all around me and*

catching up on things. I go to the bookstores and the cafes and over to the "gay ghetto," too. (I'm not sure I like the way they use that word "ghetto" again. People move words too much, sometimes, I think.) I hope we will be closer, please write or phone or even visit, when you have time.

The medication really was working. Breathing easily, Helen had returned from the time of terror, just as Shulamit persuaded herself to plunge headlong into it.

With effort, Shula ceased beating her foot on the cement path. She lay back against the bench, fixed her eyes on the easy blue sky and concentrated on the sensual afternoon. The sun warmed her limbs, the wind cooled them again. She listened to gull cries wafting from the field behind the hospital and waves of traffic rolling behind her. She wanted the wind to blow through her mind, to scatter the images of terror and destruction. She yearned to see only resistance and survival, to glimpse the vibrant culture of Ashkenazi Europe. She pictured the majestic stone menorahs that braced the ruins of the Great Synagogue of Warsaw on Tlomachie Street, dynamited on ss orders after the Jewish defense of the Warsaw Ghetto in 1943. Let the wind carry the ruins away, show me the synagogue whole and proud, Shulamit wished. Show me those menorahs alive again with Jewish fire.

She thought of Hannah Senesh and her mother, Catherine, tracing letters in the air, disrupting the lethal silence of the women's section of the Budapest German Police Prison. Hannah raising a cut-out alphabet, letter by letter, to the high narrow window of her solitary cell, her resilient woman's body atop a tower of chair, table and bed. Simple messages to Catherine growing into "news reports" for all the imprisoned women. Let the wind free her, Shula wished, let her drift skyward in her British army parachute before the execution.

She pictured Frieda Jurman diving to block ss bullets fired at her daughter Alicia, late on a May afternoon on Kolejova Street in Buczacz, Poland 1944. Dying at her daughter's feet as Alicia was rearrested by the Germans, who had retaken the city. Alicia crouched and sprinting, zigzagging to dodge bullets from the firing line, across the Fador, starving legs running for the pine saplings, the river, the hollowed tree with only an underwater entrance. Run Alicia, let the wind be your legs, swim Alicia, let the water give you breath. Crouch in the hollow tree as the footsteps of the Jew-hunters fade away. Hide Alicia, hide and live.

She tried to imagine Zivia Lubetkin and Vladka Meed in the Warsaw Ghetto Uprising. She strained to see Auschwitz in her mind, to peer into the Pulverraum in the summer of 1944, where the precise hands of Regina Saperstein, Esther Wajchlum, Genia Fischer and Rose Meth pilfered two teaspoons of gunpowder a day from their forced labour on v2 rockets. Gunpowder sewn into a tiny, precious pocket, sometimes tipped onto the ground when a search began, other times given to the hands of couriers Anna Heilman and Alla Gaertner, and then to Roza Robota, who passed it to the male Sondercommando. The Sondercommando hoarded the dark grains, spoonful by spoonful, until word came down of their pending execution. On October 7, 1944, teaspoons of gunpowder blasted Auschwitz Crematorium 4. Shula pictured an explosion, then willed the wind to blow, blow history away.

Shulamit refused to ruminate on the execution of four young women for the explosion. Instead she remembered that Anna Heilman was liberated in her seventeenth year, Rose Meth in her twentieth. Teenage girls who resisted, and survived to tell their stories. She recalled an interview she had read with Rose Meth, who reported that she, like the others, hadn't cared about the danger. What she wanted was a chance to fight back.

To fight back, Shula thought, to defy the genocide, then realized that defiance was her birthright. Daughter of survivors, existing, persisting. Shulamit, they gave her death, and you, you got her life. Isaac's mother, Shulamit, Shula's namesake. And his sister, Raizel, her story never told. Shulamit Weiss, once, twice. Suddenly exhausted, Shula let the residual fear ooze from her body, slake from every pore. Her body cooled and relaxed. Gulls flew overhead and a raven soared high above, black and free in the blue sky. She breathed fresh, oceanic air wafting on the breeze, the scent of a white rose bush blooming by the chronic care unit.

Shulamit closed the book on her lap, gazed up at the window of the room occupied by Sarah S. Wise, half expecting letters to appear, the beginning of a message from the bedridden woman. HELP, or better still, HELLO. A coherent, appropriately placed greeting would have been more than welcome. She rose from the bench—a great bear returning from a distant journey, sometimes leaden, sometimes unburdened—sighed and strolled toward the chronic care unit. She was doing it, this time, dredging up monsters and submerging in ugliness. The route out, she was beginning to suspect, was narrative, the story-paths Helen and Isaac had travelled. And that of her aunt, Raizel. Perhaps the time had come to ask questions, perhaps this new Helen might provide answers. Or Isaac, on a good day, in the right mood, would tell a tale or two. Shula shrugged as she caught her reflection in the door to the chronic care unit. Put it away, she thought. Focus on medicine.

The fourth floor nurses' station seemed deserted.

"Hello?" Shula called tentatively, still shell-shocked.

"Hello," a husky woman's voice responded from below the counter.

Shula leaned over. "Oh, hi, you're Dr. Weiss, right?" Shulamit faced a weathered, forty-fiveish, pearl-skinned woman with spikes of bleached hair. "Justa sec, gotta talk to you, somethin' just came in," the woman added, standing.

"Have we met?"

"Oh, no, sorry. You're just, well, recognizable, in this surrounding."

"Like a sore thumb, eh?" Shula laughed, relaxing.

"Could say. It isn't exactly the West End of Vancouver here."

Shula laughed again and raised an inquiring eyebrow. "No, not me, straight and sorry. But my sister's a dyke, so I'm no Anita Bryant. I'm Del, Delores Whitewater." She offered a lean, well-manicured hand to Shulamit.

"Shulamit Weiss, pleased to make your acquaintance."

"So listen, something came in." She rifled a stack of papers. "I mean your Sarah Wise, there, now, she's dead."

"Dead?" Shula gasped. Ghost horrors quickened within.

"That's what Ontario is telling us. That's why they're so slow to come up with anything. They haven't fully cross-referenced deaths and health-care numbers."

"Dead? Why wasn't I—"

Del cackled, "No, doll, your Jane Doe 12-93 is down the hall, alive and pretty much ready to kick a little butt, I'd say. But Sarah S. Wise, that name we sent to Ontario, she's long gone to the other side. Hadn't seen a doctor since '82 so they ran a possible fraud cross-check with the registrar of births and deaths— anything to save a buck these days, eh? And sure enough, deceased, March 24, 1983. 'We will not be responsible for any health-care costs incurred where the insured is deceased' unquote. It's all here." She handed Shulamit a rumpled fax.

Shulamit read the fax slowly, to calm herself. Why did she care so much about whoever she was, anyway? Opening the past didn't do a helluva a lot for perspective and stability, she mused. "So it's back to Jane Doe. Didn't the police ever bring round her clothes and things? I called and explained weeks ago."

"Well, nothing showed up here. The clothes she wore coming in are still around. I think she has the top on, along with some sweatpants fished out of the lost and found. You should see her, she looks pretty spry. Noisy, too. Could almost swear she's saying words. But I can't make sense of it. Happens that way with the strokes, eh? Sounds just like a sentence, except for the words. You feel like you know what they mean, but really you just know they mean something. Frustrating as hell, I'd say."

Shulamit nodded and handed back the fax. "Thanks. Good to meet you. I'll just have a look in on her."

"Yeah, see you again, doll. I'm here now, long term." Del winked.

Jane Doe 12-93 dozed in a green hospital recliner wearing a brown knit top Shula recognized from the evening of her stroke. Her eyes fluttered open as Shula entered, the attentiveness in them startling Shulamit. For the first time she seemed aware of her surroundings. Her eyes narrowed.

"Dr. Shulamit Weiss," Shula said immediately. She had said it each time she approached the woman's prone body and probed for the human inside. "I'm the doctor supervising your care. We've met before."

The woman nodded in agreement.

"You know that we've met before."

Again she nodded.

Delight swept Shulamit. "And you understand you're in the chronic care facility of the Royal Jubilee Hospital in Victoria, B.C. You're here because you suffered a stroke."

The woman sat nodding, encouraging Shulamit to continue.

She's coming back, Shulamit thought excitedly, struggling to maintain a professional demeanour. "I was there," Shulamit explained, "when you had the stroke. That's how you ended up here. By the sea wall, on Dallas, Holland Point." The woman's head stopped moving. "I found your motel key, we went there to get your things, my friend and I, but the clerk wouldn't give them to us. The police were notified, but apparently they haven't brought anything here yet, I don't know why. I'll have the hospital call them again."

As Shulamit talked on the woman seemed to shrink with fatigue, and lose focus. Shulamit hoped she was still following the information, but if not, at least she had been clear for a few moments.

"Your name in the motel register was Sarah S. Wise." The woman flinched. "You're not Sarah Wise, are you?"

Jane Doe turned away from Shulamit. She raised her movable arm to shield her face and crumpled into herself. Shulamit heard muffled crying, then moaning, as she stood awkwardly at the end of the bed and the recliner. A caring bedside manner did not come easily to her. She had to know someone well before she wanted to soothe, rather than solve, them. Adrift in the residue of genocide, Helen had never been physically demonstrative. Shulamit had learned physical affection from Isaac's burly body. Her vocabulary included a firm handshake, a playful punch on the shoulder, a supportive pat on the back, and a crushing bear hug, none of which seemed appropriate to the situation.

"Aaaa-raaah," the woman wailed. "Aaaarrraaahhh." Shulamit laid a thick hand on the woman's small curved back. Jane Doe clutched Shulamit's medical coat with her mobile hand.

Shulamit's breath caught. She leaned over, slid one arm behind the woman's back, another under her thighs, and picked her up. Shulamit lifted Frieda Jurman from the stones of Kolejova Street, she lifted Hannah Senesh from the floor of the interrogation cell in a Budapest prison, she cradled Anne and Margot Frank as the typhus drained the last strength from their bodies, and laid them all carefully on the bed.

"Sssssss-aaaaaa-rrrraaaaaaa," the woman whispered, love and longing breaking on her battered breath. And Shula heard, as she tucked a blanket around her frail body. Shula listened to the sorrow and the joy that inhabited the name Sarah. As Jane Doe drifted to sleep, Shulamit slumped back into the reclining chair. She wasn't Sarah Wise, but she certainly knew her. Her belongings must be somewhere. With the police, at the motel, maybe lost somewhere in the hospital, between the medical ward and this chronic care unit. And she could talk. Could understand, briefly. If her health held, therapy could do wonders.

Shulamit made a number of deductions from Jane Doe's reaction to the name Sarah Wise, dead for a decade. This woman knew her and loved her. One more plus on the lesbian theory — let Crow reduce *that* to wishful thinking. Shulamit's foot began to drum on the polished tile. Therefore, Jane Doe had access to long-term memory. She clearly identified a woman she hadn't seen for a decade. She called to her. All of which was not unusual in a stroke patient. Childhood memories quite commonly survived or resurfaced after a stroke. Many stroke patients spent more time visiting the past than alive in the present. Not necessarily irrational, Shulamit thought. The memories were probably infinitely more pleasant than hemiplegia in a barren hospital room. Her next guess was that the woman did not remember the sea wall, or the motel, and perhaps never would. It was entirely possible, however, that she knew who she was and where she lived, and if not, that someone related to Sarah Wise did. Nowhere to go but up. It was time to locate Todd and schedule her in. And a speech therapist. One garbled name wasn't speech, but it was a start. Only time and work would tell.

Del seemed sufficiently unorthodox to climb on board Shulamit's pet project: the recovery of—of who? Shulamit rose from the chair. It was difficult to revert to calling her Jane Doe. Although her name was once again unknown, she didn't seem anonymous. She was very present, and somehow, very necessary. The unknown civilian, the wounded who could be cured, the dying who might be rescued. And she had been Sarah's lover, Shula was convinced. She laid her large hand briefly over gnarled knuckles and hurried away to spin the wheel of fate.

"It's not her recovery, it's yours," Jane said over the phone late that evening, as Shulamit fried chicken, carrots, snow peas and ginger in a well-used, but not well-cared for, wok in the house on Toronto Street.

"No, it's hers," Shulamit argued back, "but maybe she's mine. Whatever strange way it configures into my personal trip, she will definitely see some improvement from where she is now. I don't know how far she'll get, but it will be her recovery. It's just odd to be so wrapped up in it, so volatile."

"You've always been volatile."

Shulamit slid the chicken dish onto a steaming plate of rice and licked her lips. "No, not swearing and cursing volatile. This is different," Shulamit insisted, carrying the plate and the telephone to the table. "It's like, depressed to ecstatic, round and round, but maybe, maybe the cycles are smaller each time."

"And you're really reading stuff?"

"Yeah, really. And there's been an incredible change in Helen. She's finally snapped out of her comatose condition. She even acknowledged that she's been gone all these years. And, get this, she writes to tell me she goes to the 'gay ghetto' in Toronto, only she doesn't like that they call it a ghetto. I think she's trying to tell me that she thinks I'm a lesbian."

"Well, you *are* a lesbian."

"She doesn't know that." Shulamit lifted a forkful to her mouth.

"It seems she does. Did you ever tell Isaac?"

"No. You don't tell Isaac things. Isaac either knows or he doesn't know, it doesn't matter. I think the possibility of my existence always seemed so unlikely to him that whatever I do is astonishing, whether it's eating a piece of bread or finishing medical school."

"So you never came out to your parents at all?"

"Not exactly."

"What's not exactly mean?"

"It means I never said, 'Helen, Isaac, I'm a dyke.' But I never hid anything either." Shulamit leaned back, opened the fridge door, and rooted for a can of Cascade beer.

"Listen, I, I'm glad. You sound so much better."

Shulamit wrapped her hand around cold metal and shoved the fridge closed. "Well, it's mostly up and down, but when it settles, yeah, it's better. I think I'm gonna go see them. Maybe the High Holidays. I have to see what's happening here after this locum. I don't know if Killock's coming back or not yet. Have to know soon, though."

"Listen," Jane tried again, "can I talk to you for a sec."

"You mean can I shut up and listen? Yeah, sorry, I just get flying." She popped the top of the beer can and poured it into a dark red mug to let the gas run off. "What is it?"

"Marie."

Shulamit drew a deep breath.

"I think Marie and I are calling it quits."

Shulamit lifted the mug and drank deeply.

"Shula? Are you there?"

She swallowed. "Yeah, I'm here."

"Well?"

"Well, there's lots I could say, lots I would say, but I think, first, I have to declare a conflict of interest."

"What? A what? A fucking conflict of interest? What does that mean?"

"Hold on, hold on. It, it means everything that I have being saying for the last while about you and Marie not having that old spark still goes, but now my feelings are such that I'm not to be trusted on advising you with regard to that lovely little Crow."

"Jesus H. Christ. Well, fuck you, too, Shula. Fuck both of you."

Shulamit sat at the table sipping her beer and nibbling the snow peas out of her dinner, listening for Jane. Finally, she heard Jane's voice. "Shul? Not now."

Shula held the receiver away from her face, drew a deep grizzly breath, and howled raw and ragged, "*I LOVE YOU.*" Electric words hurtling across the Strait of Georgia and over the coastal range, up into the Rockies and down the foothills to the prairie, ripping from the receiver into the dark starry lakeside night, mingling with aurora and moonlight, in a resounding affirmation of her vitality. Shulamit furiously insisting that desire conquer fear, that she, daughter of Helen and Isaac, namesake of the murdered Shulamit, could defy the genocide and relish her existence.

Jane hung the receiver back in the cradle. Shula drained the beer mug and slammed it on the table.

Hollis Sigler & Donna Murdoch

"WHEN SHE LOST control, she only wanted it back," Marie whispered the words as her bike tires zipped along the sea wall between the dense green of Stanley Park and the greying harbour. The August rain was fresh and light, beading gently on her skin. Her feet pressed the pedals down and round, she felt her calf muscles strain and strengthen. "When she lost control, she only wanted it back." Marie had read the phrase a half-hour earlier on a vibrant pastel drawing that summarized her fears and desires in radiant hues.

She had set out late morning for a relaxing Sunday ride through town, thinking that the journey might include a visit to the Sylvia Hotel, on the chance that the night-dancing ghost women might return to English Bay. Her first stop was the bright pandemonium of the On Lok restaurant, for steaming wonton soup. Cutting across to downtown on West Hastings, with a pit-stop among pigeons and aging white men to drop a parcel at Co-op Radio for a friend, Marie had noticed the windows of the old Woodward's department store. Damp wheels slid through the brake pads. She bounced thick Doc Marten heels off the pavement to slow the bike, jumped the curb and rolled up to the display window, staring at the drawing hung there. Mustard, lime and turquoise framed a scarlet woman in a cage. Bracing the cage were pairs of potted plants, dinner tables for two, trees propping up a thin white banner. In the deep background a fiery sunset lit a brown burial mound. On the banner, Marie read "The illusion was to think she had any control over her life." She locked her bike to a stop sign and entered the oddly housed gallery.

Inside, a dozen more drawings scintillated with intense colours. Marie faintly remembered Shulamit referring to this style as faux naif, though she saw nothing false in the depiction of disturbing and dislocated images—a dress surrounded by knives, women's clothes scattered on a hillside, drowning stoves and televisions—in exultant tones. The colour celebration resonated with the energy of Mazie's conjurings, the images echoed the messages.

All the pieces flew banners. One said "Some days you feel so alive," another, "Trying to maintain an air of normalcy." Farther on Marie read "What does the lady do with her rage?" and "Walking with the ghosts of my grandmothers." Marie shuddered and absorbed it all, a sea sponge in a soul bath. If the accompanying short texts had not repeated facts and statistics about breast cancer and quotes from writings on the disease, Marie would have assumed it had all been conjured for her. That the artist, Hollis Sigler, had created it to ease Marie's mind, help her straddle the distance between her reality and the world everyone else perceived. As she gazed and wallowed, Jane's voice came back to her, and Marie understood how important it was to salvage their friendship.

Marie circled the exhibit again. She knew that pursuing Shulamit could make reconciling with Jane a long process. It could easily prove too close for comfort. Somehow, her role as initiator of change called into question the unimportance of flings that were, really, unimportant. But long-distance love just didn't seem to do the trick. Marie liked to hold a body, touch skin to skin, more often than every few months. She paused in front of a brightly framed rainbow. A yellow staircase lead to a door bearing a large red question mark. Below, it read "She really feels she has nothing left to lose." Even though the risk was unnerving, Marie wanted to plunge into the firm ample soul of Shulamit Weiss. If her penchant for wandering was spawned by character, well, Shula was still a ferry ride away. There was room for a mistake or two. She studied the painting before her. Paneless windows of a grass-floored room opened onto a barren landscape of sand mountains. Above the window a banner read, "The future moves in much closer." Marie grinned.

Before leaving the gallery, Marie gazed languorously around the cavernous space, drinking deep on the multi-coloured courage of Hollis Sigler. She would come back, while the show was still hanging. Come back with Shulamit. Shula could paint, if she would. And if Shulamit would paint for her, then everyone would see Mazie's women.

Marie cycled happily along the sea wall, emboldened by the verification she had received from the art, imagining the small catalogue in her knapsack glowing with spirit. Like the wheels of her custom-painted five speed, life was spinning forward, and forging ahead was increasingly attractive. Ending her lover status with Jane lifted a previously unnoticed weight. As the drizzle waned Marie acknowledge the strain of sustaining four years of intimacy across the second-largest country in the world. She saw the burden of guilt she had carried for her little trysts, because her sweet moments had bothered Jane, even though Jane intellectually accepted non-monogamy. Variety was just not the spice of her life. Luck of the draw, Marie thought, everyone you love can't be just like you. Maybe Shula would prove less vulnerable, or more adventurous. Rounding the point where the harbour opened to the ocean and English Bay, the last binding twine snapped and Marie rolled to a stop. The plain ache it left behind awoke an itch in her hand, the longing for words to mark the love and the loss, the familiar yearning to write. Without cataclysms or tidal waves, visitations or hallucinations. Without Mazie. The pure, uncomplicated desire to write. Marie sighed and pedalled again, toward the benches along English Bay where she could sit and scribble through the late afternoon.

By early evening Marie was back in her apartment, pinning the colour reprint in the Hollis Sigler mini-catalogue to her tiny black kitchen bulletin board. She flitted about the apartment, a bee buzzing with plans. The Association of Ontario Midwives had replied, explaining that a three-year training program would begin in September. Admissions were limited and closed for the year. Did she want to move back? Anything seemed possible, but her first priority was a collection of these magic writings, the cri de cœur of ancient voices. *The Freewomen's Chorale.* She imagined a chorus of live flesh and blood, touch-and-you-can-feel-them women, echoing through the same cavernous art gallery, encircled by canvases Shula had painted. Women dancing on a water horizon. A star canopy swirling above the night city. *Ia Orana Maria* kissing lifeblood in a forest of green. Shula loomed before her, presenting infinite possibilities. Friend, collaborator, lover. Without hesitation, Marie lifted the phone and dialled Shulamit's number. She would seize life now, squeeze sense out of it, rather than wait to be seized. She would visit Toronto and weigh whether midwifery was worth three more years in Ontario. She would—Shulamit's recorded voice announced no one was home and listed a variety of ways to reach her in an emergency.

"Hi Shul, it's Marie. Got your message. Sorry Jane hung up on you." On impulse she addressed the unspoken. "I guess it's just too close. She loves us both and, well, you know. Anyway, I'll just keep calling now and then until she wants to talk, but she'll talk to you soon, I'm sure. Call when you get a chance. How's that Jane Doe of yours, your lesbian granny, or should I say bubbe? Yeah, your lesbubbe? And uh, when was the last time you visited Vancouver? Hint, hint. Ciao, chica."

The following Friday a nervous Shulamit sat on the fold-out futon couch in Marie's claustrophobically crammed living room as Marie finished a late-morning shower. Shula had caught an early ferry from Victoria and driven up from Tsawwassen while Marie dreamed blissfully of nestling in thick arms and full breasts. Shula had an afternoon consultation with a geriatric stroke specialist; Marie would work twelve to eight at the co-op. The prospect of the evening together generated a nervousness in Shulamit that almost equalled Marie's excitement. Marie's phone message had opened the door, but Shulamit was loathe to roll blithely ahead while Jane was still ignoring her calls. And then, well, it had been a long slumber. Years, she admitted to herself, of sexual hibernation.

Shulamit heard the shower stop and squeezed her thighs together defensively. The ensuing rush through her genitalia warned of the possible demise of her career as a celibate. Shula rose and paced the small space, a spring bear in an unfamiliar cave. Her embarrassment recalled the awkwardness of high school gym class, the keen physicality of girls verging on sexual lives. She picked up and put down a collection of poems, fiddled with dusty shells lining the edge of a shelf, then noticed a small, surprisingly new television set tucked behind an aloe plant. A remote control lay on top. Exactly what she needed—televalium.

Returning to the small zebra-striped couch, Shula flicked on the mute and let her thumb do the walking through the channels. The rent must include cable, Shula mused. She couldn't imagine Crow paying to enter the multi-channel dimension. The Jays might be on. TSN had be there somewhere. Community access, CBS, BCTV, NBC, the Knowledge Network, the Parliamentary channel and a familiar face. Donna, Dr. Donna Murdoch, Shula's Hamilton friend. In a courtroom. Shula remembered the item on the radio news when Crow visited Victoria. Shula flicked the mute off and pressed for volume. *Inquiry into the Treatment of Children & Adolescents at St. Jude's* flashed across the bottom of the screen. She listened to her friend, her mentor, talk about her role in the aborted 1962 investigation into the convent school and orphanage near Cochrane, Ontario.

"I had been in practice in the town a number of years," Donna

Murdoch answered the lawyer's questions matter of factly, "and I didn't usually see the children at the school. But their regular doctor was away in Toronto and this teenage girl, she needed treatment. One of the nuns phoned and I agreed to see her."

"And what did the girl need treatment for?" the lawyer asked calmly. Shula heard the handle turn on the bathroom door and concentrated on the television set. Feet shuffled quietly behind her.

"That's my friend," she said over her shoulder, "my friend Donna Murdoch. Remember, the inquiry about that school near Cochrane, Ontario?" Shula turned, smiled and blushed. Marie stood in the doorway in an oversized T-shirt with drooping arm holes, towel drying her buzzed hair. Shula's eyes drank her in.

"She had been complaining of lower back pain," Donna Murdoch answered evenly. Shula turned back to the television.

"And did you discover the cause of her lower back pain?" the lawyer continued. Marie sat down beside Shula on the couch, still rubbing her hair vigorously. *Inquiry into the Treatment of Children & Adolescents at St. Jude's* flashed across the bottom of the screen again.

"That's the school Thérèse hates," Marie said quietly. They stared at each other. Marie perched on a corner of the couch.

"Yes," the doctor answered. "Once the nun left us alone, the girl revealed that she also experienced pain on urination. To my unpleasant surprise, examination and subsequent tests revealed urinary tract, bladder and kidney infections, as well as serious internal and external bruising, arising from repeated, forced sexual intercourse."

"And did the girl tell you anything about these acts of sexual intercourse?"

"Yes. She told me—"

"Objection." *Tony Ferucci, lawyer for St. Jude's* flashed across the screen. "This is hearsay."

"But this is not a formal court of law," the judge countered.

"Dr. Murdoch, you may tell us what you recollect of the girl's story, but it would be better if you did not name anyone who might be liable to criminal charges."

Donna Murdoch nodded and continued. "She told me that she had been living at the orphanage for three years, since her family died in a house fire outside a nearby town." Marie stopped rubbing her head. Stopped breathing. Clenched her fists. A familiar jolt slapped her spine. The woman on TV multiplied like an Andy Warhol silkscreen. The faces spoke in unison, chanting *died in a fire, bald-faced liar, died in a fire, bald-faced liar.* Marie closed her eyes and rolled into Shulamit's shoulder. Concentrated on dense, secure, surrounding flesh.

Shula tensed, listening as Donna Murdoch continued.

"She was very reluctant to speak, but after I explained that she was too ill to return to the school immediately, and would have to be hospitalized in Sudbury for a few days, she told me that she had been forced to have sexual intercourse by an adult male connected with St. Jude's on a regular basis for some time." She nodded at the judge.

"What did you do with this information?" the lawyer asked.

"Well, first I thought about it. Then, I decided to call one of the local constables, with whom I felt I had a good relationship. After she was settled in the hospital, I called the constable. He felt there was little we could do. That no one would take the word of a teenaged orphan against . . . against someone so highly placed in the clergy. He thought it could be arranged that she not return to the orphanage, but would still be allowed to graduate, as she had just a few months left."

"What happened to the girl?"

"The constable had a widowed sister in Toronto with a small child. The girl became her nanny, at least for a time. I lost touch after the . . . after a time."

"You lost touch after the what?" the lawyer probed.

"The birth," Marie whispered into Shulamit's soft T-shirt. Shula squeezed her.

"I just lost touch." Donna Murdoch smiled.

"The birth," Marie repeated, as Donna Murdoch's kind face fractured across the television screen. Marie jumped to her feet. The room filled with figures, closing around her, women pushing and shoving, grunting and squealing, babies crying and howling, wave on wave of voices crashing around her, water flooding from all angles. Marie spun and spun, pushing them back, then suddenly, whirling and dancing, joining their chants, dancing on the water, riding over the waves, soaring out where sun and sky are a continuous element, spinning and repeating:

> *Bred in pain*
> *born of the earth*
> *a price was paid*
> *it's what you're worth*
> *bred in pain*
> *child of the earth*
> *daughter of the water*
> *forgive your birth*

And Shulamit, stunned at first by the abrupt change in Marie as she rose, trancelike, fury and grief under skin and bones, suddenly scrambled for a pen and paper. Crow whirled in the small room. Shula sketched and scribbled as Crow spun on, thin limbs in a manic cycle, feathers flying in all directions, words rising and falling. A lone voice articulating a choral movement, and beneath, Donna Murdoch calmly refusing to disclose the name of the girl whose story she had told.

"If I must protect the guilty, then I shall protect the innocent." She rose from her chair as the judge reprimanded the lawyer for St. Jude's.

Gradually, Crow slowed and quieted. As she came to a stop, she teetered. Shulamit leapt to break her fall. She carried the broken Crow to the bedroom, pulled back the leopard-print sheets and gently laid her down. Shula checked her pulse—still racing—felt a fever breaking into fine sweat on her brow, and went to the kitchen to put on the kettle.

The television droned on. Donna Murdoch was gone, but Shula knew where to find her. Marie was in no shape to go to work. Shula was tempted to fill a prescription for a heavy tranquillizer, but it would have been too much of a betrayal of Crow's holistic principles. She rooted in the kitchen for an appropriate herbal concoction, eventually brewing a heavy mix of valerian and St. John's wort. Finding Marie's work number on the bulletin board, she called in sick for her, then dampened an orange handtowel and laid it across her forehead. Marie stirred slightly, but continued to sleep. Her pulse had slowed to resting. Shula left the sedative tea sitting on the freestanding chrome ashtray that served as a bedside table.

House keys dangled from a cowgirl boot fridge magnet. Shulamit went out, strolling Commercial Drive to clear her head. The bustle of life on the Drive was calming. Young punks and aging bush hippies hanging out in the park. Dykes on bikes and motorbikes, laid-back het couples brunching at noon, strollers and gawkers, panhandlers and hawkers. She smiled at the graffiti punctuating the walls. Nothing like a buzz to calm a caged bear. Shulamit ruminated as she walked. It was difficult not to link Marie's visions with the information revealed today, especially as it so clearly prompted a journey into the land that only Crow visited. Some deep part of Crow's psyche had been working on this all along, Shula speculated. And probably asserted itself from time to time because it was getting so little conscious attention.

Shula paused to get her bearings in front of a stationers' with journals and sketchbooks in the window. It was only then she remembered sketching Crow as she whirled, scribbling the sounds, the words Crow seemed to be speaking. Her fingers tingled. Her eyes teared suddenly, she blinked, and reached for the door handle. A small bell rang as Shulamit stepped inside the shop.

An hour later she was back at Marie's, her large palm cradling Crow's sharp chin as Marie slurped liquid sedation. Crow's frightened eyes darting about, Shula's calming hand pressing each cheek.

"Sleep, Crow, everything's taken care of. Drink this, and sleep as long as you can. I'm going to keep my appointment, but other than that, I'll be here. You sleep now, and then we'll talk."

Meekly, Marie kissed her hand. Shula was here, strong and calm and loving. Shula would know. Crow was too tired for any more flying. Crow was scattered feathers on a bed of down. Crow was sinking away, into the quiet deep, and the deep quiet cave would be safe. The bear was on guard.

Shula took the mug to the kitchen. Began emptying the bags of groceries she had bought. Stress enhanced her appetite. A large omelette would do nicely, and fresh coffee with milk and honey, toasted bagel on the side. She sliced vegetables, thinking of how many times she watched her mother, Helen, do the same. On top of the fridge lay a pristine sketch book and a variety of leads. Could she draw Helen from memory? Capture that now-vanished creature before she met the butterfly that had emerged from her cocoon? Shulamit whistled. So much to do, and so interesting. What made life suddenly come alive? Why did everything sometimes seem an interesting challenge, other times a road littered with insurmountable obstacles? Love? Maybe. But maybe it was more than that. Maybe it was every-thing—the challenges, the changes, the twists and turns. The love. Maybe it was grabbing on to life with vigour, plunging in with all four paws and not holding back anything, from the grunts of pain and frustration to the growls of lust and celebra-tion. Maybe it was all about living fully as the bear she was. Shu-lamit Weiss, once, twice. Almost thirty-five, she takes her own advice: "Company, contact, caring. Touch can be a great healer."

13

Masha Cammen-Courchene

& The Queen of Hearts

JANE FROWNED AT the naked shoulders of Prime Minister Kim Campbell gracing the Muddy Water *Free Press,* a photograph of the one-time minister of justice standing behind, rather than wearing, judicial robes.

"It's only daring insofar as it's a photo of a federal justice minister," Jane addressed a monarch butterfly fanning its wings on a file folder. "For women, undressing has always been the easiest way to get attention. Nude has meant woman for centuries. So now," she paused her rambling to sip warm coffee, "the prime minister is a nude. Feh, as Baba used to say. Keep your clothes on in public, Kimmy."

The morning sun intensified, Jane slipped out of her saffron sweatshirt, head emerging as a flashy pick-up pulled into the top of the driveway. Masha's unmistakable auburn locks were followed by a tumbling toddler, Micah. Four now, born out on Manitoulin Island the summer Jane reopened the cabin, listening to reports from the Aboriginal Justice Inquiry and obsessively cutting caragana.

"Microbe! You've grown," Jane called, strolling up toward the truck. "Got your message, Mash, but you never called back with the number."

"I tried you in the city a few more times, but when you were never home I figured you must be here. Tell her you're too big to be a Microbe now, aren't you, Micah? Thought I might just drop in." Masha freed the struggling child to run in the long grass.

"Hey there, little sweetheart, gonna come and see your—your what? Oh, yeah—your first cousin once removed." Jane crouched low as he giggled toward her. Auburn hair blowing back in the gentle breeze, his father's gentle, crooked smile breaking into a low chuckle. "You rumble like your old man, Micah, I haven't heard that in a long time." Micah stood in front of her, grinning. "Didn't bring Dad along, did you?"

"No," Masha absorbed the landscape where she had frolicked through exquisite childhood summers. "Not today. But Charlie sends his greetings. He's up at Kenora for the grand opening of the new casino. He did the plans, couple years back. 'Course now he's worried about the effect on the community."

"Well, they'll make a lot of money, anyway." Jane relished the firm, tiny grip as Micah took her outstretched hand. She led him toward the cabin. "Want some watermelon, Micah?"

"He'd love it. He's already sucked down all the juice I brought for the trip. They'll rake it in hand over fist. It's just a question of from who. And of course, how they spend it."

"That's the crux, isn't it? How to spend communal funds, especially in a small community."

The screen door slammed behind them. Micah settled in at the kitchen table as Jane heaved a large watermelon from the fridge to the counter. Masha wandered into the living room. Sweet memories crowded down the years—rainy-day card games, chilly late-night swims, Aunt Sophia stoking the fire to warm their shivering bodies, yellow flames toasting Masha's back as she dripped on the fireplace hearth, now occupied by Jane's table, cluttered with papers and files.

"You're really working," she commented.

"Yeah. Almost finished. Just need to sort everything into chapter files, then settle down at the computer and write." The long knife blade pierced the watermelon, green rind split into soft fuschia. Watermelon sugar oozed onto the counter. Micah watched, fascinated.

" 'In watermelon sugar the deeds were done,' " Jane quoted

Richard Brautigan's prose, magical to their ears twenty years earlier.

" 'And done again as my life is done in watermelon sugar,' " Masha echoed. "Where's the computer?"

"Mine's in town. I leased a laptop rather than lug it back and forth. Power failures, rowdy middle-class teenagers who like to break into cabins . . ."

"Like Gene's friends." Masha laughed knowingly. "So much is the same here. Phil's ugly old stuffed fish still sitting on the mantelpiece there. Wow, Micah, that watermelon's pretty juicy, isn't it?"

"Pretty watery," Micah answered, both hands reaching for the slice in Jane's.

"Want some, Mash?" Jane asked, handing her a dripping piece. "So, you're not staying long in Kenora?"

"Well, it's all up in the air now. We've been moving ever since Charlie graduated—project to project. It's been hard but really good. I worked so much when he was studying, I haven't minded just taking care of Micah and managing the travel. Where haven't we been lately? Cities, I guess." Masha stopped to bite into the watermelon.

"Come on, let's sit on the dock and spit seeds in the water," Jane suggested. "Make a watermelon lake."

"You're wasted on adults, kiddo," Masha observed. "Anyway, I've had enough of moving us around all the time. And Charlie's interested in an internship with Douglas Cardinal. Which could mean moving west." Masha held the front door open, Jane took Micah's hand, and they child-stepped, one stair at a time, down to the little path. "Micah needs to settle into a school, and I'm ready to, well, I don't know what exactly. I'm not interested in going back to bookkeeping, but I want to work. It's time to put down some roots. Maybe Charlie will come and go if he has to. I'd like to head out to B.C. before too long."

"Can you swim?" Jane asked Micah as they inched down the rocky path and onto the old dock.

He nodded.

"Some," Masha corrected.

"Let's sit here then, where it's shallower."

Masha slipped off Micah's runners and socks, his feet stretched toward the water.

"Marie's in Vancouver, isn't she?"

"Yeah, but—"

"Micah, if you want to go wading let me pull those pants up. Or take them off and go in your shorts." Micah had scrambled over to the little beach and hovered, toes edging into the cool water.

"I'll do it." Jane stepped barefoot onto a dockside rock. "But we're splitting, I guess. I mean we've split, Marie and me . . . Marie and I. A short goodbye." Hopscotching from rock to rock, she arrived at a giggling Micah and helped remove his turquoise sweatpants.

"Oh, sorry." Masha spat a seed to ripple ten feet away.

"Nice shot . . . Yeah, and I think she's going to take up with my friend Shulamit," Jane studied her reflection in the water as Micah waded in.

"Ouch." Masha observed Jane's distraction and decided to extend her visit. Kenora could wait.

"They've both been leaving messages." Jane pitched a stone out into the bay.

"You're not speaking to either of them?"

"I know it's a bit childish but . . . I'm pissed off. Well, at Marie, anyway. She always does what she wants, she always gets who she wants. She wouldn't recognize a consequence if it spat in her face. I feel like I spent four years waiting for something that wasn't ever going to happen."

"Maybe you did—Micah, don't go past that rock," Masha admonished. "Maybe you didn't, though. You never thought Marie was going to move to Muddy Water, did you?"

"Uh, I guess not." Jane flung another stone. "No, of course not. I might have wished it that first fall when I bought the house and was setting up. But, no. For more than three years I knew she'd never move here."

"Nu?"

Jane laughed. "Nu, I guess I got what I settled for, as Oprah's sexperts say. Lots of time to myself. No fusing of psyches and souls. Romantic trips to Vancouver . . . I met a lot of great folks there. Muddy Water's all right. It's home. But Muddy Water suits me a lot better when I can pop off to Vancouver every couple months." She watched Micah splash toward a school of minnows. "Especially in winter. What a relief. I'll miss that."

"You don't have to," Masha countered. "We'll probably be out there soon. And, you know how it goes. You and Marie could end up friends."

Jane dipped a foot in clear water. "I miss Shula already. We haven't been in the same city for a while but we've always been in touch." Quartz pebbles sparkled beneath the shimmering surface. "Marie pisses me off though. All those affairs, now she has to go after Shula? It's not like Shulamit's the only available woman she knows. She wants to be taken care of, and Shula will do it, easily. Piece of cake." She paced the water's edge, cooling her toughened feet. "Well, I'm not giving up my friend just because Marie's got the hots for her. Fuck that noise—Oh, sorry."

Micah grinned. "Fuck you, fuck off, fuck it, fuck them, fuckin' bi—"

"Thank you, Micah. We've heard them all before. It's much more interesting to think of new things to say, isn't it?"

"Wee-nuk!"

"What's that?"

"Micah, that's enough. I don't care if you know these words but I don't feel like hearing them any more today." She turned to Jane. "Penis in Ojibway. He's discovered swearing. Listen, would you like to take a trip with us?"

Micah bent to splash Jane. Jane waded in, ready to return fire. Micah let fly with both hands.

Jane squatted to retaliate. "A trip to where, Mash?" Micah sprayed her again.

"Petroforms. Bannock Point. Up the old highway, hang a right before the goose sanctuary. I hear it's amazing but I've never been. Folks have been having ceremonies out there again. I just want to walk around, introduce Micah while he's still young."

"Really? I had no idea. I'd love to go." Micah waded over to a red plastic bucket half-buried in the sand.

"We could stay over and go tomorrow, if you'll lend us something to sleep in." Masha looked at her son. "He's had enough driving lately. Just need to call Charlie and let him know."

Jane dug deep in the water, soaking Micah as he retrieved the bucket. He rippled with delight. She backed away as he submerged the pail. "Have to go to the pay phone across from the beach." Jane shrieked as the water hit.

"Janulah, you could get a phone."

"Janulah. No one calls me that any more." She enjoyed a moment of nostalgic calm. "Guess I'm a bit of a Luddite, Mash."

"Guess so. It's still 1968 in there. Micah, not me, I'm not playing." He strode steadily toward her, a tugboat tyke dragging a loaded pail. Masha scrambled to her feet.

"Except for the laptop. Well, hangin' in the past has been good for my historical research. But maybe you're right. I could shove all that bric-a-brac in one memorial corner and bring down my own stuff. A woman has a right to her own tacky junk."

With a heave Micah poured sand-laden water that sluiced down his mother's calves. "That's it. You've had it now." Masha plunged into the shallows.

"Sock 'im in the nuts, Mash." Jane burst into laughter.

"Can't—he's my kid." She hoisted Micah. He tilted the pail. "Oh, gross," Masha squealed as sandy dregs sluiced down her neck.

Micah giggled. "Oh, gross," he mimicked. "Sock 'im in the nuts, Mash."

"Time for bathing suits." Jane waded to the dock.

"Ours are in the knapsack. I left it on the kitchen table."

"Back in a sec," Jane sprinted lightly up the path to the cabin, warm in the afternoon sun, wondering if she'd been waiting for time, when the real trick was to keep pace with it. Perhaps contentment lay in letting go of holding patterns and long-distance lovers, and splashing forward into the present.

Morning dawned scarlet. Jane squinted at the blazing silhouette of the eastern shore and slipped back to sleep. By eleven the sky was a noncommittal grey, and Jane was riding comfortably in the new truck, high above the aging highway as they bounced between pines and lakes. At the goose sanctuary, wide wings fanned into graceful two-point landings amid choral honking. Jane rifled the shelves of the interpretive centre for pamphlets and maps on the region. As they drove north, she read aloud from the government brochures.

" 'Man's presence'—of course they mean human presence, can't beget a man without a woman, eh?—'in the Whiteshell Provincial Park has been traced to about 3000 B.C. . . . a few clues around Jessica Lake point to an even earlier date . . . About 1800, the Cree left the area, moving north and west, and the Saulteaux . . . moved here from the vicinity of Lake Superior . . . It is not known whether it was the Saulteaux, Cree or one of their predecessors who left the mysterious petroforms in the Whiteshell.' "

"Not known by whom?" Masha snapped. "They certainly weren't slapped together a hundred years ago . . . Moved north and west, sure, Europeans pushing the Saulteaux, Saulteaux pushing the Cree. The European intrusion created one helluva land pressure. We're all g.d. immigrants, us Euros."

"G.d.," Micah whispered, nodding off to sleep.

Masha rolled her eyes and patted his head.

" 'The name "Whiteshell" appears to be related to Migis,' " Jane continued, " 'a white shell that symbolized spirit power and was an important part of initiation into the first level of the Midewiwin or Grand Medicine Society of the Ojibwa.' "

"Jesus fucking Christ Almighty." Masha clenched the steering wheel. Micah's eyes popped open. "Nothing worse than the government trying to explain what they don't understand. Can't they just be respectful and back off. I'd like to see them write up Christianity like that."

"It appears to have been brought to the continent by wayward travelling men, unwanted in their birthplaces," Jane began, "and intent on convincing the inhabitants of Turtle Island to worship the image of a man nailed to two pieces of wood placed at right angles and to sing in an ancient language no longer spoken."

"Domini, domini, domini," Masha intoned, "we're all Christians, now."

Jane picked up another pamphlet, skimmed it silently. *The area containing the petroforms is Manito Ahbee, the place where God sits. It is the site where the original Anishinabe was lowered from the sky to the ground by the Creator.* "Manito Ah-bee," Jane repeated aloud.

"Where god sits," Masha responded.

"Gottisfeld," Jane mused, "god's field or god's land."

"Here." Masha announced, turning right off the road into a gravel parking lot.

Jane saw the same mix of poplar, pine and birch that surrounded the cabin. "Manitoba." She opened the truck door and hopped down as Masha unbuckled Micah. "The place where god sits," she said quietly.

A metal plaque beside a well-tended path read "Boulder Mosaics" and offered another rambling, uncertain explanation of the petroforms' origin.

"Never mind that stuff," Masha said. "Let's make our own interpretations." She bent down to Micah. "Where we're going now, Micah, is very special. You'll be able to tell. And it's really important that we're very careful while we're here. Everything is exactly where it's supposed to be, and we want to make sure it stays that way." She showed him a small plastic bag of tobacco. "We'll leave some of this in thanks for our visit. You can help me." She winked at Jane as Micah grasped her hand.

They walked expectantly along the path to a spacious clearing. Bedrock open to the sky, a plain of rock broken only by small stands of pine. A perfect quiet descended. The low cloud ceiling stilled the air. Jane strolled to the right, toward a rock outline on the ground. Masha led Micah over to a small grove, where Jane saw her place tobacco in his hand, take some in hers and close her eyes. Jane continued on.

To the left, a large turtle, in outline. Farther on, an ancient snake, twenty, thirty feet long, Jane estimated, pale pink granite covered with mint lichen. Jane searched her memory. Lichen takes hundreds of years to grow, can be thousands of years old. Thousands of years. To the left, the form of a fish. Twice Jane's arm span in width, thrice her height in length. Jane walked around it, tracing the outline, imagining human footsteps wearing the rock smooth over thousands of years. She followed the fish form, again and again, inhabiting the quiet, not a ghost terrain swarming with imputed spirits, but an empty temple whose stone pews bore traces of centuries of worship. That's what Masha meant by our own interpretations, Jane thought, turning to see Masha and Micah approaching from behind.

Jane surveyed the ancient, stark beauty, relishing an elusive physical echo, the resonance of every foot that had smoothed this stone. A place where she could feel the history of the land, this place where god sits. She pondered the vastness of life before the Europeans arrived, striving to remake Europe on another continent. Life before shingles and bricks, petticoats and top hats, before industrialization transformed forests into planks, cliffs and valleys into gems and minerals. Ahead, she noticed tracks of a long-unused road.

"Imagine what they drove over," Masha said, beside her.

"It's amazing anything survived."

"Thank god," Masha scooped Micah up, nuzzling face to face. He wrapped his arms around her neck.

They wandered comfortably, commenting on the different forms, snakes and turtles and fish, human figures and Medicine Wheels. At the path both women turned back.

"It's like suddenly learning that the Wailing Wall, or a sphinx, has been sitting in my backyard all my life," Jane said.

Masha nodded.

"Got any tobacco left?" she asked Masha. "I don't know what to say or anything but—"

"Some in my purse pocket," she leaned away, jutting the bag out behind Micah's leg. "Just say whatever you feel, and be respectful. I don't think it can hurt."

Jane nodded, shy but determined. She walked over and placed a pinch of tobacco inside a circle of stones. At first no words rose to her tongue, then she leaned back and gazed at the sky. "L'chaim." Her voice was clear. She stood, light and strong, and followed the mother and child out of the clearing.

Even Micah was quiet on the return drive, stilled by the silent splendour of the petroform site. They drove by the old bakery, where the road bordered the open water of the lake.

"Who knows, maybe you'll meet someone," Masha suggested.

"Yeah . . . Remember the cinnamon buns." Jane rolled down the window and leaned into sweet air. "Just gotta get out in that thriving Muddy Water dyke scene."

"Blueberry pie." Masha licked her lips. "Even I know it's not that bad."

"I suppose," Jane grumbled. "No, I know. Besides, I'm a bisexual . . . It's only been—what?—five years I've been with women. Almost six since I've been near a guy. Fuck—" Micah turned his head sharply. "Oh, sorry. That would be weird."

"I've read a story about migis." Masha ignored her son. "If I recall rightly, Nanabosho made clay figures of a man and a woman, and the Creator blew life into each through a migis—a shell."

"I've never seen a shell here."

"They're small and white. I'll find the story for you. A lot of our books are stored at my folks'. "

"Somebody named this park, and not so long ago, either." Jane rooted through the pile of pamphlets. "Yeah, here . . . 'in 1931 the province established the Whiteshell Forest Reserve . . . in 1961, the Whiteshell became a provincial park . . .' so, in 1931 someone thought there was a good reason to call this area the Whiteshell."

"Maybe it's always been called that, and the government just translated it into English."

"Yeah, maybe so. Migis Park. The name never changed, just the dominant language." The Pine Cone Bar came into view. "How about an ice cream? My treat."

Time slowed and lengthened after Masha and Micah left. Jane felt newly alone as early shadows cloaked the cabin, conscious of Marie's absence after years of living with the expectation of contact. Dependent on a habit of mind, she realized, that more than a thousand miles away, Marie expected her, to call or to write or to visit. A habit she now had to break. Jane knew Shula deserved a lover, and that she wouldn't just slip one on like tight jeans for a night on the town. She stepped deliberately into the twilight. The uncut grass bristled as she walked up the driveway to the pay phone across from the beach.

"Hi," Jane blurted when she heard Shulamit's voice. "I miss you. I have to admit I'm lonely."

"You've been lonely for a while," Shulamit answered quietly.

"Ever since Sophia died. I guess it's time I let her go." Jane twisted the phone cord.

"You will when you're ready," Shula said evenly.

"I'm ready as I'll ever be. Most of the research is done. You know, in some ways it's been fabulous. They've all come alive in my mind, Sophia and crew. What a bunch, what a time. I love it." She suppressed a desire to bawl like a baby.

"I'm sorry."

"Don't be. I couldn't stand it if you were sorry. I expect you to be happy." Jane heard the hiss of a beer can opening.

"Well, don't marry us off yet."

"Shula, you may be measured and sensible. Plodding, even, if you don't mind me saying so, when it comes to flesh and emotion, but I know Marie better than that. She'll have your big heart wrapped around those lovely fingers of hers and you won't know which way to turn." Jane struggled against a bitter tone. It didn't really matter. "Shul—"

"Yeah?"

"Don't hide your love away," Jane whispered. "I'll call soon, and we won't have to do this again."

By the end of the week the files were organized and the laptop had swallowed months of research into a concise introduction. Jane shut the machine, slumped back in the thick armchair and listened to the distant, echoing wail of a loon calling mate or loonlings. She cupped her hands and softly copied the sound. Heard the melodic answer of the loved one. Most loons mate for life, she remembered, but overwinter separately. She had read that spring reunions were elegant, romantic water waltzes.

"Loons and wounds and lousy deals," she sang, rearranging Joni Mitchell's classic, remembering Sophia's love for the song. Sophia had re-emerged through the summer, sprung to life again as the activist Jane wished to document, and the long-gone, longed-for mother. Both needed to be resolved and resealed. Writing the thesis would process Sophia's public life. The rediscovered hooks of Sophia in the private sphere, unforgiven mother-daughter ties, an easily rising sense of abandonment that led her to the edge of the chasm, those Jane needed to face, alone and directly. Urgently even. She stood abruptly.

In the kitchen she opened the bottle of Johnny Walker Red bought the week before in Muddy Water, and poured a large drink over ice. As the liquor coursed through her veins she pictured Sophia, bent over the coffee table in the living room of the house with the fossilized front, weeping marital distress into a glass of scotch. Pictured the before-dinner drink by the electric frying pan as Sophia cooked through the sixties for the family. Rounds of gin-and-tonic downed with Niamh at the cabin. Sophia and Bob visiting adult Jane in Toronto, sending her to the liquor store for a case of white wine and several forty-ouncers of gin. "No tonic, thanks, just a little water, tonic's too sweet," Sophia's velvet cigarette voice. Glasses of water abandoned in odd corners of Bob's and Sophia's friendly home by the Atlantic becoming tumblers of gin when sipped. Sophia dozing after wine with lunch, starting again with gin-and-water before dinner. Jane stared at the glass in her hand. The invitation of the sour-sweet liquid. She staunched the tears brimming in her eyes, set the glass back on the counter and thought back to the last weekend she spent with Sophia and Bob.

They had dined overlooking the lights of Mahone Bay. When Bob, having climbed temporarily on the wagon, declined a drink before dinner, Sophia nervously requested a gin-and-water. Jane quietly watched her hand shake until the first sip slid down. You're addicted, Jane thought. But she only asked the same question she posed each visit.

"Seen a doctor lately, Soph?"

"Certainly," Sophia answered, lighting a cigarette. "Clean bill of health."

"Hadn't seen a doctor for three years," Bob admitted eight weeks later, after her sudden death. "Last visit, the doctor told her to quit smoking and drinking." Bob shook his head. "She never went back."

Sophia's distrust of doctors was a legacy of her marriage to Phil. She let bunions twist her toes sideways rather than face another orthopedic surgeon. Orthopedics was Phil's specialty. No doctor was going to convince her that she couldn't take a drink or have a smoke. That was how she lived. Jane lingered at the sink, where Sophia had stood so often, chatting, washing dishes, decoding the world news coming in on the old radio, infusing each day with a great flow of life. Jane thought of

Georgia, Sophia's first Canadian friend. Georgia lived for decades with arthritis. When her doctor asked how much she drank, Georgia answered, "As much as possible," and bellowed gales of laughter retelling the exchange. When failing health forced her to quit smoking, Georgia interrogated smokers. "What brand do you smoke? Gonna have one now, as soon as you leave? Well, have one for me. God I loved to smoke. Smoking was just the best thing." Her broad smile, eyes wide and lively, a tank of oxygen in the corner of the warm living room that last winter. Her home comfortable and inviting, furniture Jane had sat on as a child, while the owl and the pussycat headed out to sea in a beautiful pea-green boat.

"You know," Georgia confided to Jane in the cold doorway, "Bob came to see me, just before he died. He'd married that woman. You know, the one who looked him up after Sophia died. Company, I guess." Jane assumed he had, but he never mentioned it and she didn't care to inquire. "And she didn't want him to see any of their old friends, any of Sophia's friends, any of you kids, ever. She was so wrong. So bloody wrong." Georgia wagged a wise hand, "Love isn't like that. Love is elastic." She paused for air. "I loved those two." Her tone was wistful. "I loved your mother."

Jane saw Georgia straight-backed at the shaky grey card table in the living room, smoke wafting from a newly lit du Maurier, eyes narrowed as she analyzed the possibilities of the dummy hand laid out across from her. "Get the babes off the street!" she announced, and threw the ace of hearts onto the table.

"You're awful," Sophia rejoined. "That's trump."

"That's what I said," Georgia howled. "Get the babes off the street!"

"It'll never work." Niamh took a long indulgent sip of an icy gin-and-tonic. "You drink everything so cold here." She covered with the five of hearts. "It's all this incessant refrigeration."

"Aargh," Sophia pouted. "Well, there, you have it." She

threw down the queen of hearts and slid out a Cameo menthol. "For all the good it will do you."

"A singleton queen." Georgia turned to Niamh. "You must be holding a mittful of hearts."

Niamh hid behind her cards. "You'd even chill a stout, wouldn't you? Put it in the refrigerator next to Mr. Labatt's Blue or that horrid Canadian." As Georgia sank back to revise her strategy, Niamh mouthed, "Five little ones to the jack," across the table at Sophia. Sophia smirked behind her cards.

Jane studied the glass on the counter. She often had a drink in hand when she thought about Sophia. It helped close the chasm when it yawned unexpectedly. Now she wanted to plunge all the way in, then climb out, permanently. She imagined her mother's face. In less than twenty-four hours Sophia had slipped from a flu-like illness to a coma and death. "Doctor said it was a gram-negative blood infection," Bob reported, missing her too thoroughly to fuss over facts.

"Blood poisoning," med student Shula explained, years later, in a wee-hours chat.

"Can boozing cause it?"

"I think so," Shula guessed, "want me to research it?"

"No. That's enough."

"If you say so."

"I do."

If booze killed Sophia, Jane reflected, poking the ice in her drink, it wasn't booze alone. A way of life killed her, after sixty years of living it. Not enough, but not so bad, really. Jane left the glass on the counter and walked out the front door.

Outside, deep blue dimmed leisurely to black. The moon lit the southern treeline. Venus glittered. Jane heard a noise to her right, glimpsed the outline of an animal the size of the neighbours' dog. As her eyes adjusted to the darkness, she realized a small fox stood at the bottom of the steps assessing her. Jane stared back.

"Hello, fox," she said in a friendly tone, "would you like to hear my confession?" The fox sat down expectantly. "I'm no Catholic, but I suspect neither are you. It's nothing grandiose, so don't expect much. However, it seems necessary for me to divulge it to someone, and it looks like Masha's Creator has sent me you and Venus, and—" she leaned back and watched the moon rise above the poplars, "and Luna. So, there was once, not so long ago, a very spirited woman, who knew all about hearts. She knew how to warm them, lighten them, how to open them up and climb right inside. When I was troubled, she'd let me climb right in and nestle in kindness till my pain was soothed.

"As I grew from child to woman, she aged from a strong, loving mother at work in the world into a traveller, companion, lover and grandmother. She was neither more nor less kind than she had been, but she was more distant, less fluid, more tired. She spent a lot of time in a small pleasant house by the ocean. The less she ventured out, the more she relied on television and radio to inform her about the world. Well, news reporting is mostly politics and disasters. Cars crash, boats sink, planes careen out of the sky. A space ship exploded into white smoke and vast blue. A nuclear power plant melted the earth. Everyday life melted the ozone. The woman became afraid.

"I didn't want her to be afraid. Without realizing it, I developed the habit of trying to restore her confidence. I let her in to my heart, to nestle in warmth and kindness." Jane hesitated, her hand reaching for a glass, her tongue watering for a sip. "Maybe she'd walk out her door into the front bumper of a careless driver, or nod off to sleep in the lower berth of a train as the wheels leapt the track. And maybe not. I didn't know. I just didn't want her to feel afraid.

"One sunny Saturday morning in May the phone rang. I was washing the dishes, mulling over plans for the afternoon. I dried my hands quickly, hurrying to catch the call, and there was her voice, small and troubled. She was supposed to be flying to Europe and she was afraid to get on the plane.

"I encouraged her to set her fears aside. I said everything

would be all right, she'd be safe, and the trip would be good. She cheered enough to go. But it wasn't safe. Two weeks later she died so quickly I couldn't even fly over to say goodbye." Jane clenched her teeth against desire to walk back inside for a swig of scotch. "I told her it would be all right and it wasn't.

"Ever since, I have wished that instead of reassuring her, I had just told her she didn't have to go. Maybe if she'd been at home, they could have saved her. Maybe . . ." Jane faltered. Moonlight crept across the black lake. Wind hushed through the trees. The fox sat expectantly at the bottom of the steps. "Mea culpa," Jane muttered, slipping back inside the cabin. In the kitchen her hand wrapped firmly around the cold glass of scotch. She returned to the steps and raised the glass high.

"Now, Ms. Fox, I want to forgive myself and let the Queen of Hearts rest in peace. So I'll say, sorry, Soph. I probably couldn't have changed anything, but I'm sorry I didn't tell you to stay put. I miss you and I'll always miss you." Jane brought the glass to her lips for a symbolic sip, then tipped the drink, anointing the ground.

The fox rose and trotted out of view around the side of the cabin. Jane stared at a beautiful diamond cluster low on the eastern horizon. The radiant Pleiades graced the smooth black neck of the night sky. Jane's spirit raced on a surge of relief. Tomorrow she'd pack Sophia's papers away forever, or maybe until a child of hers became curious about the unknown grandmother. A child of hers. Micah splashing in the shallows, honking at the geese, carefully studying rock snakes, fish and turtles. A child.

The fox peered back around the cabin, silhouetted in a ray of moonlight.

"For love of her children."

Jane heard the words clearly, without hearing any voice. The fox fixed her with an impertinent gaze.

"For love of her children," she heard again. The answer that had eluded her for months. The breeze danced tree shadows across the moonbeam. Pacifism, a mother's steely promise to the infants she birthed. Jane remembered a line from Ruby Gottisfeld's eulogy—*she tried to provide a better world for her children.* Bats flew silently above the porch light.

The fox was gone. Who needs booze, Jane thought, deciding it was bright enough for a night swim. A quick cool cleansing on a diamond night.

14

Georgia O'Keeffe & Aunt Raizel

SHULAMIT WAS FLYING. Out over the Pacific, rounding and banking, cruising above jagged snow shaded peaks of the coastal range. The Rockies, foothills yawning to plains as Shula flew east into history and mystery. The rock-hard roots of Crow, the ambiguous identity of lesbubbe Jane Doe 12-93, Helen's renaissance, the shaky renewal of her friendship with Jane, all rolled through her rambling mind as she settled into cross-country sleep.

Donna Murdoch had answered warmly when she heard Shula's voice, though her tone chilled when Shula mentioned the inquiry. Her reaction to the possibility of Shulamit visiting the brick house high above Hamilton harbour was an unqualified "delighted."

Shula quickly asked if she could bring a friend.

"Oh, a *friend*," Donna said knowingly.

"Well, okay, more than a friend, but only just," Shulamit admitted. Crow, too, had migrated east a few days earlier, seeking some confirmation before she faced Thérèse in Montreal. Since that Friday afternoon, Marie had cycled through storms, gathering and venting, psychometric pressure rhythmically building and dropping. Through four hurricane weeks, Marie sought relief in the smoothness of Shulamit's skin, the sure strength of her embrace, the expanse of her luscious body opening to burrowing hands and tongue. Deep in the bear's soft folds Marie roused animal passion, waves that ripped through her tightwire tension, spreading Crow wide as liquid sky.

Shula nearly drowned in the flood. Years of avoidance buck-led and crumbled, rigid behavioural patterns melted beneath Crow's nimble body and lithe spirit. She scurried back to Vancouver whenever work permitted, back to the tender Crow's nest, where long-buried intensity erupted sexually, sensually and creatively.

The morning after tucking the broken bird between her leopard-print sheets, Shula woke on the living-room futon, ablaze with desire. The big bear shuddered as Crow's electric tongue licked passion higher. Molten soul ruptured fissures and cracks in stone emotions, the Weiss wall melted before life lava with no desire to cool. Standing under the fine spray of a late-morning shower, Shula silently apologized to Jane, soaped her arms, and felt entirely in and of the world. The water rinsed away the last of those silent lessons absorbed at Helen's side, the cautiousness that preferred to let life slip by a few lanes over. Her body had warmed to a lover's touch, bursting awake after grieving hibernation. Her hand curled again around a pencil, and described what it saw. Wise old hands, talking back to the world. Shula flexed her fingers under the flow, scrubbed each digit carefully with chamomile oat soap and rinsed them high above her head, a prayer of thanks to the unknown provider.

From that moment life possessed more than a purpose. Will animated Shula, demanding that everything be done, immedi-ately. Love, sex, drawing, laughter flooded Shula's senses the morning after. Rich coffee fumes mingled with steam escaping the bathroom. In the kitchen Crow sat perched on the high stool between the counter and the telephone, negotiating for time off work.

"Well, unpaid leave then, and you know just how easy it is to do without two weeks' pay." She glanced at Shula. "Coffee's ready," Marie whispered covering the mouthpiece and chewing on an unlit clove cigarette. Shulamit plucked a bright yellow Tweety-Bird mug from the shelf and lifted the espresso pot. Coffee steam hissed from the spout. Shula watched the vapour magically dissipate, inhaling deep aroma.

"I'd be happy to make up shifts when I get back," Marie started in again. "No problem. You know that's not a problem." She rolled her eyes and tossed the cigarette aside, flashed Shula a thin smile. "Great, fine, I'll book my ticket and let you know . . . Two weeks—why not put me down for anything that opens up this week? . . . Yeah, anything, might as well get those hours in now. You're a peach, Dean, maybe even a nectarine . . . Yes, I really do appreciate it . . . Family stuff . . . Sure, of course I'll be back. I love it here, I love the store, I love all of you . . . No, I'm not lying, would I lie to you?" She directed Shula toward a lime cream pitcher.

Would I lie to you? Shula sang Annie Lennox. Soft white cream poured from green ceramic, thickening java to warm gold.

"Okay, bye, Dean-o." Crow flipped the receiver back onto its hook on the wall. "Good shower? Good coffee?" She spluttered, hunched on the chair, head tucked beneath shoulder wings.

"Good everything, little one." Shula rolled the thick coffee on her tongue.

Marie tipped her small head to the side, smiled softly beneath distraction.

"Going somewhere?"

"Oh, yeah. The phone call." Bird eyes narrowed. "Yeah, I am. I'm going to find out."

"Anywhere in particular?" Shula sipped Marie's intensity like warm caffeine, fuelling up for a vigorous day.

"East. You know." She stood behind the stool and rocked it.

"Well, I know . . . and I don't know," Shula answered lazily, amazed by her own detachment. Crow was lost in turbulence, yet she felt no compulsion to diagnose, soothe and solve. The coffee was delicious, Crow was deliciously intense, morning was electric. Shula hummed, *Would I lie to you?*

"Take me to see her," Crow squawked. "No, call her!" She whirled the stool around.

Shula took another sip. Crow's anger was delectable. She set Tweety down, walked over and placed reverent hands heavily on each of Crow's hunched shoulders. Spun Crow back to face her. "Now?" she asked. "Who? Donna Murdoch? Long distance? Your phone?" Shula leaned down and kissed, a slow, beautiful drink. *Would I lie to you?* she hummed, watching Crow's face.

"*YES!*" Marie shrieked, still pinned by forceful hands. "*YES!*" she screeched. "*I WANT TO KNOW!*" Her voice was frenzy.

Shula studied the pores on Marie's face. The freckles across her cheekbones. The black shimmer of her irises. Of course she wanted to know, Shula thought, though it seemed she already did. And investigating might not bring her any more certainty than she already had. No one here needed to deny her assumptions, or demand proof through verifiable facts. Perhaps she'd be happier with unchallenged convictions, with instincts and visions. Shula studied her lover's face again.

"Okay," Shula said, "I'll see what I can do. I'll call Donna."

Marie's tension slackened. She relaxed into Shula's breasts, listened to the bear's heart pound. Shula cradled the soft bristles of Crow's small head, leaned down to sip soft lips, sparking again that unlikely duet of bear and crow. Again they rocked in leopard sheets, Shula's ardent hands pealing layers of ripped fashion black to reveal quivering white fury. Wise hands teasing righteous anger into ripe sex, an eager tongue lapping revenge fury into hard, honest lust. Crow seared, soared, subsided. And they slept.

They woke again to afternoon calm, to talk and sort and plan. Marie was still determined to travel east, certain that knowledge would sustain her more fully than assumptions. Shula listened and advised, as images of Toronto danced in her mind. Helen and Isaac celebrating the High Holidays, on couches freed from plastic, sharing a shvitz and a swim with a mother freed from illness, observing Rosh Hashanah or Yom Kippur with family. When, late in the afternoon, Donna

Murdoch hesitated to discuss the inquiry on the telephone, Shula decided she, too, would visit her birthplace. Shulamit remembered that Marie hadn't seen her drawings.

"Would you like to?" she asked after a hasty explanation.

"Are you kidding? The immovable object shifts and you want to know if I'm interested? Of course I'm interested."

"But it's you, you know. I drew you, as you spun out."

Marie nodded quietly. Interest in persuading Shulamit to paint her visions outweighed nervousness. The wall had cracked, an opening existed. She and Mazie and all that spawned her had burst through.

They sat in the living room, touching casually. A bony foot rested on a muscular calf, hands played with a dangling chain. Shulamit lay the sketches on the floor in front of them. All motion, multiple lines depicted wings, elbows, knees, feathers flying. The vacantness of Marie's expression matched the blankness of her memory after the images splintered. No waves to ride, no chanting, no far horizon sunny and razor-edged. The Maze had swallowed her, then disappeared, leaving only a void, the instant nothing she conjured in childhood to imagine complete nuclear catastrophe. There it was on her face in Shula's drawings, a disquieted blank. She kissed Shula, lay her head on her lover's shoulder, and cried quietly, unwinding.

Shula hugged her, the old friendly bear hug. "Are you—?"

"Yeah, I'm fine," Marie whispered. "Just overwhelmed. That's exactly what it felt like. After."

"After what?"

"Well, when I really took it in, the television screen split in multiple images, like rows and rows of negatives, the same face, across and down. And then blank. Not that I don't remember, what I remember is a great nothing . . . Somehow, that's what you captured on my face. That feeling of nothingness."

"A little bit of Sartre in the soul, eh, Crow?"

"Huh?"

"You know, *Being and Nothingness,* major Jean-Paul tome."

"Shula, I don't know that shit."

"Yeah, well, I wouldn't recommend it. Out of date. Everyone underestimated how heavily his thinking was influenced by living through the destruction of Europe. Of course they became existentialists . . . Never mind." She paused, suddenly aware that she was speaking her own legacy. "Anyway, you've been there."

Marie smiled. "We've all been there, Big Bear. I act therefore I am, no?"

"Yeah. Sort of"

"Only it seems that really we *are,*" Marie continued, "whether we do anything or not. Like I jacuzzi, therefore I exist. I couch potato, channel hop, numb out, and I still am."

"Ah, but if you are a potato, are you human?"

"I am Crow, no?" She lay back on the refolded futon. Stared at the ceiling, then lifted her head and looked directly at Shulamit. "Paint for me."

"What? For you?"

"Yeah. I mean, what I see. I mean, I'd like to take the writing that's come from the visions, hallucinations, whatever, and pull it together as a collection. I'd like other people, other women in particular, to hear what I hear, and I'd like them to see what I've seen." She paused.

Shula studied the pile on the black carpet.

"Would you do that for me, Shul? Try and paint what I've seen?" She meant to wait for an answer, but anxiety rushed on. "There's this great new gallery space in the old Woodward's department store. Cavernous. There's a fantastic show there now about breast cancer," Shula looked up, intrigued, "and I can just imagine it hung with those glorious dancing women. The Freewomen's Chorus echoing off canvas . . ." Marie sighed, carried into daydream.

"The Freewomen's Chorus?" Shula grinned at Crow. "Is that the title?"

"No, well, the women are The Freewomen's Chorus, but it's a collection of their chants, so I'm thinking it's *The Freewomen's Chorale.*"

"Not c-o-r-r-a-l, eh, Crow?" Shulamit spelled out her joke.

"This ain't the lesbian rodeo, lover. I checked the big fat Oxford, and," she closed her eyes and strained to picture the entry, "a chorale is a metrical hymn, set to music, recited in unison . . ." It wasn't exact but it would do. She shrugged at Shula. "Aside from the music bit, it's perfect. A metrical hymn recited in unison. They're like hymns, well, maybe hers. And there's something . . . sacred about it, like a feminist liturgy. Liturgy. Now I have to look *that* up. Anyway, it's my way down below the ocean stuff. I'm scraping the primordial sea of my genesis here." Black pupils intensified.

"Well, Crow, I don't know if I can do it, but I'm willing to try," Shula answered, startled by a jolt in her hands, an electric desire for brushes and canvas. "I guess I could set up in my other room at the house. It's still just a pile of boxes. And with that south window, the light's not bad, just need to take down those hideous drapes. Get some brushes. Probably do some pencil sketches first."

"Those drapes are hideous." Marie slipped into Shula's lap, skimming light fingers across her brow. "You will, won't you? You really will." She knotted her hands on the back of Shula's neck.

"I'll try," Shula whispered, passion closing her throat as she felt Crow's smooth cheek on her own. She rolled back onto the floor and let Crow slide onto her belly. Felt her T-shirt slip up and groaned as her left breast was eased from her decaying sports bra. Soft lips suckling, a nimble foot wriggling between tightening thighs. "Oh Crow," she groaned, succumbing, "we'll never get any . . ." A hand slid down her belly.

"I'm gettin' somewhere." Marie eased the bra up on the other side. "In fact, I think I'm going all the way."

Shula groaned again, arching her back to meet Marie's small body, less shocked at Marie's avid lovemaking than at her own pleasure in it. Opening over and again like a night-blooming flower, spiralling the length of O'Keeffe's calla lilies. She could love, she could touch. She would paint. Marie's tongue slid down her belly. Paint glorious women. Dancers, singers, howlers, lovers. Whatever frenzy Marie described to her. It was easy to be willing, sometimes.

In the intervening weeks Shula shopped at art supply stores in both cities, though her mind kept returning to the two boxes remaining in Helen and Isaac's basement. After so long, could there be anything of use in them? Still, she knew she would open them, extract and examine every article inside. She yearned for openness. For breezes blowing through her studio window, cloudless skies as August wound into September, long walks by sea where she had first encountered Jane Doe 12-93.

As the jet engines shifted to descend Shulamit woke with an image of the Jane Doe in her mind. Thin grey hair, skin loose on her knuckles and wrists, that generous half-smile she offered. Over three months had passed without her identity being clearly established. Once the Ontario bureaucracy declared Sarah S. Wise dead, the hospital administration took a livelier interest. Their phone call to the police pried her belongings loose from the vigilant Mrs. Donald. But no wallet or identification had been left behind in the room. She had to have dropped it on her walk, perhaps a wallet, falling unnoticed from a pocket, knocked aside as she struggled uphill. She must have been disoriented, minutes before a major stroke. With any luck she would be speaking clearly soon, and the guesswork would be over. But there might be a way to investigate while in Toronto, Shula thought, releasing her chair back into the upright position. She strained to see the lights of the city without engaging the straight-suited man in the window seat, imagined Helen and Isaac waiting beyond the glass doors of Terminal 2, and grinned like a prodigal returning home from a long exile.

To Shulamit's surprise, only Helen stood waiting outside the glass doors to the baggage carousels. She looked firm and fit, tiny yet resilient. The picture of middle-age health, Shula thought, amazed. It was almost as if a stranger answered her "Hello, Helen," as Shula gazed about for Isaac.

"Shululah," Helen breathed her name like a blessing, then collected herself and dangled the car keys. "He's not here," she answered the question on her daughter's face. "I drove myself. But I'm not that comfortable on freeways so you might as well drive back." Their hands grazed as Helen handed Shula the keys.

As they strolled through the airport, it became obvious that baseball fever had gripped Toronto.

"Meshuge for baseball, eh?" Shula said.

"Even your father," Helen nodded. "Not me."

"No."

"You?"

"Definitely." Shula gave her a deliberate beaming grin, meant to reassure.

"Maybe you and Isaac could go," Helen suggested timidly.

"Great, but I'd really like to spend some time with you," Shula ventured.

"Oh, yes," Helen gushed. "I'd like to go for a drive to Niagara Falls."

"Great," Shula agreed "We'll go."

Helen pointed to the parking garage. The door had eased open, both women wanted more.

The city was feverish. The Blue Jays were closing the season leading their division, heading into the pennant race, eyeing a second consecutive World Series title. Non-fans crammed sports bars and memorized the magic number: how many more games the team needed to win to clinch the division. Fans jammed the Skydome, second-guessed every strategic decision from base-stealing to pitch-outs. Manager Cito Gaston was everybody's man. Cool, collected, reserved, his public face allowed even political types, like Shulamit, to hustle whole-heartedly onto the bandwagon. One of a few Black managers in baseball, managing a multicultural, multi-racial team. Players from the Caribbean and Puerto Rico, stars like Joe Carter, Robbie Alomar, Juan Guzman. Or so Shula argued to an intransigent Marie after a few increasingly comfortable days at home with Helen. She had turned down Marie's invitation to a poetry reading at The Women's Common to join Isaac at a ball game.

"Ball scratchers and gobbers," Marie argued back, "rich boys who don't have to grow up, just play a game. Pro sports is so male." Marie had not flown onto the bandwagon.

"Hey, I wouldn't turn down Martina if she came calling."

"I'm not sure you'd turn anyone down right now, you're so goddamned happy."

"Hey, lovers can be friends, you know. Don't get shitty with me."

"Sorry, you know. Too much pressure." After the startling visit with Donna Murdoch, Marie's cycles stalled in a heavy low. Steely focus on her Freewomen Project—inputting the contents of her notebook at self-serve computer centres, contacting old friends involved in publishing and art galleries—kept her moving through choking Toronto streets.

"I know. So, go. See Thérèse. If you want me, call, and I'll come. But I have to be back in Victoria next weekend, so if you want me in Montreal, it has to be soon." Shula remained firmly on her own course, enjoying the fine eastern fall, early maples bursting to brilliant red, bushels of tomatoes and corn lining roads of the lush Niagara peninsula. She and Helen had spent an afternoon driving through the valley, past orchards, vineyards and wineries. They joked about crossing the proverbial Jordan River, indulged in a night at a charmingly restored nineteenth-century hotel in Niagara-on-the-Lake. The next morning,

perusing designer paraphernalia in the bourgeois tourist bou-
tiques, they shared an easy familiarity. In an oak-lined bookstore,
Helen bought herself a signed, hardcover copy of *The Robber
Bride* and insisted that Shula accept a magnificent coffee table
volume of Georgia O'Keeffe's western work. Shula's hands slid
across the glossy pages, seeking the brush strokes of each creation.

"You know I'm working again," she said quietly as the shop
door closed with the faint tinkle of a brass bell.

"I guessed. You spent so long sorting those boxes." Helen
paused. "Maybe it's not my place to say, but you don't have to be
Florence Nightingale or Marie Curie. Shulamit Weiss will do. I
like her just fine."

Embarrassed, Shula narrowed her focus and studied Helen.
Freed from years of absence, she saw an older woman, very present and very perceptive.

"I'm not so sure about the haircut, though," Helen reached
for the cowlick on Shula's brow, halted and then gently tugged
the thin tail-like braid that trailed Shula's otherwise short hair. "I
think of rodents, the rodents of Europe."

"It's hip, you know, radical," Shula explained. "Think of me
as a radical rat. Jewish, Euro-Canadian. An English-speaking
Ashkenazi rat."

"Okay, my hip rat. Drive on to the great waterfall." She
handed Shula the keys at the big old Buick. Shula unlocked
Helen's door, then her own. "Though I always thought of you
more as a bear, like Isaac. Everything big and strong with life, so
sure of life, in his body. The first time I touched him I felt that
confidence. I wanted to scoop it up. To never let go. A source of
life . . . What they call 'a natural,' helped him through his years
as a labourer, I guess, and then after, an athlete of sorts, teaching
in England and playing every sport . . . " Helen hesitated, distracted by the sheer pleasure of opening to Shulamit. "You
always seemed that way too," she continued as Shula slid into
the driver's seat. Helen slipped into the car.

Shula started the engine, pulled out onto the street. "I think

Marie sees me that way. Strong and sure," she said quietly, watching the road ahead. It was awkward, then comfortable to introduce her lover as a subject of conversation. "She's having some difficulties now, and I'm, well, I'm not. I'm doing fine." Then Shula laughed comfortably and reached spontaneously for her mother's hand on the seat beside her. Helen grasped her fingers tightly, desperately crossing the lost years.

"If you love her, that's good." Helen spoke haltingly, ignoring tears dampening her cheeks. "But, you know, no Florence Nightingale."

"Yeah. I know. But she ain't heavy." Shula followed the parkway paralleling the Niagara River, high above the water.

Helen gave Shula's hand a parting squeeze. "So, are you painting or drawing?" Helen asked. The conversation rolled along the willowed road, Shula describing Marie's visions fervent with the incredible release of creating, Helen finally folding into her daughter's life with an ease that surprised both.

The road curved away from the hazardous beauty of the whirlpool, a treacherous plunge that lured the lost and abandoned. Ahead lay the city of Niagara Falls, tourist clutter and majesty of nature framed by the Nabisco factory and international bridges. The air was thick with mist from the falls. Shula wound her window down and fingered the fine spray. Helen focussed on the rim of the horseshoe, where the water stopped for an instant before tumbling over.

"Nu?" Shulamit asked, pulling into the parking lot across from the souvenir store.

"The falls?" Helen mused. "It rushes so fast, yet it doesn't move at all."

Shula chuckled. "Very nice. Yes, I see it. Constant change— is it changing or constant?"

"Both!" Helen answered, stepping out of the car, sighing in the damp air.

"Over here," Shula pointed above the falls, hooking her arm protectively under Helen's as they crossed the road. "I like to

watch the fault line where the water begins to fall, the line of
the rock underneath."

Helen nodded, enjoying Shulamit's firm grip, the same solid,
rooted-in-life energy that flowed from Isaac's flesh. A vast
rumble engulfed them as they reached the stone wall where
river verged into falls. Eroding bedrock, visible beneath the
river, formed a dark edge separating forward motion and
freefall. Shula leaned over the guard rail, immersed in the con-
trast between the impenetrable blue riverbed and the transparent water hurtling over it. Occasionally she followed a twig or
leaf cascading in stop-motion into the mist below. Helen
absorbed her daughter meditating on the flow, ever the child
with her own ways of seeing. Remembered how she would sit
for hours after an outing, reproducing images so the viewer saw
not the object, but Shulamit's experience of it. Helen had mar-
velled at such uncanny power in a young girl, but, one day, Isaac
remarked off-hand that his sister had been like that, too. Helen
drew a long, moist breath.

"You've never asked Isaac about your aunt, have you?" She
pitched her voice above the clamour of the water, words tumbling over the lip that mesmerized Shulamit.

Shula watched a tree branch careen off two rocks and plunge.
She faced Helen. "Can I?"

"Who knows?" Helen shrugged. "You know your father.
He'll either tell you everything, simply and calmly, or it's as if
the question never touched your tongue."

They gazed at each other.

"But," Helen continued slowly, "I know a little. Bits and
pieces I've gathered over the years. Believe it or not, he talks
more now than he used to . . . " She paused. "Anyway, I've
threaded together a story of sorts."

Shula stood transfixed, then nodded.

"Let's walk then, it's too loud here," Helen suggested,
ambling along the river, away from the precipice. Shula trailed
behind. "From what I know, she looked like you—not the face,

your face is mostly my family." She smiled thinly. "But her body, she was tall and strong, built like Isaac. She drew, you know, before . . . everything. We told you that when you were young."

Shula nodded, remembering.

"Until recently Isaac thought that none of her art survived. So much was lost, who would think a child's drawing would survive?" Helen shrugged again. "Apparently though, a friend of Isaac's saw a drawing in a memorial exhibit in Israel. A travelling exhibit, you know, 'Children of the Holocaust.' " She hissed the word. "It's supposed to come to America, sometime." She wiped mist from her brow. "Isaac knows more. He can tell you . . . So there is another, smaller piece of her. In addition to you."

Shulamit watched the *Maid of the Mist* tour boat struggle upstream toward the falls, laden with blue-slickered tourists. She swallowed, throat dry. "You never met her, did you? She died in the Shoah?"

"In the Shoah, in the catastrophe." Helen scratched the back of her head. "More or less. The war stopped before the Shoah ended, if you know what I mean. Some went back to claim their houses and were shot on the doorstep. Some perished of starvation and disease. Even now, some commit suicide because of those days. War doesn't end, just because it stops. And genocide," she lowered her voice to an angry whisper, "well, look how it goes with the original people here . . . suicide, prison, violent death . . ."

Shulamit listened with surprise, never dreaming that somehow, across silence and absence, it had been Helen who had delivered the message of social responsibility. Below, the *Maid of the Mist* chugged valiantly past the American falls.

"Your aunt. I'd say the Shoah killed her. In the beginning of the end. After the war, she and your father met . . . somewhere—France, Germany, Hungary—I don't remember. Isaac wanted to come to North America, away from it all. Raizel, your aunt, she wanted Eretz Israel—Palestine then. She wanted to found Israel. One of those convinced that Jews would be safe only in a land of our own." Helen sighed and unconsciously slipped her arm through her daughter's. Shulamit felt the comforting weight. She motioned downriver at a stand of glowing red maples, embers of the fire fuelling their quiet conversation.

"And in Israel Jews are still at war. Just on the other side, now," Shulamit blurted, thinking of the Intifada.

"It's not the same," Helen countered. "But you're right. It's not good and I doubt it's what your aunt died for—so Jews could force Palestinians into camps."

"Raizel, she died for Israel? A fighting Zionist?" The *Maid of the Mist* swayed in churning water near the bottom of the falls.

Helen opened her palms, hunched her shoulders. "Well, Yitzhak said she was very thin—everyone was thin—the last he saw her. She had very short hair and she insisted on getting his papers copied by someone. Then she used them to pass as a man. As Yitzhak Weiss. He heard she hooked up with the Brecha, moving Jews out of Russian-occupied areas through Austria or Belgium to France and onto boats for Palestine. Someone saw her in Budapest, then Vienna, I think, then in Marseille. They would tell him, you see, a month, a year, a decade later, 'I met your brother, he saved my life.' Finally, it seems, she got on a boat herself. The British refused them landing. There was a hunger strike. Some tried to swim ashore, some pushed off in lifeboats. And those were the last rumours Yitzhak ever heard of her. Not her, of course. His 'brother.' How she managed the hiding, who knows? I always wondered why exactly until . . ."

"Until now," Shulamit interrupted. "Until me."

"And what I've learned in the last year. Now it seems that there could have been lots of reasons. She could have just been hiding, passing for safety. Many did it. She could have been trying to get more respect in the Brecha than she could have as a woman, though that doesn't seem as likely." Helen had released Shulamit and paced beside the railing. "Or—"

"Or, she could have been a lesbian," Shula interrupted. The *Maid of the Mist* laboured to turn in taut water, straining at a full throttle standstill.

"Eventually, not long before we met, Yitzhak heard of someone living in Tel Aviv under his name. And he went—in '52 or '53. At first this other Yitzhak insisted the papers came from a friend, Yitzhak, but when Isaac told his side of the story, this Israeli man Yitzhak said *she* had been a friend of Raizel's, and Raizel had given *her* the papers on the boat. She said Raizel was tired of hiding, and wanted to arrive in Eretz Israel as herself. According to this Yitzhak, Raizel left the ship in a lifeboat, cut it loose in the night hoping to reach land on her own, after five days of hunger strike. No papers, no identity. Never turned up again. The ship was escorted to Cyprus, and this Yitzhak never said anything because well, you see, she was passing as Yitzhak . . ." She continued to pace.

Shulamit wrapped her hands around the steel bar atop the stone fence.

"And that, as best I know, is how your aunt disappeared in the Shoah." Helen concluded.

Below, the current caught the *Maid of the Mist*. The boat rocked to starboard. Helen spoke to Shulamit's back as Shulamit listed toward sorrow.

"She would have been seventeen or eighteen," Helen guessed.

Shulamit imagined a figure like her own, sneaking into a lifeboat late at night, slicing ropes and crashing into the Mediterranean. Lights flashing in the darkness, bullets resounding overhead. The *Maid of the Mist* completed its manoeuvre and skidded downstream on a swift current. Shula released the railing. Helen started toward her, then stopped. Shula turned, wiping her eyes with the cuff of her sleeve.

"That was me, a generation ago."

"This is you," Helen answered firmly. "Here and now. Raizel lived her life, then. You live yours now." She took her adult daughter by the hand. "We are all here and now. You, me, Isaac." Helen turned back toward the car, leading a dazed Shulamit by the hand. Shulamit let herself be led, watched the boat's swift progress downstream, thinking about how it had barely moved forward as it chugged toward the waterfall. One turn and suddenly it raced.

"A show?" Shulamit murmured, following Helen.

"Mmm-hmm," Helen answered, "someone has put together an exhibit of art by children who didn't survive the Shoah. Your aunt was a child when it started."

"And I can talk to Isaac about it?" she asked, stepping more solidly.

"Sure. He's trying to find out more himself. Ask him when you're together, at the baseball game or something. It's easier for him to talk if he's partially distracted."

Shula knew the comment described her as well. She threw her free arm around Helen's small, muscular shoulders and squeezed. "Let's walk back to the top of the falls for a minute," she urged. "I like to stare into the oncoming flow."

"You certainly do," Helen laughed. "And not just rivers. But not too long, I'm getting soaked and you know I'm no spring chicken."

"I'll buy you the nation's worst hot chocolate after," Shula promised.

"Such an offer," Helen chortled, marvelling at Shula's protective grip as they strolled upstream.

Two nights later Skydome was jammed. The Jays were hosting the California Angels, Dave Stewart pitching against Chuck Finley. Bottom of the fifth, no score, Jays batted with two out and catcher Pat Borders at second. Shulamit and Isaac sat side by side, twenty-six rows from the third-base line. A time-softened baseball glove covered her left hand with familiar worn leather. Isaac laughed each time she punched it with her fist.

"How many years have you had that?" he asked slowly, eastern Europe vaguely present in his pronunciation.

"You don't remember? I bought this with Bat Mitzvah money," she answered, as Devon White stepped to the plate.

"Of course I remember, that's why I gave you the money. I just don't like to think about how many years have gone by since."

Finley threw wild and high.

"Come on, Devo," Shula yelled. "Then I won't tell you. Is Weiss related to Wise?"

"Spell it." White sliced a grounder left. "He's out," Isaac announced.

"W-i-s-e. No, he's not!" Shula shot back as the throw from the Angel's shortstop pulled the first baseman off the bag. "Safe!" She punched her glove.

"Safe. And here comes Molitor. I like this player. He's smart. Mature. Plays like a mensch—for the whole team. A good buy. Why do you ask?"

"Ya gotta like Winfield though—all class . . ." Shula referred to the designated hitter replaced by Paul Molitor. "I have this patient, this Jane Doe, sorry, I mean this elderly woman." Finley threw. "Holy shit." Molitor connected, bringing the crowd to its feet as the ball sailed over the fence. "Yes!!" Shulamit was up, glove raised in jubilation. "All right, Molly!!"

"Three-run homer." Isaac guffawed. "Great player, this Molitor. Second-best average in the league, at his age—"

"They call him Molly," Shula explained to Isaac, reclaiming her seat. "Anyway, she had a stroke and can't speak yet, though I think I understand some of what she says. No identification on her when she was found, and the name she'd signed at her motel was Sarah Wise, Toronto."

"Molly the mensch. Why Jane Doe?"

"Ontario government says Sarah Wise died in 1983. I think they're related, or friends or something. I think she used her friend's name when she signed in. Either that or there's more than one Sarah S. Wise, and she's not from Toronto."

"Friends?"

"Friends, companions." Finley retired the side with a pop fly. The Jays took the field. "I think this woman was the companion of Sarah S. Wise. It's the only discernible sound she makes, the name Sarah. And it's barely discernible. But I guess it's become clearer to me over the months. She seems to be calling it, not offering it as her name—trying to summon someone. She says it in her sleep a lot."

Dave Stewart threw to Chad Curtis.

"Well, I'm a sports psychologist, not a detective, but I can ask around. You looked in the phone book?" The pitch was high and outside. "Pull him, Cito," Isaac muttered. "He's fighting an injury, needs rest."

"He's still got something left . . . Dozens of Wise in the phone book. Nine with the initial S. Then Saul, Sidney, Simon. I even called an S or two . . . And the phone book said 'see also Weiss.' "

"You called?"

"Yeah, I called. I said I was Dr. Shulamit Weiss, and I asked what the 'S' stood for. You'd be amazed how many people will answer a question just because a doctor asks it. One Sam, one Sharon."

"Sam Wise . . . sounds familiar. Look, another ball. Pull him before it's too late. I'll ask around. If she was really from here, somebody will know her family. How old would she be?"

"Her friend is easily seventy-odd. So sixty or seventy, probably."

"That generation, everybody knows somebody, so somebody should know."

"But are they related, Weiss and Wise?"

"In a lot of Europe, Jews had to adopt last names a century or two ago. Depends where." Curtis hit to left field, Rickey Henderson backed up to the fence, but the ball was up and over.

"Okay, Cito—pull him," Shulamit hollered, along with half the stadium. "Adopt names?"

Isaac laughed. "Now she yells. Last names. Before that it was son of, like David Ben-Gurion. People got names in lots of ways. My Zeda told a story about his Zeda. In his town there were four names for Jews to have—Klein, Gross, Schwartz and Weiss. Little, Big, Black and White. So the whole town was cut into four pieces, like a pie. Still one pie, Zeda always said. Gants Ashkenaz iz eyn shtot. All Ashkenaz is one town."

"No shit?" Shula digested the casual mention of her great-grandfather. "And Wise?"

"Who knows, depends on what it started out as. Could be a transliteration of Weiss. Could be something shortened, could be invented coming through immigration."

"See also W-e-i-s, W-e-i-s-e, W-e-i-s-s, W-y-s-e," Shulamit quoted the Toronto phone book.

"Exactly. Or Wiseman, Weisberg, Weisbrod, Himmelfarb, even."

"So it's connected? We could be connected?"

"We could all be connected, Shulamit, if you believe. Thirteen tribes, one lost in the Christian wilderness . . . Or maybe Koestler was right, maybe we Ashkenazis are all Khazaks converted in the twelfth or thirteenth century. Maybe there is no blood tie between us. Does it matter? I don't know. I like Zeda's pie. Gants Ashkenaz iz eyn shtot, it's true for me," he admitted. "There are many peoples in the world. All human. Maybe I'm just a little more like these people than like others. I'm theirs and they're mine. The shmucks and the shlemiels. They're mine. The momzers and the mensches. Same pie. But, you, you'd really like to know?"

"Yeah," she agreed, "I'd like to know. I'd . . . I'd also like to see Aunt Raizel's art if you find out where that show is. I'd go with you if you're going."

"Sure. We'll all go, whenever. You, me, Helen. The whole pie."

Shula quieted. It was rare for Isaac to talk so freely. Yet she knew him to respond when he was ready. She longed for a glimpse of her aunt's childhood creation. What mysterious stranger had saved it? And why? Now there was a story.

"Heads up!" Isaac yelled with a distinctly American accent.

Shula glanced up at a foul ball arching toward her. She shot her gloved hand up and left. Leapt from her seat. The ball slapped smartly into old leather. Shula snapped the glove shut. Raised both arms. Isaac patted her on the back. And there on the big screen at the north end of the stadium were father and daughter, triumphant. Yitzhak and Shulamit, living well, almost fifty years later.

15

Buffy Sainte-Marie & Grand-mère Latouche

On her third evening in Montreal, Marie waited nervously beneath a canopy of elms at a restaurant patio across from Thérèse's Outremont apartment. The neighbourhood was green and stately. The comforts cherished by long-time Québécois and newly arrived Hassidic residents usually discomforted Marie, but on this trip she harboured little energy for rebellion. This once, she enjoyed the calm. Enjoyed the heavy silverware on the linen tablecloth in front of her, garlic and wine permeating the cooling fall air as she anxiously anticipated her mother's arrival. Insulated Outremont felt safe, and though she would never choose insulation for herself, Marie took solace in the cocoon it provided Thérèse. She wondered whether the charms of the neighbourhood, bolstered by thirty-plus years of denial, would prove sufficient to stifle the echoes of the St. Jude's inquiry.

Marie sipped a slightly chilled glass of Sauvé and fingered the title printed on the booklet in her hand. *The Freewomen's Chorale.* In the course of three days she had brewed thick morning café au lait for Thérèse, arrived laden with white roses for lunch at a café near the CEGEP where Thérèse taught, sautéed fillet of sole almandine, broiled fresh salmon steaks with dill and lemon, fried bananas with brown sugar and cinnamon and dripped them over vanilla ice cream. When she offered to pop out to the video store after a sumptuous meal, her mother laughed aloud.

"Okay, ça suffit," she said, leaning back in an over-stuffed armchair. "I'm completely content. Totally satisfied. Either you have bad news or you need something. I feel like you're still a teenager and you've either smashed up my car, or borrowed my favourite necklace and lost it, though how you could do that in Vancouver I don't know." She sat up quickly. "You're not pregnant?"

Marie flinched. "I'm a thirty-year-old lesbian, Maman. If I was pregnant it wouldn't be unwanted, would it?"

Thérèse relaxed. "But still, there's something, isn't there?"

"Mostly just to see you . . ." she stalled. "But I want to show you something, some writing I've done . . . Tomorrow. I'll get it printed nicely tomorrow, like a chapbook."

"Oh, very nice. But does this nice never stop?" Thérèse laughed. "Suspicious old mother. Okay, tomorrow. I'll buy you dinner across the street. La Moulerie, very nice little place, lots of fish for your Vancouver mouth."

Marie arranged for a simple layout and the printing of a half-dozen copies of *The Freewomen's Chorale*. She resisted placing the subtitle, *or life with Mazie,* on the cover.

On the soothing train ride from Toronto, Marie had conceived a plan to present her writing to Thérèse, and explain its genesis as a prelude to unravelling her own. Rolling through golden countryside between the freeway and the silvery shore of Lake Ontario, traversed countless times after Thérèse first departed for Montreal, Marie had slowly sorted her feelings. While Buffy Sainte-Marie buried her heart at Wounded Knee to electric guitar pounding through earphones, Marie settled consciously into a depth that had evaded her since the advent of the mind maze. She realized Mazie had vanished as abruptly as she had come, ending magic tricks and mystical trips. Buffy's voice walked across searing lyrics—*silver burns a hole in your pocket, gold burns a hole in your soul, uranium burns a hole in forever, it just gets out of control.* Marie's mind followed. Forever, she thought, for ever, I will be Marie Latouche, daughter of Thérèse Latouche. And only Thérèse Latouche. Stubbornly, her mind looped back to lunch with Shulamit at Donna Murdoch's. Her right thumb rubbed the woolly fabric of the train seat. She recalled the expression on Donna's face when Shula introduced her.

"And this is my friend, Marie, Marie—" Shula began.

"Latouche," Donna interjected, and the sadness in her eyes belonged to a much younger woman. "I believe I knew your mother, briefly."

Marie stretched out a hand, but as her small face crumpled Donna Murdoch wrapped her in seventy years of arms that had tended humanity. Like a boat entering a canal lock, Marie slipped into the certainty of those few words and waited to sink. She didn't see Shulamit mouth, "She never told her" at Donna Murdoch, nor Donna Murdoch mouth back, "I thought that's why you called." But she did hear Shula say clearly, "Marie wanted to know."

Donna released Marie. "Come sit in the back—I roused myself and shopped for a gourmet lunch. Maybe you'd like a beer or a sherry?"

Marie opened her mouth, struggling for the word *sherry.*

"Beer would be great," Shula answered behind her.

"No—sweet, please," Marie managed as Donna led them through the house. "I mean I'd prefer sherry, please. Something sweet. My mouth is bitter."

"It'll pass," Shula whispered, and laid a hand on Marie's shoulder. Their fingers entwined as Marie reached eagerly for a lifeline. Donna opened the back door wide and gestured toward a set picnic table.

Marie sipped two full glasses of sherry and nibbled at carrots, celery and crackers while Shulamit enjoyed two cobs of sweet corn, red potato salad, cold cuts and marinated mushrooms.

"Excellent meal," Shula wiped her mouth with a serviette. "It's good to see you."

"Best take-out Hamilton has to offer," Donna explained. "And medicine? Does geriatrics suit you?"

"It's really a general practice with a geriatric population. I guess I don't really know yet. The doctor whose locum I just completed is reluctantly on the verge of retirement. He's post-poning by offering me another three months. I'm not eager for a permanent position yet, so I'm leaning toward taking it. There's a lot I like about my life right now——"

"I look like him, don't I?" Marie interrupted suddenly. "Oh shit, I look like him." She hunched into sharp Crow shoulders, her gaze questioning Donna Murdoch.

"What?" Shula followed Marie's sight line to Donna, pale white woman greying to ashen.

"*Him.*" Marie spat.

"The unholy ghost," Donna muttered eerily. "May he burn in the hell he preached."

"Oh shit," Marie repeated, "oh shit, oh shit, oh shit, oh shit. I hate being alive." *All those years she looked at me and saw that old bastard,* she thought.

Shula pulled a pencil from her breast pocket, slid a napkin from the pottery holder in the middle of the table and began to draw.

Marie stood and paced. "Oh *shit,*" she snarled, spinning abruptly to change direction every five or six steps. She pulled her jacket collar up, hid behind it. Shoved her hands deep in her pockets. "Oh shit." She whirled.

Confused, Donna Murdoch watched the thin birdwoman pace, watched her lover sit and draw her as she walked.

"Oh shit," Marie moaned. Shame was a river, a current she could not resist. Grass bent beneath her feet. The horizon would not open. No one danced. No one chanted. No water flowed. In a silent world blades of grass screamed and broke, a bush leapt in front of her, "Oh shit," she muttered and pivoted. Some bastard in a cassock raped your mother. *Raped your mother,* the leaves rustled. "Shit!" she screeched, stamping a heavy boot on the ground.

Shulamit's pencil paused.

"Help her," Donna urged Shula.

"She doesn't like pharmaceuticals," Shula said calmly, "so there is no point in trying to sedate her. Besides, this isn't so bad. She used to totally trip out. I bet she's still here with us, in the yard."

"Listening to every shrieking blade of grass," Marie hissed. "And I'd really rather be anywhere else, but I can't seem to get there any more. Mazie, my guide, has fled. Back to where the women dance their sorrow into strength, out where the ocean meets the sky, the far herizon where justice seethes and swells."

Shula scribbled as Marie spoke. "Herizon—how do you spell that?" she asked abruptly.

"What?" Donna blurted.

But Marie focussed and answered. "H-e-r-i, wait, no . . . H-e-r . . . new word," she said slowly, pausing to smile, "H-e-r, new word, r-i-s-i-n-g. It's amazing, isn't it?" She grinned at Shulamit. "Her rising. I guess Mazie is still here, she's just donned a new form."

"Whatever works," Donna Murdoch whispered to herself. "I think I'll have a sherry now." She bent and kissed Shula's head as she passed on her way into the house to fetch the bottle. "Still have that tail, I see."

"This must be anti-tail week," Shula mumbled. "You okay?" she addressed Marie, who was standing in the yard, drifting again.

"Okay? I don't fucking know. I'm pissed. I'm sad. And I'm ashamed to say it, but I'm ashamed. And I'm pissed that I'm ashamed. What did I do to be ashamed? What did Thérèse do?"

"Survived." Shula shrugged, sipping her beer.

"Your parents."

"That's right, Crow. What did they do? They were children, too. Like Thérèse. Hold your head up. Raping your mother doesn't make him your father."

A Crow wing wiped a tired eye. "I don't have a father. I've never had a father. And I certainly don't need some bastard rapist in a cassock, even if I do look like him."

"Sherry?" Donna asked coming through the door. "You assumed you look like that unholy ghost because I recognized you."

"Yes," Marie answered, "and yes, a little more sweet poison."

"I can't deny that there's something there. But it's certainly not enough to recognize you as related. I met you, years ago. You were a curly-headed darling, four or five. I ran into you and your mother in Toronto one day. I was moving from that god-forsaken town to here. Just saw you on the street. If Shulamit hadn't been asking about the inquiry, I don't think I would have made the connection."

"So I don't look like him?"

"I only saw him a few times. After Thérèse's disappearance, I didn't have much interest in his bloody church. But I see Thérèse in your face too."

"I see why Shula says you're kind. Well, it's a nice lie anyway," Marie growled bitterly. "I bet he had sandy hair, with lots of curl."

"Bald as a billiard ball. Carefully trimmed grey beard. Too careful, you know? Now your grandmother, I saw her once or twice, shepherding her flock of kids around town. I would've guessed those kids were Cree or Ojibway if I hadn't seen her green eyes and blond curls. She was a natural beauty, your grandmother. And she loved those kids. The talk was that she could've saved herself after she got Thérèse out, but she went back to help Anselme with the rest and the oil burner blew. Terrible." Donna grimaced. "Maybe it wasn't Anselme. Something with an A. I think if you had any hair, you'd look just like her."

Marie rubbed her bristles self-consciously. Maybe she'd grow it, for a while. Let it curl. A bit of bleach might be fun. She sat and sipped the sherry Donna had poured, too sweet now, with the bitterness settling. Fire. There had always been fire, somewhere in her mind. Smoke and burning, human hair turning, high flames licking. Thérèse, petite and boyish at thirteen or fourteen, standing in slippers on melting snow, standing in a pine clearing, waiting for someone, for anyone, to emerge from a small, charred house. Waiting.

"How many were they, the children?" she asked quietly.

"Five or six, I think," Donna answered sadly. "I think six counting your mother, at least three boys. I remember them skating at the rink, three young black-haired boys with new hockey sticks."

"I would've had uncles," Marie mumbled, picturing a white snow-banked river crowded with hockey-playing Latouches, skidding up the ice, small and fast. "Cousins, maybe. And grand-parents." She bowed her head.

"Yeah," Shula agreed, "but would you have ever been born?"

"Shit." The happy crowd vanished behind the robes of a bald priest. Marie jolted from her chair. "Nice, Shula, very nice. Thanks." She paced again.

"I know it's fresh news to you, but you're not the only one to look back in anger. If it weren't for a history I'd rather disown, I wouldn't exist. But I do, I am. The good that sprouted from evil. And so are you, Crow. So are you."

Marie stopped her itching feet, let Shula's words turn her back around. "Do you think she'll be able to talk about it?" The question hung in the quiet yard, echoed as she sat on the train and invented her grandparents, a Euro-Canadian woman and a vaguely Indigenous man.

The question still hovered as Marie sipped the chilled Sauvé and rose to greet her mother with a kiss on each cheek.

"You always did that, didn't you?" Marie asked quickly. "Kiss on both cheeks."

"Oui." Thérèse paused and drew a breath. "C'était l'habitude dans ma famille."

My family's way. Marie knocked her wine glass, then caught it. "You never, ever mentioned—"

"No, I never did," Thérèse conceded. "Things come back now, sometimes. Just pop out, whether I want them to or not," she said warningly. "Maybe someday you'll get your big wish, but it's very hard, remembering. I've stopped reading the papers entirely."

Something's getting through, Marie thought, guiltily fingering the weave of the tablecloth. "My big wish?"

"You think I didn't see, all those years, that you were dying to know. And now, what is worth a trip from Vancouver, fresh café bol three mornings running, that wonderful salmon—I'm glad you've learned something out there, not just idling away in your health store and chasing women—you don't even know, do you? You always pampered me before you asked about the past. Always. It took me a while to realize that you were at it again. I might have guessed, what with the news." Finely manicured fingers lifted Marie's tender chin. "I can't," Thérèse whispered, "I can't picture their faces." She stopped.

Marie waited.

"Family is you, for me, just you. And I gave you all I had. Me." She leaned forward as a waiter placed a sliced baguette and iced butter on the table. "Merci," she nodded automatically. Then whispered, "I just can't, Marie. It would drive me crazy. Break me into little pieces."

Marie plucked a piece of bread and mashed butter onto it. She clenched the cool stem of her wine glass, swallowed an acidic gulp. Fortified, she shoved the booklet of poems across the table and bit into the yeasty loaf.

Thérèse reached in her purse for frameless bifocals. "*The Freewomen's Chorale,*" she read slowly, and turned to the first page, "à Thérèse." She gazed over her eyeglasses at Marie. "Is it all about the silent mother and how she deprives the poor daughter of her history?" Thérèse flipped hastily through the pages. "The mothers of intention . . . No, I see it isn't. But rhyme? What, are you a white lesbian rapper?"

"Are we," Marie hesitated, "white?" She whispered the word.

Thérèse's mouth opened, but nothing came out. She gestured at the waiter for a bottle of wine. "Why, is that important?"

"Maybe." Marie stared at her.

"Well, we know we're assimilated francophone Canadians. That's someone to be," Thérèse said.

"But what if there's more?" Marie asked.

"What if, will it matter to you?"

The waiter quietly uncorked the wine and poured it. "Would you like to order?"

"Ah, oui François, comme d'habitude. Et le même pour ma fille. Je vous présente, Marie . . . Marie, François . . ." They nodded as Marie pondered her mother's question, then shivered involuntarily. Too much new, too much true.

"I think it would," Marie said as François departed. "Everything seems to. At least to me. Everything matters, and everything . . . everything affects everything. Flows from the same source, floods together like all the waters of the world. That's what that's about." She pointed to the booklet.

"But why rhyme?" Thérèse, teacher and translator, sipped her wine.

"Well, it's not like my other work . . . I didn't write it so much as hear it." Marie sucked her breath in sharply. "It's because of the past, I think, secrets. I had a period of visions, or hallucinations." Thérèse leaned forward intently. "At the time I thought they might be real. Maybe they are. Maybe the Free-women are dancing somewhere, tossing star canopy graffiti above cities. But I can't find them any more." She hesitated. "Not since I saw Donna Murdoch testifying at the inquiry on television. Not since I met her." Her voice dropped quietly.

Thick garlic essence prefigured the return of François with a heaping tureen of steamed mussels. With swift movements he tidied the bread-crumbed table, set the main meal, tossed and served Caesar salad and departed with a "Bon appétit."

Thérèse was silent, staring. Bumping against solid rock memory that had offered protection for decades.

"Let's eat," Marie urged, hastily spooning mussels onto her plate.

Thérèse still didn't move. Marie laid her hand over Thérèse's. "Maman," she whispered, "come back." For a moment they were worried child and lost mother again, for a moment Marie whispered with ten-year-old lips across a veil of memory, to lure her mother back.

"Let's eat," Marie repeated as Thérèse's eyes focussed on her. She handed her mother the spoon. Thérèse accepted it, smiling weakly. "We don't need, I mean, I don't need to talk any more. Maybe you should talk, to somebody, but that's your choice. As long as you're okay . . ." Marie scrutinized Thérèse. She was the same compact, capable woman Marie had known all her life. That bereft, abused teenager dwelt in Marie's mind and, perhaps, in some inaccessible realm of her mother's thoughts. But not in the present.

Thérèse's hand shook as she served herself mussels. Marie refilled her mother's wine glass, handed it to her. Thérèse took a long sip. As she drank, Marie heard Buffy Sainte-Marie word-walk over pounding drums. *Rape burns a hole in forever.*

"And I am the good born out of evil," Marie whispered.

"And I am no longer the sole survivor," Thérèse whispered back.

All days followed that one. With tender nurturing Marie coaxed information from Thérèse. Single words, swallowed syllables, nods of the head became a garden that flourished in Marie's imagination.

"Des sœurs?" whispered from behind. An affirming nod. A single digit held up in silence.

"Des frères?" Marie ventured another morning, as Thérèse dressed for work. Later that day Marie noticed the number three scrawled on the notepad by the telephone.

The garden sprouted a family. Parents, a sister and three brothers for Thérèse, three uncles, an aunt and grandparents for Marie. Marie imagined playful children living the northern life, skating and swimming outdoors, learning how to bait a lure, fillet trout and pickerel, learning the harvest seasons of wild raspberries and blueberries. She struggled to visualize a caring father, with strong, worn hands that laboured for a livelihood and a traditional mother, baking, sewing and knitting for a brood. All exploded in winter smoke, burnt out of time, frozen into memory. Comprehension of her mother's loss dissipated Marie's childhood resentments. The family, as she invented it, played on in Marie's mind, a yellow-tinted super-eight film, joyously living out lost seasons. The family Latouche.

Saturday morning they lay on Thérèse's large bed drinking café au lait. Thérèse played with the hair sprouting on Marie's head.

"It will start to curl soon, Chou." Thérèse smiled.

"Like your mother," Marie answered.

Thérèse sat upright. "Marie Latouche." Placed a hand on her pounding chest. Sweat beaded above her lip.

"Maman?"

Thérèse took a long slow breath. "Marie Latouche," she repeated, "ma mère, ta grand-mère, Chou." She stroked Marie's bristles and stared at the white wall straight ahead of her. Whispered again, "Marie Latouche, ma mère et ma fille." Words barely audible.

Marie stroked her mother's hand.

Thérèse slowly brought Marie into focus. "C'est tout, Marie. That's all. I'm exhausted." She slumped back against the pillows and let her eyes close.

"I'm sorry, Thérèse." Marie stroked her tense brow. "But thank you. Merci, merci, merci."

"Talk about something, Chou," Thérèse asked with quiet urgency. "Tell me about your life."

"Well, actually. Jane and I gave up. Remember Shulamit?"

"No, really you gave up? Of course, who could forget Shulamit? But you're seeing her? Not very adventurous. It's like another point on the same triangle."

"I'm thirty, Thérèse. I'm slowing down."

"Thirty—that's not so old. When I was thirty . . ." She changed the subject. "No chasing girls at the bar?"

"Well." Marie smoothed the cotton spread. "Maybe not. When were you thirty, actually?" Marie asked, suspecting Thérèse had never been quite honest about her age, wanting to disguise her youth at Marie's birth.

"Ah, Chou, does it matter?" Thérèse tapped her hand in gentle admonition. "Is Shulamit still an artist?"

"No, she's a doctor. There, see I've gone completely respectable. I'm dating a doctor." She picked up a flowered throw cushion and batted her mother's leg.

"Garde, Chou. Le café."

"But she's going to do some art for me. For the show. I want to have a show, and a launch for the poems. I want others to see my Freewomen. Shula's already started work. You must come!" Marie pictured the big gallery filled with friends. "You must."

"Okay." Thérèse hesitated, unsure she wished to tread further into memory. "Send me an invitation in lots of time. It's not scheduled yet, I imagine."

"No, just dreamed, like so much . . . I think I'm going to become a midwife."

"So many dreams, Marie. Poet, midwife, clerk. Doctor's wife."

"Very funny, Maman. No, not clerk. Just poet-slash-midwife. They have courses in Ontario. I was checking it out, but I never followed up. Things got too crazy. I got too crazy." Thérèse flinched. "I think I'll see what I can do in Vancouver. Maybe I can train through apprenticing. Or volunteer. Just get some experience. You know what I figured out?"

"What?" Thérèse sipped the cooling coffee.

"Well, it sounds obvious, but when you find something you want to do for the rest of your life, it doesn't so much matter how long it took you to find it. It just matters that you start." She paused. "I have to go, you know. They're already freaked at the store that I took extra time."

"I know. When?"

"I'll take the train tomorrow and fly out Monday."

They were quiet, each examining the changes in herself, pending emergence from their garden of renewal. Rolling over to face Thérèse, Marie smiled.

"Forever, I am Marie Latouche, daughter of Thérèse Latouche, and only Thérèse Latouche."

"Like I always said." Thérèse nodded, grateful to be closing the doors of memory Marie had nudged open.

"You always said," Marie agreed.

Worried child, fragile mother, planted a garden, nurtured each other.

Ethel Chartrand & Miss Beatrice Brigden

SEPTEMBER SUNLIGHT FILTERED golden through ochre leaves. Jane's worn leather bag dropped in the dust, her hips slid onto the wide strap of the swing. Thirty-seven-year-old feet pushed off sand into seven-year-old rhythms. Strong summer arms pulled on thick chains, legs strained up into wide Manitoba blue. The swing arched, at the apex, that childhood urge to leap lay in wait.

Jane and Gene kicking shoes up and away, launching agile bodies skywards, swings crashing behind.

"Beat you."

"Did not."

"Did so."

"Rematch."

The long backyard behind the old house, the hole behind the swing set through the earth to China, sour-apple tree branches beckoning small airborne bodies. Parachuting off the garage roof into a mountain of raked leaves, climbing snowbanks, tunnelling snow forts, lying spread eagle to fan snow angels into existence, staring up into black, star-studded eternity.

"Gene, how big is the universe?" Arms crunching rhythmically on the hard snow as they move.

"Bigger than everything. Infinite."

"What's at the end?"

"There is no end. It just goes on and on."

"Like Dad's war stories." Breath thick in the air. A thousand thousand crisp white gems in the dark. "You believe that?"

"Well, he was in the war. There's a German luger in the trunk behind the furnace." Whispering over the snow. "He took it from a dead man."

"No, not the war. The universe, going on forever."

"It's just a definition. The universe is everything, so it can't have an end. Everything can't end." Angels in the winter night.

Pushing the heavy oak door open, into the warm house, tossing boots, snow pants, parkas and mittens in the hall. The rustle of newspaper means Phil is reading in the living room, not yelling about the air lock and keeping the hall door shut. The clink of dishes under running water says Sophia is loading the dishwasher, a cigarette burning in the ashtray. The distant sound of a Hollies' song—Owen is on the third floor, blasting the latest hits. And this is the universe. This is everything, and everything can't have an end.

Jane swung through those close childhood years that were everything and still ended. Leaving her with this park slumbering along the slow muddy river, echoes of Sunday morning strolls with parents and brothers, after-school bike rides with friends, swings that sliced through time in the curve of an arc. Jane let her feet drag on the hard-packed sand. She stood, reached into her weathered bag and retrieved a bound manuscript—her thesis—and a large envelope in Marie's handwriting, postmarked Toronto.

Earlier that afternoon Jane had delivered another copy of her thesis into the hands of Judy Rubin, her supervisor. Sitting back on the swing she flipped through the pages, enjoying the weight in her hands, a physical realization of her ideas. She slipped the thesis back into the bag, withdrew Phil's fish-filleting knife from the front pocket and paused.

Marie's envelope had arrived a week earlier. Jane ignored it until that afternoon, when she tossed it into her bag as she left for the cross-town drive to the university. The high of finishing the thesis might carry her through Marie's missive. Rocking between resentment and curiosity, she opened the wood-handled knife, slit the envelope and tilted. A booklet and a thick, handwritten letter slid out. *The Freewomen's Chorale.* Laying the booklet on her knee, she fingered the unopened letter. Swung, dragging her feet in the sand, unfolded it and saw a note in Marie's precise script:

> *Sorry. Please don't be too pissed off to read this and my Chorale. Please, please, just read. After you finish be pissed again if you still want to. And if you want me to, let me know and I'll just leave you in peace. If you want me to.*

Cautiously, Jane continued reading.

An hour later she was still sitting at a picnic table in the clearing behind the pavilion. Marie's letter and booklet lay open on brown wood. She had read and reread, reflected and absorbed, denied and believed. As shadows swayed in fading light, distance replaced anger, the separation stretched farther than the thick white sixteen-hundred-mile trail behind a passenger jet, disappearing at five hundred miles an hour. Marie, Jane's ex-lover, had transformed into the woman who wrote these poems. Revelations, Jane thought. Peel the onion of life, cry the tears and become. Her eyes played with the flickering shadows, divined the shape of the woman who had roused love and fury. As yellowing leaves blew easily from autumn branches, Jane let memory's Marie shift in the wind, imagined Marie riding those wild visions to know her own history, Marie sparking Shulamit to love *and* to paint, Marie orchestrating a celebration of her journey in images, sounds and words. Jane felt the crisp chill of frost on the evening breeze, packed the papers away and strolled back through the swings. Shedding trees whooshed in the blackening blue. Fresh wind whistled through her thoughts, revealing a crystal image of Marie, alone in her apartment, shimmering with plans. Salut, 'Rie, Jane thought, feeling the last sparks cool.

Jane slid the key into the ignition on a surge of joy. The exhilaration of freedom flared; old chapters closed cleanly as she rolled out of the quiet park and down the broad avenue along the river. Without hesitation she turned right, up the majestic street where the fossilized house stood, braked and gazed at the warm glow radiating from the hearth of another child's universe. After a moment, she shifted her foot to the accelerator and cruised away, patting the bag that contained her thesis "The Guts & The Gall: Socialist-Feminist Roots in Muddy Water 1955–70."

Jane checked her watch as she crossed the river toward downtown, dropped her foot a little harder on the gas pedal. Masha, visiting the city for a few weeks to finalize plans to move west, had mentioned a meeting to nominate a candidate in the federal election. Sophia's old party. Ethel Chartrand, whom Masha knew, wanted the nomination. Jane had heard Ethel's name around the community centre and was aware of her involvement in the new Aboriginal schools in the north end. She could be the first Indigenous woman to represent the city in Muddy Water's century of existence, Jane thought, heading north on the route Phil had driven to work for thirty years. Phil racing in and out of traffic, always racing. The first light was green. The rest were synchronized. Jane cruised all the way to the railway yard. As the sign "Welcome to the north end" came into view on the shingled roof of the auto body shop, she giggled. "I'm okay, Phil." She saw Sophia's wide eyes glowing with anger and with love, and honked the horn perfunctorily as her tires rolled off the bridge and up Salter into the home stretch. "Love you, Soph," she whispered, closing the whole book. "And I always will." The address of the meeting was pinned to her kitchen bulletin board. If she hurried, she could be there by 8:30.

There was a reasonable crowd in the high school gym. Jane waved at Masha across the room and took a seat at the back. A tall, clean-cut white man called the meeting to order as Jane looked around for other familiar faces. She nodded to a few board members from the centre. Without her job, Jane realized, her life in Muddy Water would have been wholly a tunnel of memory, thought and fantasy. Sophia and life at the old house, theories of women's organizing, a lover conjured in the mind when desire burst the gates of purgatory. She glimpsed a profile that seemed familiar. A guy about her age nodded with the man beside him. Ricky Solomon, grade ten, blasted on pot in the back row, giggling his fool head off with smilin' Mike Costello. Jane laughed at the memory, as he turned and recognized her. He crossed the gym smiling.

"Jane Cammen. Twenty years later, and you're still laughin' at me." He offered a hand, she stood up and shook it.

"Actually, that laughter was twenty years old. You were always so ripped."

"True enough. What brings you here? I thought you moved east years ago."

"I did, but I've been back a few years now. I live up here, work at a community centre. I wanted to make sure Ethel gets the nomination. Yourself?"

"Oh, I travelled some. Taught in a few places, you know, working my way along the gringo trail. Exploring exotica. Still ripped. Finally landed. I teach elementary. Inner city mostly, so I ended up moving back up here to the parents' childhood turf. Less travel. Ethel's great. I'm starting this fall at the Aboriginal elementary school because of her. Hell, there wouldn't be an Aboriginal school without her. And of course the Reform Party surge is scaring the shit out of me."

"No kidding. Who's that at the mike?"

"Haven't a clue. I thought you'd be immersed in local politics."

"Grew up that way. Been more into grassroots feminist politics for a while now. Not so much electoral."

He eyed her sideways. "Married? Kids?"

"No and no," she admitted, musing that he'd grown up nicely. "Lesbian. Mostly, anyway." Handsome, almost. Attractive, that was it. She was watching Ricky Solomon's face and finding him attractive.

"Ha. I always said so. Costello owes me a sawbuck. And twenty years' interest." He had a sly smile.

"And yourself?" she asked, enjoying the light rush of adrenalin.

"There's Fanny Mae, the love of my life. Turned six this spring. Her mother, Rachel, well, we're together again now. Been a little rocky from time to time, but that's all my fault for sure. Rach is great."

"Rachel? Would I know her?"

"Maybe, she sings at the Blue Note sometimes. It's a small town, this city, isn't it?"

"Actually, I've been a bit of a recluse. Working, studying. Spend a lot of time at the lake. I just finished my masters thesis . . . But I intend to get around more now."

The room had settled down. The man at the mike called the meeting to order.

"Good to see you." Ricky patted her shoulder.

"Yeah, you too."

"Catch you on the campaign trail," he called out, backing away.

"Sure thing," Jane agreed, remembering the rush of excitement that infused Sophia at election time. Days and nights at the campaign office, on the streets, knocking on doors, analyzing the other candidates' moves and digging for the mood of the electorate. Sophia at her public best, pulling community together, encouraging everyday folks to vote on issues, not personality, and to force candidates to take positions.

Ethel Chartrand spoke briefly and passionately. No one opposed her, and the meeting rose as one to endorse her candidacy. Jane returned a wave to Ricky Solomon as she made her way through the exiting crowd to Masha.

"Glad you made it. Come and meet her," Masha commanded. "Wasn't that tricky Ricky Solomon, major pothead?"

"Yep. He's teaching at the new school."

"My, my. Some white boys do grow up. Just a sec, I have something for you." She dug around in a nylon knapsack.

"If you wait long enough, I guess."

"You still have a crush on him? Here——" She handed Jane a book.

"Well," Jane smirked, "to be honest, he does seem to have that effect on me. Guess I'm part het after all. Anyway, he said he always thought I was a dyke." She looked at the book. "*The Mishomas . . .* that's grandmother, isn't it?"

"Grandfather. It has the story about the migis that I was telling you."

"Really? Great, thanks for remembering, Mash." Jane squeezed her cousin warmly, burrowing in soft hair and bottled essence of lilies.

"You're welcome. Now come on," Masha urged. The crowd around Ethel Chartrand had thinned.

"Ethel, you're on your way." Masha hugged her. "This is my cousin Jane. Born in a back room, weaned on elections. Put her on your team, she's got time on her hands."

"Yeah, I do," Jane agreed, shaking hands. "And I'd love to get involved. Can I leave my number somewhere?"

Jane stayed a while, chatting, enjoying Ethel's sharp political cracks and easy rapport with friends. She volunteered for the election planning committee and asked if the canvas organizer had been hired. Working around the clock in a campaign office could be just what she needed. A woman was leading the party, and a scoundrel was arousing the people's worst instincts, suggesting fear as a basis for voting. Freed of many encumbering layers, Jane suddenly itched to plunge into the fray.

Walking through the front door she hollered, "Hello, house," and flipped switches until the entire first floor glowed warm and yellow. A dog wouldn't be out of place, she decided. If you didn't have a Marie or a Micah or a Fanny Mae. A dog would welcome you home. There were no message lights blinking on the answering machine. She grabbed a bottle of mineral water and climbed the stairs two at a time.

Upstairs, Jane lay the thesis on the desk, gave a thumbs-up to Sophia's best campaign photo framed on the wall. One last pile of research material remained to be filed. Jane flipped through it, hesitant to return to a work tunnel, yet not wanting to waste her excitement surfing television. The hour in the park nagged. She opened the file drawer, then picked up the phone and dialled Marie's number. The answering machine clicked on, Martha Reeves and the Vandellas dancing in the street.

"Well, I read it. Uhm, peace, yeah, for a while, anyway. I'd like us to come out of this friends, but I'm gonna need some time, well, just some time. I'll let you know. Salut."

Chapter notes, clippings, the text of a speech by Sophia, a partially torn photo of Sophia and Ruby Gottisfeld in Montreal. Jane sorted quickly, creating new files as necessary. A sheaf of photocopies from the provincial archives lay at the bottom of the papers, including letters between Miss Beatrice Brigden— later, Aunt B. to the Voice of Women—in Brandon and Dr. Albert Moore of the Social Service and Evangelism Department of the Methodist Church, in Toronto. Ongoing correspondence covering arrangements for Miss Brigden's evangelical travels through rural Manitoba and Saskatchewan between 1910 and 1920, as working people radicalized and organized. Ending in 1920 when Miss Brigden—who Jane remembered as a small, serious, seventyish woman in a wool suit, sensible shoes and a matching hat—emphatically supported efforts to create a labour church, while Dr. Moore strongly disagreed.

Jane reread Miss Brigden's letter of July 26, 1919, just over a month after the end of the 1919 General Strike. "The Labour crisis through which we have just passed affected the people of the West in a very decided way . . . Even more than the war did this crisis make our people think," Beatrice Brigden wrote in response to a request from Toronto for information. ". . . for vituperation, reviling and unreasonable wrath," Miss Brigden continued, referring to established church reaction against the creation of a people's church, "a parallel would be hard to find." Jane read on, hearing Miss Brigden, young and righteous, riding trains through ripening grain, seeking the pulse of the people, beating the path that would be followed by T. C. Douglas and Stanley Knowles, from college in Brandon to leadership of Canadian socialism. Old Miss Brigden, Sophia called her, marvelling at her strength and determination. Jane pictured Old Miss Brigden outside the brick walk-up on Westminster, Sophia in the driver's seat on the way to or from an event. Boxes of her papers were stored in the provincial archives. Jane read on. Citing exhaustion and sexism obliquely as her reasons, Miss Brigden quit the Methodists within a year of the strike. "I am obliged to earn my own living and if possible provide for my own old age. Being just a woman, I am fully aware that the church will not interest herself in such practical matters." If the church really was female, she would have, Jane thought. Miss Brigden's true reasons appeared in an earlier argument with Dr. Moore. "The hope of the church then is to stand for justice for all," she had written. "The preaching of a full-ordered morality alone can meet the demands of the common people."

Jane closed the letters, picked up a pen and labelled a new file—"Just a Woman: The Prairie Life of Miss Beatrice Brigden" —and slid in the copies. She would write again, another woman's story. Without a tunnel, this time, she admonished herself. Without hiding in history or suckling on sorrow. Peel the onion, shed the fears, plunge into life and revel in the years.

17

Marie la Deuxième & Rose of the Ashes

MARIE'S EYES SCANNED microfilmed pages of the *Sudbury Star,* the decades-old editions of the daily newspaper that might have reported a tragic house fire in Smooth Rock Falls. She had a rough estimate for the date of the fire that swallowed her ancestry. Passing hours heightened her tension and strained her vision. She was determined to secure official validation, if only a brief, matter-of-fact account of the event that precipitated her conception. "Rise from the ashes, child of fire, all that you lost, burning desire," Marie muttered, then scribbled in an open notebook. *Phoenix, many years risen, seeks a family. Seeks life in death. Names, dates, faces to fill the vacancy.* Personal ad, place it anywhere. Her left hand wound the film ahead.

There they were. Arriving, like all anticipated events, the moment she was distracted. Marie bit her lip as she read the headline "Family Dies in Fire Tragedy" on the front page of the second section. She focussed on the burnt shell of a house in a beautiful clearing. Black earth visible around the structure, April snow re-encroaching. Down the page, those dreamed-of faces blurring and fading. Awkward school snapshots of Luc, 11, Marc, 9, Guy and Chantat, both 7. Sharp black crow eyes, long extinguished. Antoine, big burly father with a thin mustache, holding a first-prize pickerel at the local derby. Marie, mother and never-to-be grandmother, in a crowd of women presenting an unidentified petition to the local school trustee. And Thérèse—*sole survivor.* The caption echoed in Thérèse's adult voice—*and I am no longer the sole survivor.*

Marie swam in the images. She felt Luc's child-soft skin, heard the giggle behind Guy's cockeyed grin, twisted her fingers through Grand-mère's blond curls. Antoine bellowed and belched, rubbed his sons' heads with rough affection, rocked a sleepy Chantal and coaxed a bedtime hug from an embarrassed teenage Thérèse. Grand-père's deep black eyes, Grand-mère's light blond curls. Marie Latouche, la deuxième. Cree? More likely Ojibway. Never know. Throw away a true heritage, or adopt an inappropriate one. Marie sighed. Maybe, maybe not. She knew how to live with uncertainty. Better a maybe than an ignorant wannabe. Perhaps Mazie would return to guide her through new discoveries. More likely she would weave these faces into her imagination, invent their lives in poems and stories, beg Shula for portraits of the adults they might have been. Somehow, in those threads, she would find her way, respectful of a heritage, that she, like so many others, might have lost long before birth.

Marie picked up her pen to complete the form for photocopies of the page. She would take her family home to the co-op apartment off Commercial Drive. Invite them to breathe her breath, flow in her blood, sweat through her skin. To live in those vacancies in her imagination. Rose of the Ashes, sparked by a fire, digs in black earth and fulfills her desire.

18

Wise Sister Sarah & The Firmament of Women

SHULA WAS AT HOME. At home in her house, in this small, easy city where landscape absorbed the tensions of life, resting her churning mind on the warm green chest of its streets. A city slow enough to induce Shula to reflect, after so many years of careening forward, a wild bear charging target after target. Instead of revving from waking until collapse, she occasionally idled. She strolled. She painted, calmly birthing Crow's celebratory daymares on canvas. The small second room shimmered with cavorting figures, incandescent sunlit horizons, curling waves of high tide.

She did office hours and hospital rounds, visiting Jane Doe early, and sometimes, on clear mornings, wheeling her out to sit in a livelier world, among green grass, yellow benches and still-flowering beds. Each time they teetered on the verge of conversation, Shulamit listening for a halting voice to whisper, "Hello, I'm Bertha Rosenbaum" or "Eva Schwartz" or "Betty Brown." But the words only danced in her head. Jane Doe 12-93 offered half-smiles and a knotted hand to hold. She nodded a vigorous, angular "yes" of her lean, grey head each time Shulamit mentioned the name Sarah Wise, closed her right fist and laid her right arm across her hollowing chest. Shula smiled and nodded in return.

Helen, Isaac and Toronto still resonated. The Blue Jays had clinched the division, the pennant would be a cakewalk and a second World Series title was entirely possible—or so Shulamit and Isaac speculated as September closed. Her parents phoned weekly, the three chatted of world events, books and movies, chewing on morsels of everyday life. Helen's quiet enthusiasm for Shula's return to painting was a nourishing stream. For the first time in decades, the river of life flowed easily between.

"You asked about Sarah Wise," Isaac said one evening.

"Yeah," Shula answered, lolling on her back on the studio floor. "Any luck?"

"I think so. Sam Wise, I did know him, years back we golfed together a few times. Ran into him at a rubber chicken dinner last week. He had a sister Sarah. Much older than him, more like an aunt, he said. I asked one question, he talked for twenty minutes. Apparently his mother died when he was still young, and his sister mostly raised him, out west. They both moved here. Sister never married, became very political. 'Always against something,' Sam said. She had what he called a special friend. Died in 1983, you're right . . . Enough?"

"Yes. Great. Thanks. Nothing about the special friend?"

"Nah, made him nervous. I didn't press."

"But, Isaac, you said you thought he meant a woman," Helen added on the extension.

"Yeah. Definitely. Made him nervous."

Shula spun on her back, staring up at a canvas sprinkled with pencil lines, sketch stars in the firmament of women. Crow's pantheon. "Add one for Sarah S. Wise," she whispered as Helen offered an analysis of women's relationships in *The Robber Bride*.

Mornings dawned later and cooler. The Sunday after Isaac's news, Shula bought a thick lilac cardigan at a garage sale. She buttoned Jane Doe 12-93 into it before their Monday breakfast stroll. They sat among the yellow benches, red geraniums fading in autumn. Shula talked of Sarah Wise and her brother Sam. Jane Doe nodded, half-smiled, nodded again and laid her right arm, fist closed, across her chest. She breathed out the sleep-wail Shula recognized as "Sarah."

"Sarah Wise," Shula repeated. "You are not Sarah Wise."

No, the woman nodded, repeated the sound and again, crossed her right arm across her upper body, fist over her heart.

Shula imitated the gesture. Left fist closed, left arm across her chest. No, the other one — right fist closed, right arm across her body. Jane Doe's eyes narrowed, she nodded encouragingly. Shula crossed her right, then her left arm over her breasts. Jane Doe clapped her free hand on chair arm. It wasn't a gesture, Shula realized, it was a sign. The sign for love, in American Sign language. Jane Doe grinned a thorough, lopsided grin and a strange, mirthful sound bubbled from her thinned body. Laughter.

Shula's months of patience imploded. She bent and kissed Jane Doe's cheek, spun the wheelchair abruptly, wheeled her unravelling mystery into the hospital and over to the small gift shop.

"Paper," Shula blurted.

"Bottom shelf on the wall," a small woman answered from behind the cash register.

Shula whirled, bent, grabbed a blue airmail pad and tossed it on the counter.

"And this." She pulled a chewable Bic pen from a jar beside the register.

"Five twenty-nine." The clerk faced her.

"Five twenty-nine?" Shula began to argue, then dug in her pocket, threw a five and coins on the counter, opened the pad and picked up the pen.

My name is Shulamit Weiss, she wrote.

Jane Doe nodded in agreement and pointed a thin finger a Shulamit.

Your name is _____ , Shulamit wrote, and handed Jane the pen. Jane Doe clasped a wobbly hand around the transparent plastic and scratched at the page. Vertical lines, horizontal lines, some nice rolling curves decorated the blue page. Still can't write, Shulamit thought, probably permanent. Del and Todd had both told her. Shula's left heel drummed on waxed linoleum. The aphasia might also be permanent, she thought, after almost four months of not permitting the heretical thought. But she *knows*. She knows my name, she must know her name. And a whole lot else. Retaining some language function without speech was uncommon, but entirely possible. And she had sign language.

"Who is Sarah Wise?"

Arm across the heart. Love.

Shula beamed. If you got the question right, she could give you an answer. She began multiplying, twenty-six letters in the alphabet, times how many letters in a name? And no clues. Absently she picked up the pad and pen, slipped them in her white coat pocket and began pushing the chair toward the elevator. The right answer lay in determining the right question. The elevator doors opened. But a name could not easily be discerned by a process of elimination. Shula watched the floor numbers light up one at a time, black numbers in small raised boxes.

"Scrabble!" she shouted as the door opened on Del's face.

"Might be one in O.T.," Del said calmly. "Why?" She strolled into the elevator and laid a long, silver fingernail on the open button.

"Spelling," Shula said excitedly, still standing in the elevator. Abruptly she focussed on Del, now patiently indicating the open elevator doors. "The problem is she can't write. Maybe she can spell." Shula rolled her patient into the hall.

Del followed Shulamit out of the elevator.

"Weiss, why don't you let me settle her and you find your Scrabble. We'll be right down the hall."

Shula was back in the elevator before Del finished speaking. "Seen Todd recently?" she called as the doors closed.

"No," Del called over her shoulder, wheeling Jane Doe along the corridor.

Todd was in the cafeteria finishing an unscheduled coffee break. He was easily cajoled into rifling the occupational therapy cupboards for a Scrabble game. "Haven't used it in a while," he said mildly, "Don't get too many who can spell but can't speak or write . . . Here."

"Excellent." Shula whisked the box from his grasp and hustled back to the chronic care ward, her mind spinning possibilities. If Jane Doe could pick out letters in Scrabble, she could pick out letters on a keyboard. Speak through a computer. She had some mobility. If she had heavy insurance, she could leave the hospital, live in a nursing home of some kind. Maybe there was family somewhere. Maybe she would travel home, Shula at her side, wheeling her off an airplane into the bosom of waiting well-wishers. Shula paused in the doorway to Jane Doe's room. Family? Too Disney. Any attentive family would have found her by now. Calm down. This is, this was, a woman for whom spending months "out of touch" was normal, or close to normal behaviour. Independent, Shula thought, without dependents.

Shula sucked in a lungful of air and entered the room. Took what she hoped was a last look at Jane Doe as an anonymous elder, so much thinner than when she entered the hospital, yet still sinewy and determined. Grey hair sprung in all directions. Alert eyes tracked Shula as she crossed the room. Her right hand reached for the Scrabble box as Shula lay it on the bed. She lifted the lid, tipped all the letters into it and began turning them over.

"You're bored out of your mind, aren't you?"

If a wink could holler, Jane Doe was shrieking in agreement.

"Okay. Hold on. Let's not play. Let's talk." Shula's breath quickened. "What is your name?" she asked.

Jane Doe cleared a space in the lid. Her fingers shifted letters slowly into place. I, T, O, L. Shula strained to read. D, Y, O, U, A, L. In a flourish she added R E A D Y.

"ITOLDYOUALREADY. I TOLD YOU ALREADY." Shula read aloud.

Jane Doe giggled, high and lively.

"You told me already?" Shula stared at her.

Jane Doe grinned and nodded, then swept aside the words. Shula did not breathe as the hand picked out five letters and laid them down one at a time.

"So you did." Shula barely restrained a bone-crushing hug. "Pleased to know you."

AND YOU, the woman spelled back, eyes shining. Six letters speaking below the five that had spelled her name: HONOR.

"Y-o-u a-s-k-e-d w-h-o i a-m, D-r W-e-i-s-s," computer keys tapped a single stroke syncopation. "S-o I'-l-l t-e-l-l y-o-u." White lettering lit a small blue screen, shadows caressed a face rapt in concentration. "I am a woman born of a woman, seventy-eight years ago, in a long-vanished house that once stood at the corner of Spadina and Dundas in Toronto. I was born on a short, hot summer night. My mother laboured long and loud, from suppertime Wednesday until she heaved me from her body as twilight waned on Thursday. My grandmother and my aunts agreed that she spent herself in the birthing. They never tired of repeating that she named me Honor Ellen, cradled me, kissed me and slept away from life. I suppose it was all of a piece with their desire to have me know her, for there seemed no end of tales passed on about her doings. Tales aside, I believe I missed her each day since, in ways small and large, though the longer I live, the more those stories seem like ancient mysteries. Yet her absence shaped the story that is my life . . ."

Acknowledgements

This novel was born of living in a women's world. Its genesis belongs, in a general sense, to all the women I have worked with, been educated, influenced and nurtured by—obviously a list too long to reproduce here. I hope I have expressed my thanks and acknowledgement along the way. There are some, though, whose friendship, guidance and ideas formed a wellspring for the writing of this book. They include: Una Decter, Irene Buncel, Donna Friesen, Dena Decter, Carole Geller, Dorothy Bolton, Rebecca, Leah and Maryam Decter, Jacquie and Penny Buncel, Niamh O'Connell, Lucille Roch, Angela Robertson, Ruth Mandel and the women I have worked closely with, at and through Women's Press in Toronto.

I have also relied on published and unpublished work for information and perspectives, including, in no particular order: the files of the Voice of Women and of Beatrice Brigden at the Manitoba Public Archives; Hollis Sigler's show *Breast Cancer Journal: Walking with the Ghosts of My Grandmothers* at the National Museum of Women in the Arts in Washington in 1993; *Alicia: My Story* by Alicia Appleman-Jurman; *Hannah Senesh: Her Life & Diary* by Hannah Senesh; *Hidden Children: Forgotten Survivors of the Holocaust* by André Stein; *When in Doubt Do Both: The Times of My Life* by Kay MacPherson; *Children of the Holocaust: Conversations with Sons and Daughters of Survivors* by Helen Epstein; *No Burden to Carry: Narratives of Black Working Women in Ontario 1920s to 1950s* by Dionne Brand with the assistance of Lois De Shield and the Immigrant Women's Job Place-

Acknowledgements

ment Centre, and *Different Voices: Women and the Holocaust* edited by Carol Rittner and John K. Roth. In addition, I'd like to thank Mairin Nic Dhiarmada of the Celtic Studies Program at St. Michael's College for her assistance with the Irish language.

I am grateful to the women of Press Gang—Barb, Della, Val and Emma—who offered assistance from the early stages of the work, and to editor Jennifer Glossop for a challenging and rewarding editorial process.

And finally I want to thank those who listened and read, answered research questions, offered places to sleep, shared research excursions, provided technical assistance, nourishment and encouragement while this book was in development —Angela Hryniuk, Derry Decter, Heather Guylar, Mona Oikawa, Leah Decter, Hana Aach, Marian White, Rebecca Decter, Sam, Nora and Riel, Lillian Allen, Karen X. Tulchinsky, Loreto Friere, Michael Decter, Lucille Roch, Lois Fine and Gene Long.

Sources & Credits

ANN DECTER is author of the novel *Paper, Scissors, Rock*. Her writing has been published in numerous anthologies and periodicals including *Plural Desires: Writing Bisexual Women's Realities* and *Fireweed: The Jewish Women's Issue*. A co-editor of two recent anti-homophobia anthologies—*Resist!* and *Out Rage*—her earlier publications include the prose poetry volume, *Insister* and a children's book, *Katie's Alligator Goes to Daycare*. Ann has spent a decade in feminist publishing, including five years as co-managing editor at Women's Press in Toronto. In 1994, she co-founded McGilligan Books, where she acts as publisher. She teaches creative writing to women independently and through George Brown College. Born and bred in Winnipeg, after fifteen years in Toronto, she almost calls it home.

PRESS GANG PUBLISHERS has been producing vital and provocative books by women since 1975.

A free catalogue is available from Press Gang Publishers, #101 – 225 East 17th Avenue, Vancouver, B.C. v5v 1a6 Canada